ISBN 979-8-35095-866-9

# Twenty-Five Years

**S. Heather Carroll**

# Part One

## Twenty-five Years Ago

# 1.

## Spur of the Moment

Ainsley:

Honey nut Cheerios, Muesli, or Cinnamon Toast Crunch…,

Decisions, decisions. I grabbed all three boxes and started mixing them into one bowl. The sound of the Cheerios hitting the bowl was loud in the quiet kitchen of the sorority house. Most of the girls having left for the Christmas holiday, only a handful of us remained. It was almost eerily quiet for a house that usually housed twenty boisterous girls.

I opened the fridge and took out the milk and sniffed. Thank God it was still fresh. Especially since I had already mixed the cereals into one bowl and wouldn't be able to pour them back into their respective boxes. I closed the fridge and jumped in surprise at the unruly head of curls that greeted me.

"I have the best idea. You're not doing anything tonight are you?" Ashley asked. Her curly head of blond hair bouncing with excitement.

"I thought we were going to Sigma Pi's New Years Eve party with Steph?" I said as I shoved a heaping spoon full of yummy into my mouth.

"Eh, we could do that. Or we could drive to Vegas." She said, twinkling her finger tips in an arch of jazz hands.

"Continue." I mumbled as a cheerio escaped my lips and fell down my shirt into my cleavage. I fished it out and ate it anyway as Ashley hatched out her plan.

"If we leave by noon we will be there before sunset. And then we just walk the strip drinking blue drinks in glasses that are half our size, and flirt with all the cute boys."

"Just us?"

"Hailey too. We can see if Steph wants to come, but I bet she is going to stay for the Sigma Pi party, cuz you know…

'Mathew'." She sighed and fanned herself, mimicking our love-struck sister Steph, who had it bad for Mathew.

"Do we have a place to crash?"

"We won't need it. No one sleeps on New Year's Eve. We will be up until sunrise partying. Do you remember what Hailey said about last year?"

"Re... (chew, chew, chew) ...mind me again?"

"Hails said that last year it was totally nuts! The entire strip gets shut down and there are thousands of people just walking, mingling, and dancing, and making out in the street!" Ash said with excitement, repeating Haileys tales of last year as if they were her own. "She said there were show girls and some of those Thunder from Down Under strippers just walking around handing out free tickets to shows and beads like at Mardi Gras."

"Do you have to show your tits like at Mardi Gras?"

"Let's go and we can find out." She smiled encouragingly, shrugging her eyebrows up and down. "In the morning, we can hit up an awesome breakfast buffet then head home before traffic. What do you say, are you in?"

I took another huge bite and chewed as Ash watched me anxiously, bouncing back and forth from one foot to the other.

"Yeah, I'm in. Leave at noon?"

"Or sooner if we can get our shit together. Girl, we are going to have so much fun!" She squealed, spinning in a circle. I was starting to catch Ashley's excitement. A spur of the moment trip to Vegas did sound pretty awesome.

"So, what are you going to wear?" I asked, as I started to plan out what to pack.

"You know my purple off-the-shoulder with the see-through back?"

"Oh, that's sexy." I agreed as my mind ran through my wardrobe; but I was at a loss.

"What are you thinking?"

"I'm not sure" I said before shoveling another spoonful into my mouth. "I'll think about it while I'm in the shower."

"I'm going to go see if Steph's awake. If we all chip in like fifteen bucks for gas, that should get us there and back."

"Are you going to drive?"

"I'm happy to. Maybe we can take shifts driving and sleeping on the way home. Oh! Maybe we can stop at those outlet shops along the way." She jumped with excitement over her own idea.

"I enjoy a good sale." I agreed, smiling at her enthusiasm.

"I'm so stoked! We are going to have so much fun."

"Me too." I said from behind the bowl as I lifted it to drink the sweet cinnamon milk.

Mmmmmm. The best part.

Rinsing my bowl, I tossed it in the top rack of the dishwasher and followed Ashley upstairs to start getting ready while she tried to convince the rest of the skeleton crew to come along.

*** 

Standing in my towel I surveyed my closet.

Jeans were a no brainer. A pair of dark denim hipsters that did amazing things for my ass.

Shoes would need to be comfy, so I went with simple black ballet flats.

Bra: Fredricks of Hollywood, black push-up. No question.

Panties: A black thong to match.

Top: hmmmm, I have my black V neck with the plunging neckline... but no, it has what looks like a grease stain.

Shit.

Well, I have my blue scoop neck, but that is more of a day time top. I turned my head and looked longingly over at my roommate's closet. Now empty for nearly two weeks, since Cherrie left for the holiday. I miss both her and her wardrobe right now. There are many great things about having Cherrie for a roommate. But one of my favorites is that we wear the same size and she is a shop-a-holic with a high credit card limit.

A knock on the door made me jump as Ash and Hails peeked in. "Hey there lovely lady, how's the outfit selection coming along?"

"I miss Cherrie." I whined.

"Is it just the three of us?" I asked, looking at the two of them standing there. Ashley had her curls now in place, and her make up finished to a perfect Ten. But she was still in the boxer shorts she stole from her ex, and the Jimmy Buffett T-shirt she slept in. Hailey was decked out in a strappy, sequin-gold dress that fell only about half an inch below her butt. Her bed-head was raging, and a toothbrush was sticking out of her mouth.

"Steph stayed at Mathew's last night." Hailey mumbled around her toothbrush. "Said she was going to go with him to the frat party."

"Good for her. Do you think she will let me raid her closet?" I asked.

"Come with me, I have something you can borrow." Hails said, and I followed them both down the hall.

Hailey threw open her door and started rummaging through her closet. I sat down on her bed looking at all the photos pinned above her desk, when a green something landed on my head. Then something black landed at my feet, followed by a fire engine red number. I peeled the green crop top from my eyes just as a lacy number wacked me on the nose.

"Hey, careful." I laughed, as I picked this last one up to take a closer look. It was a cute, little, black lace top with a wine-red fabric underneath. Barely-there cap sleeves and a plunging heart neck line that just might look half decent with my push up bra. "I think I like this one, can I go try it on?"

"That's why I threw it at you."

"Thanks Hails."

"Do you want to take any of the others back to your room to try on, just in case?"

"I'll come back if this one doesn't work."

"Cool, see you in like forty-five minutes then. Ash said she is leaving at noon on the dot, with or without us. 'Whup-ah!'" Hailey said, miming the cracking of a whip.

"Well, we better not keep taskmaster Ashley waiting." I laughed. "Thanks again for the shirt." I said, as I headed back to my room and finished getting ready.

***

"Get in the car Bitches!!" Ashley honked from the portico in front of the sorority house. I came tripping out of the door with a little overnight bag, containing some fresh clothes, toothbrush, and Ibuprofen.

"Hails is grabbing us all bottles of water for the drive." I told Ash in response to her exasperated face over the fact that I was the only person to emerge from the house.

"Smart. I suppose I can wait for that."

"Very considerate of you." I teased.

I started getting in the front seat just as Hailey came running through the front doors. Well not really running, in her three-inch stilettos, it was more of a fast shuffle.

"Are you sure about your shoe choice for tonight?" I asked as she fell into the back seat.

"Nope. But I brought a backup pair of sandals."

"Good girl." Ash nodded, turning the key in the ignition. The radio blared to life, as Brittany Spears voice filled the little red Civic, singing 'Hit me Baby one more time.'

"Punch it, Chewie!" I yelled from the front seat, ready to hit the road. But neither of them caught my nerdy Star Wars reference, as Ashley hit the gas and we pulled away and onto our grand one-night adventure.

***

"Okay ladies, we have fifty-six minutes to eat, pee, and shop." Ash commanded.

"10/4 boss. But I think I'm going to skip food. This dress looks better on me when I'm hungry." Hailey commented from the back.

"Dear lord, Hails." Ash rolled her eyes. "You need to eat something or you are going to die of alcohol poisoning by 9:00 pm."

"Fine." She moaned, as we pulled into the In-n-Out parking lot. Three double-doubles and an Animal Style fries to share later, left us with only twelve minutes to shop if we were going to stay on Ashley's timeline. So, we unanimously decided to save the outlets for the drive home, and hopped back in the car for Vegas.

"Okay girls, here's the plan." Hailey announced. "Tonight, let's kiss all the cute boys!" she said, excitement permeating every word.

I laughed, "All of them?"

"As many as we can." She nods. "Or at least make sure we have three cute boys nearby at midnight."

"Let's kiss them all!" Ash agreed. "Come on Ainsley, you've been a prude since you and Jake broke up last year."

"It has only been two months." I corrected.

Two months exactly. Halloween. I was a cat and Jake was a doctor. Unfortunately, I caught him giving a pelvic exam to a slutty nurse only thirty minutes into the party. I haven't really felt like jumping back into the dating pool since then. And with finals and now winter break, it's not like there have been many opportunities knocking on my door. I started to feel my energy darken as feelings of inadequacy reared their ugly head at just the thought of stupid Jake.

"Sorry Ains." Ash looked over at me sympathetically, "Don't let that prick get you down. Tonight is about having fun. Letting your hair down and your boobs out! No strings, no commitments. Just a little making out here and there. You know, sowing some wild oats."

"Can women sow wild oats? Is that really how that saying works? Aren't sperm supposed to be synonymous with the 'Oats'?" Hailey piped up from the back.

We spent the last fifteen minutes of our drive debating oat sowing. But once Ashley hit the turn signal to exit the freeway, we all grew silent.

# 2.

## Vegas

Ainsley:

The sun is still out, but all the lights are on so bright and loud that you can feel the energy of this shining gem from twenty miles away.

"Vegas!"

We all screamed and clapped our hands as we broke the crest of the hill to see the neon city in the distance. Hails stomped her feet in excitement, shaking the back of my chair, both of us laughing.

We made it just before sunset. Stopping at the Welcome to Las Vegas sign, we posed for at least twenty selfies before jumping back in the car to find a safe place to park. Bally's hotel was the spot. Free parking garage right in the heart of the strip. The Bellagio fountains greeted us as we rode down the escalator that dropped us off onto Las Vegas Blvd.

Standing at the corner of LVB and Flamingo, we looked around not sure what to do now that we were here; when a throng of drunk dudes, already stumbling down the sidewalk, passed us. They were carrying three-foot-tall blue drinks with glowing ice cubes.

"I want one of those!" Hails pointed.

Ash didn't miss a beat. "Hey hot stuff," she said, slapping one of the guys on the ass.

He turned, looking ready to punch her, until he noticed her boobs. "Hey baby." he slurred and stumbled slightly.

"Where can my friends and I score drinks like that?" she asked sweetly, batting her eyelashes.

"I'll buy you one for a peek at your boobies."

"I'll need to finish one of those drinks before I do that." She giggled coyly.

"What if I throw in some beads?" he asked, holding up the cheap twenty-plus, plastic bead necklaces hanging around his neck."

"Like I said, I'm not drunk enough for that yet. Actually, I'm 100% sober.  But, if you would be so kind as to tell me where I can buy one of those fancy drinks, then you'll stand a much better chance of seeing my 'boobies'." She replied in a way that seemed to put him in his place while still being flirty.

Ash had mad flirt skills.

"Dude, Brock. Don't be a douse." One of the drunk guys said. "We got them right over there, by that pink umbrella." He pointed.

"Thank you." Ash said giving drunk guy number two her best smile, then flashing him in thanks.

Everyone but Brock saw.

"Aw, baby. I missed it, do it again, come on… I asked first." Brock begged as the other three drunk dudes showered Ash in beads laughing at their friends' mis-fortune.

"I can't believe you flashed them." I whispered as we walked back the way we had come towards the pink umbrella. Ashley divided up the half-dozen beads around her neck and passed them out between the three of us to share.

"You could have gotten a free drink out of it, if you had flashed the first guy." Hails contributed.

"I can buy my own drinks. He was gross, and wouldn't answer my question. I don't reward bad behavior."

"It's important to have standards." I nodded my agreement.

***

The line for three-foot-tall glowing blue drinks was twenty people long and took fifty minutes to get through. In that time, Ash and Hails had both kissed the two guys behind us in line, and were 90% of the way to convincing me to kiss them both too.

It is New Year's Eve after all.

"Just kiss me then." Tyler said, pushing his brother behind him.

This had been their game for the past five minutes. The fact that I was still holding out on kissing either of them, despite my friends, seemed to make me the most desirable woman on the strip in their eyes. The attention felt good. My ego needed the boost after Jake. I wanted to feel free and fun like Ashley and Hailey. But the fear of rejection still lingered enough to keep me from saying, yes.

Tyler and Ben were brothers from Iowa. They started their road trip going to New York City. Then turned their truck around to head for the West Coast, 'cuz, why not? They were cute and funny and seemed like nice, normal guys. And the more they fought over which one of them I should kiss, the more I actually wanted to kiss one of them.

Or both.

It was finally our turn, and all five of us walked up to order together. "Three of the tall blue guys and two of the giant pints of Miller please." Ben said as Tyler handed over his credit card, before we three girls could get a word out.

"That was nice. Thank you." I said turning around to Ben and Tyler with my best smile.

"Aw, Come on Ains, you can give them a better thank you than that." Ash nudged me.

So, I did. My first kiss of the night was with Ben. It was more than a peck on the lips, but no tongue. It was nice.

"That's not how you kiss a girl, Benny boy!" Tyler said, grabbing my hand and spinning me in a circle and into his

~ 14 ~

arms, before practically mauling me. It had the potential to be amazing and romantic. Like something from an '80s movie. But it was just wet and kinda messy. I had to dry my chin when he was finished. Ben was definitely the winner of the brother kissing contest, the three of us agreed as we walked towards the Flamingo hotel.

"Okay, so now that you popped your kissing cherry for the night, you have to play along too, Ains."

"Alright, I guess. What's the game again?" I asked, feeling brave.

"If you see a cute guy, just go up to him and say "Happy New Years" and kiss him. Easy. We will keep count and see who kisses the most guys." Ash said.

"Really, we are still on kissing every cute guy here? There are like a million people here tonight. We will all go home with Herpes."

"Herpes and a good story."

"Ash, you need therapy." I laughed.

"I go to therapy twice a month, thank you. I am very self-aware. Seriously Ainsley, what are you so worried about? It's one night of PG reckless abandon."

"Well, when you put it like that you make me sound like a prude."

"You are a prude!"

"Mean." I pouted.

"True."

"You're not a virgin are you Ains?" Hailey whisper-yelled loud enough to get a laugh from the group passing us.

"No!" I glared at her. "There was Jake."

"So, one?"

"Yeah."

"And you're twenty-one years old?"

"I am."

"You're behind by over half." She rolled her eyes at me.

"What?"

"Ashley's right" Hails chimed in, thumbing her approval of what Ash was saying. "The average is one a year once you lose it."

"Really?" I asked doing the math in my head. 19, 20, 21... Yup, I should at least be over two by now.

After kissing Ben and Tyler, I realized that just a kiss in celebration of the New Year, didn't have to involve emotion. Perhaps this could be a good character-building experience for me. I could get all my rebounds out in one night. Maybe even an interesting study in human mating rituals. I bet I could use this experience for a paper! The nerd in me starts geeking out a little over the idea.

At twenty-one years old, I am still trying to figure out just how to be human. That's why I'm studying anthropology. I think it's interesting how people behave based on the way they were raised and their life experience. I grew up in a bubble. My parents keeping me safe from the outside world and all of the bad influences of MTV and the Simpsons. I never knew what the other kids were talking about, because I wasn't allowed to watch or listen to anything not on PBS.

Moving away to college, I have felt like an alien on a foreign planet. All my friends seem so sure and confident in themselves. They know what they want while I barely know what's out there. I admire their confidence from afar, while I try to fight off the mean little voice in my head that tells me, since Jake found me lacking, every other guy will also.

I wish that little voice would just shut the fucking hell up already. Perhaps I can drown her with this blue cocktail? Which is surprisingly strong, considering it came out of a premade spout.

Despite my trepidations of not fitting in, I was starting to get into the flow of the evening, loosening up, and having fun. Finding my confidence.

"Does that average work for both of you?" I asked.

"Yup. 100% accurate for me." Hails nodded.

"I'm an overachiever." Ash said with a wink.

"What she means to say is she's a slutty, slut, slut." Hails sang skipping backwards in front of us, before crashing into a huge group of like twenty guys.

"Ooof." Boy number one said as he lost his balance and crashed into his friends. Booze went flying ten feet in every direction.

"Fuck man! What was that for?" A small handful of guys turned to look at Hailey. The booze plastering her soaking, wet dress to her young, perky tits, had the boys forgetting their anger quickly, as she bounced on one broken heel.

"You okay sweetheart?" The entire group of guys stopped to appreciate Hailey. She gave a little pout as she bent over to take off her shoes and tossed them in the trash can conveniently located only two feet away.

"Better now. Sorry that I crashed into you all."

"No worries, but you can't walk barefoot out here. There's broken glass everywhere." One of the guys told her.

"Didn't you bring sandals to change into?" I reminded her quietly.

"Yeah, but they are back in the car." Another pout.

"I think I saw a gift shop up the street. I bet you could buy some shoes there." Another one of the guys suggested helpfully.

And just like that, the three of us were absorbed into their group, and all two dozen of us walked into the 300-square-foot gift shop together; in search of size seven sandals.

As we walked into the store, the two stoned cashiers groaned at the onslaught of people bombarding them.

"Okay girls, Hailey whispered to us. Find at least one of these nice boys to pucker up with in a dark corner while we are here." And off she ran towards the apparel. I spent more time talking than kissing, and after twenty minutes, I had learned that our new companions were a group of frat guys from Arizona State. Hailey had picked out some Penis sandals, because they were too funny not to buy, and was now deciding on which shot glass on a chain to purchase. By the time we checked out, Hails and I had each kissed one more boy. Ashley, the overachiever, kissed four.

***

As we all reconvened back out on the street, Ash commanded the group's attention.

"It's a kissing contest Boys! And we three are the judges."

I looked at Hails terrified. But Hailey was nodding along her agreement. So, not wanting to be "The Prude," I nodded too. A few of the guys bowed out, good boyfriends that they were. The rest of the guys puffed out their chest, popped breath mints, or bragged about their tongue skills on other parts of a woman's anatomy.

Before I knew it, the contest had begun and a set of lips were pressing onto mine..., totally distracting me from my nerves.

Wow! Not bad number one.

Number two was a bit more subtle.

Number three used too much tongue, and boy number four tasted like cigarettes.

Number five was so cute, that I was too flustered to even remember the kiss. But I don't think it was anything special.

Before long, they all started blending into each other, and once or twice, I'm not even sure if I opened my eyes up in-between them.

"I think I need some water." Hails said breathlessly, holding the line of guys up and giving me a moment to breathe as well. I peeked to my right to get a preview of the coming attractions, when I got hung up on a pair of blue eyes looking back at me. Embarrassed that he caught me staring, I averted my attention back to Hailey, who was glugging water to my side.

"May I have a sip too?" I asked.

Wiping her lips, she passed me the bottle and yelled out

"Next!" Waving her hand in a 'Come hither' sort of motion. I took a sip, and with a deep breath prepared for the next set of lips, while thinking about the blue eyes two heads down.

Number twelve. (Sigh)

Mr. Blue Eyes stood in front of me and I had to crane my neck back to look up at him, he was so tall. His dark hair was messy in a fun way, with one small lock falling against his eyebrow. His eyes were at least three different shades of blue, with a ring of indigo around the edge. His lips were full, his jawline strong and defined. My eyes were about to take in his biceps when his lips parted and Blue spoke.

"Hi."

It wasn't much, but it was the way he said it. His voice was deep and slow and it slithered into my ears and down my spine. His "Hi" was more than just a greeting. It was an invitation to get to know him. And I really wanted to get to know him. The instant attraction and the chemistry between us were strong.

"Hi." I replied slightly flustered, my voice sounding more high-pitched than I am used to, causing me to realize that he was the first guy to actually speak to me since this contest started. Blue automatically scored bonus points.

"You have really beautiful skin." He said as he trailed a finger from my elbow, up my arm, and over my shoulder. Sliding his hand up my spine and cupping the back of my neck. Compliments get bonus points too, I decided, as his other arm wrapped behind my back. The space between our bodies disappeared, sending hot flashes over my skin.

More points, sooo many more points.

He hadn't even kissed me yet, and he was already the winner.

Mr. Blue eyes, lowered his head to mine. His nose softly slid down the side of mine as his lips inched closer. The kiss started slow, and gentle, and warm against the cool night air. My lips and blood felt like they were on fire, yet chills were running up and down my spine. I felt so much the instant his lips melted into mine that my nervous system must have gone into shock. I was light headed and practically swooning in his arms as his mouth and body consumed every part of my being.

And every other boy fell away from existence.

My hands knotted in his hair, pulling him closer, as I returned his kiss. The butterflies in my stomach taking flight. It felt like he could read my mind with the way his lips pressed against my own with just the right amount of pressure. His tongue… just a touch, promised so much more. His teeth caught my bottom lip and a little moan escaped from somewhere in my soul.

"I think Ainsley found her winner." I heard Hails say. But he didn't stop. We didn't stop. If anything, he held me a little tighter. Kissed me with a touch more desire.

"Dude, don't hog her all to yourself, this is a kissing competition, not a baby making competition." I think I heard from the next guy in line. But Blue's tongue only plundered my mouth with greater need over the interruption. I felt Blue's arm leave my waist to swat at the next guy in line as our making out continued. Making me smile through the kiss and, unfortunately, screw up our flow.

Slowly Blue pulled away, leaving multiple small kisses on my lips. My eyes finally opened, and I breathed for the first time in two months. My hand falling to my chest, atop my pounding heart. 'Calm down heart' I thought, staring into those stunning blue eyes of his. I bit the bottom half of my lip, remembering the feel of his teeth, and doing my best to hold back from kissing him again.

He growled as he stared at my lips, shaking his head in disbelief. The growl was a sexy, deep, wanton sound that went straight between my thighs. I could feel the blush rise from my stomach, up and over my chest to my neck, as it burned my flesh and stained my cheeks. Then he smiled and I stumbled.

Literally. My legs gave out and I fell into him.

Grabbing both my arms to steady me, he whispered warmly in my ear, "I like the way your skin looks when you blush even better." And I think my heart stopped. I know I lost my voice, because I couldn't respond. He gave me one last small kiss, stepped back, and number thirteen moved in to take his place.

Thirteen ended up kissing my cheek, because I turned my head at the last moment to watch Blue walk away.

"Sorry" I apologized, giving myself a little head shake to concentrate on the task at hand. "I was distracted."

He laughed and gave me a light peck on the lips. "I know when I'm beat." And walked off.

The last few guys didn't even register.

Ashley and Hailey both voted for number thirteen. I felt slightly swindled that I had not gotten a real kiss from him, to see just why he was their number one. But then again, I didn't really care. Because, number twelve... Wow! Just thinking about him made me sigh.

He stood towards the back of the crowd as Ashley announced the winners. His eyes were on me every time I looked at him, a small half smile on his face. 'He is so damn sexy' I thought. His tee shirt hugging his biceps and his broad shoulders just tight enough that I could see the shadow of his muscles beneath.

"Coming in third," Ash beat her thighs to create the drama of drums. "Contestant number one!" Boy number one walked out of the crowd, hands above his head, cheering himself on.

"Yeah, go Todd!" "You beast!" and a few other cheers went out in congratulations for Todd. Ash slung some beads over his neck and kissed his cheek.

Laughing. "Look what I earned boys." he held up the beads to his Bros.

"Show us your chest hair!" one of the guys yelled out. Todd lifted the hem of his tee shirt in mock strip tease fashion as he rejoined the group of guys to laughter, applause, and a few loose dollar bills.

"Our second-place winner..., drumroll Hails?" Hailey took over drumming her thighs "Number twelve!"

Like the parting of the Red Sea, the crowd split and Blue walked right up to me. Not up to Ashley as expected for his reward.

Standing in front of me, I took off one of the two strands of beads that Ash had doled out earlier, and hung the blue one around his neck.

"Thank you." he said quietly in that deep, slow voice that made me want to kiss him again. And I really did want to kiss him again. He took my breath away. He was the best kisser I had ever had the pleasure of swapping spit with. I bit my lip in restraint.

"Mmmmm" he sighed, staring at my mouth. A flash of lust shot hot through my veins.

Then there was whooping and hollering and number thirteen walked up to Ashley redirecting my attention from my wet panties.

Did I miss something? Did Ash just announce the winner and I didn't even notice?

Yes, that is exactly what happened.

I was distracted by blue eyes and full lips. A chiseled jawline and a sexy deep voice. I was distracted by memories of his fingers pulling the hair at the base of my skull. The way the flat palm of his hand on the small of my back, held me flush against him. I remember the heat of his hard body, and the touch of his tongue. I can practically feel the way he bit my lip turning my insides to jelly as I still hold my own lip between my teeth. Biting down just hard enough to keep myself from pouncing on him.

"Come on Cody, kiss her goodbye already." Some jerk said from the group. Pulling my eyes away from Blue's for a moment to survey my surroundings, it seemed like the party was over.

Separation imminent.

"Meet me," he said, as the pad of his thumb ever so softly pulled down on my bottom lip, releasing it from my death bite. "Paris at midnight?" His voice was a deep whisper, a secret just for me.

"Yes." I nodded and his lips replaced his thumb and he sucked my lower lip into his mouth. He licked it with the tip of his tongue before gently biting it himself. Like he was testing its plumpness.

My heart raced.

"You should have been the winner." I said breathlessly as he pulled away.

"I didn't kiss your friends the way I kissed you."

Fuck. I have never felt electric like this before. I have never felt like the prize. I'm usually runner up or sitting on the bench. But he makes me feel like I am the best thing he has ever had.

Giving me a slow final kiss, he released me. "I really hope to see you at midnight."

"Me too." I smiled as he jogged backwards a few steps, before turning to catch up with his bros. The girls and I turning to wait for the signal to cross the street to go to the Mirage.

"I can't believe we kissed an entire fraternity of boys!" Ashley beamed.

"It wasn't the entire frat." Hails corrected.

"It will be in the version of the story I tell."

~ 23 ~

"Hey," I interrupted, "can we plan to be in front of the Paris Hotel at Midnight?"

"Is that where number twelve is going to be?" Ashley teased in an ooey gooey, sappy, sing-song way.

"Yeah. He asked me to meet him there."

"He's cute. Good catch Ains." Ash said, seeming pleased with my decision to make out with a cute boy. "Paris at midnight does sound awfully romantic. I'm good hanging there."

"Oh, and it's right across from the Bellagio fountains. I want to see what kind of show they put on for the stroke of midnight. Last year it was killer." Hailey chimed in.

   "Done. Next, the volcano show, at the Mirage." Ash decided as she ushered us across the street along with the other three hundred people trying to cross also.

# 3.

## The Stroke of Midnight

Ainsley:

The street was so jammed packed with people we could barely move. We held hands to make sure we didn't get separated as we pushed through the crowds like a herd of cattle. I'm never going to find him in this. I do my best to remember what he was wearing. Gray? Or was it blue? Blue. God, his blue eyes were gorgeous, I digressed. I open my eyes wide, looking for anyone that might be familiar. Hoping, I might locate him by recognizing one of his Bros.

Inch by inch we move closer to the hotel's center. Yet, nothing.

"Ten minutes till Midnight." We overhear some girls next to us talking, as they check the time on their phones. I don't know where else to go. We are right where we were supposed to meet. But he is not. I looked around in all directions feeling anxious. Wishing that he was by my side so that he could be my first kiss of the New Year. I had been playing along with the kissing game all night, but no one else came close to Blue and the way he made me feel when he looked into my eyes. Like he already knew me and liked me just as I was. I wanted to start off this next year feeling that way. But five minutes later, still nothing.

"Four, three, two, one... Happy New Year!"

Cheers and whoops and the rush of music and water filled the air. The Bellagio's fountains erupted into the night sky, celebrating along with the rest of the crowd. Ashley and Hails were lip locked with whomever, and my eyes were still scanning the crowd for Blue.

But he was not here.

He was lost...

Stuck somewhere in the crowd...

Found someone better...

Or, forgot about me entirely… The mean little voice in my head threw in her two cents too.

***

Time inched by and I still needed a kiss. Silly that after kissing over twenty guys in one night, I still felt the need for another kiss like an addict needs a hit.

Anything to distract me from the slow build of unworthiness.

I turn around and see a familiar face coming towards us. Todd, AKA number One, and hope surges into my chest.

"Penis Shoes! We found you," he yelled out loudly to Hails, drawing the attention of a few bystanders due to the volume he yelled 'Penis'.

He said 'We' He isn't alone, I think with hope.

"Where are you guys at?" Hailey asked as I listened anxiously to his reply.

"Way on the other side. We got stuck in the throngs of humanity." Todd said before hugging Hailey and giving her a fantastic kiss.

"Happy New Years!" he said before slapping his smackers on Ash next, then on me.

Todd was inadvertently my first kiss of the new year instead of Blue.

Bummer. But whatever. I would have felt hurt if he skipped me and I wouldn't want to be rude and decline him.

"Todd, is…." I paused. I didn't know his name. Despite the fact that the volume around us was staggering, the quiet pause as I searched for what to call my new crush, felt loud.

"Number twelve" Hails filled in for me.

I nodded then continued. "Is number twelve down that way too?" I asked shyly.

"I assume so?" The inflection in his voice did not leave me with much confidence, but it was the best lead I had to go on.

~ 26 ~

"We need to get Ainsley laid, so we need to find him." My mouth dropped open in horror as I turned to stare at Ashley.

"That wasn't my goal."

'Wasn't', I had said. The past tense structure of my statement did not go unnoticed.

"No? Well, it's mine. And I'm older and therefore wiser than you. And you need to get some." She pointed at me drunkenly.

I stood there with my arms crossed over my chest, slightly pissed at Ashley. Maybe she's right that I do "need to get some". And if anyone is going to "give it to me", Blue is my choice. But for her to say this in front of one of Blue's frat brothers is humiliating.

"Yeah, Cody won't shut up about her either."

Cody.

Blue is Cody.

Number twelve is Cody.

It seemed like such a little boy name for a man like him. He must be at least 6'3" and there is nothing little boyish about the way he kissed me. Or the way it makes me feel to know that he won't shut up about me either.

Cody.

I try to remember, but I like my nickname for him better, and his name evaporates from my mind as we all pushed our way through the crowd in the direction Todd had come from.

***

Two blisters, two AMF's, and one Long Island Iced Tea later…

I hear my name yelled across the crowd and it wakes me out of my drunken wanderings…

"Aaaaaiiinnnsleyyyyyy!"

I whip my head to the right, scanning the crowd, looking for the man behind that voice. But I don't see him. My imagination perhaps? But as I turn back to my friends there he is. Swaggering up to me with that amazing smile of his, and those brilliant blue eyes shining. My lady bits woke up just looking at him and I felt the blush rise over my skin the closer he neared.

"Hi." I give a dorky little wave of my fingers. But instead of answering me back, his fingers melted into my skin as he pulled me in for a kiss so intense my feet left the earth. I was engulfed into his arms, in a Hallmark Channel, Christmas movie, type of kiss that even had Hails and Ash whooping and hollering.

"Happy New Year." he smiled, allowing my feet to reconnect with the earth.

"Happy New Year." I smile back, giddy to see him again, to kiss him, and feel his warm, hard body pressed against mine.

"I was looking for you before midnight, but there were so many people. We got trapped down by Planet Hollywood for over an hour." He apologized. His fingers playing with a loose lock of hair near my face as a shower of beer splashed us out of our lust filled trance.

After an evening of walking through sweaty, intoxicated humanity, I was filthy. He wiped the beer from my cheek, before tending to his own beer-soaked face.

"I have never wanted a shower more in my life." he laughed.

"Me too." I agreed. Immediately feeling a blush rise to my cheeks, as the image of us naked in the shower popped into my psyche.

"Where are you three staying?" he asked, ignoring the crimson color of my face.

"We're not." I shrugged. "It was a last-minute idea to drive to Vegas. We plan to leave after sunrise to beat the traffic home."

"Oh yeah, where's home?"

"Southern California."

He nodded. "You don't really look like a SoCal girl."

"No? What does a SoCal girl look like?" I asked intrigued.

"Like your friends."

I looked over at Hails and Ash, blond hair on them both. Tan skin, big boobs, 100% put together, excluding Hails Penis shoes. Overall, he was right. They were the epitome of the So Cal Girl stereotype.

Me…, I'm a little more average. Brown hair, brown eyes, average height, average build. I know I'm some kind of mutt when it comes to the genetic pool. But I was adopted, so I don't know my background. There is something beyond Anglo in here if my skin tone, bone structure, and the angle of my eyes has a say in the matter.

"Where would you guess I'm from?" I asked, enjoying the game.

"Hmmmmm," he thought…. "New Zealand."

"Wow. I was expecting you to say Texas or something more Stateside. I'm not even sure what someone from New Zealand looks like."

"Maybe Polynesia? Or Brazil."

"I don't think I have the curves to be Brazilian."

"I love your curves." He whispered in my ear. His hand sliding up my back, then down again. Following the shape of me from my waist to my hip.

He loves my curves. Dear Lord! My heart fluttered.

His fingers led to a chill that I could not hide, and a notable shiver ran up my spine. He gave me a cocky half smile in response and pulled me closer. "You're beautiful." He whispered, deep and low.

He thinks I'm beautiful, my mind buzzed dizzily.

I was at a loss for words. So, I kissed him.

Perfection.

The kiss blocked out the sounds of the people all around us. I knew nothing in that moment except for the feel of his mouth on mine. The way his tongue tasted on my lips. The feel of him, as he skimmed the edge of my teeth, teasing my tongue into his mouth where I could explore too. We were so in sync, it felt like magic. There was no knocking of teeth or slobbery chins. There were only lips, and tongues, and necks, and earlobes. My left hand wrapped in a fist around his T-shirt, while my right, held fast onto his nicely chiseled bicep. Just in case my legs gave out on me again. I pulled him closer with every kiss. Unable to get enough of him as my temperature rose, blocking out the cold night air.

We made out on the street, people shuffling around us, oblivious to all for God knows how long. It was not long enough.

***

"Hey man, we are headed back. You two coming?"

Some guy shook Blue's arm pulling him out of our make out session.

"What?" he asked frat boy number twenty-something, in a bit of a daze.

"We are headed back to the motel, you two coming or are you going to keep making out in the middle of the street?"

Blue looked into my eyes. The pad of his thumb traced the outline of my lower lip. "Come back with me?" he asked in that slow deep voice that gave me a fever.

"Yes." I said before thinking.

"Wait, where's Ash and Hailey?" I questioned as I looked around for my friends.

"Penis Shoes is making out with Todd. The other girl already went back to the Motel with Chris." Number twenty-something chimed in.

"Who's Chris?" I asked, suddenly nervous for my friend all by herself with a strange guy.

"Don't worry, I got his driver's license." Hails pipped up from behind me.

"Oh good." I released a heavy sigh of breath, along with the worry.

"What's that you have?" Blue asked Hails from over my shoulder, as she waved Chris Jenson's Arizona State Driver's License in the air proudly.

"It's our security measure," she answered. "If one of our sisters wants to go home with a guy, we make him give us his Driver's License. Or some other important form of ID with his name and picture on it. He doesn't get it back until we get our friend back, safe and sound."

"That's cool. Chris is a good guy. She'll be safe with him." Blue reassured us.

"Hails, what do you want to do?" I turned to ask her.

"I'm cold and wouldn't mind going back with the guys."

"Todd and I can switch rooms." number twenty-something said. "That way you girls can crash together."

"Wow, That's really nice of you. Thanks." Hailey beamed.

"No worries. It's nice that you girls look out for each other." He shrugged walking away.

~ 31 ~

Blue took my hand and we followed the guys up the road a block. Then, we turned down a side street and crossed a dirty parking lot.

"We're here!" Boy Twenty-whatever, announced proudly.

The outside of the little motel looked like something from a horror film and the inside felt like falling back in time into the 1970's. Everything was orange and mustard yellow. But there was a bathroom with running water and two queen sized beds. And it was warm.

"I'm about to pee myself!" Hails moaned. "May I get first dibs on the bathroom please?"

"Go for it." Todd said. "I'm going to run over to the other room and trade my stuff with Nate while you're in there. Be right back." He said, kissing her cheek, before heading out the door behind Nate. (Aka Twenty-something/whatever.)

And with the slamming of two doors, Blue and I were alone.

"Do you want to use the bathroom once she's done?"

"Sure, Thanks. What to make out in the meantime?" I asked, feeling confident.

"Hell yes!" he grinned. Holding my face in both of his hands, he studied me for what felt like an eternity, but was probably no more than two seconds. Then the outdated 1970's room disappeared as the warm pressure of his kiss replaced its image with that of fireworks in my mind.

Stumbling into the dresser he twisted us, pressing my back against the wall. His hands weaving through my hair at the base of my neck, protecting me from bonking my head against the door. My hands moved to his ass as I pulled him closer. Excited to feel his length bonk against me. One of his hands scratched down my back, pulling me tighter against him, and my head buzzed pink. I could feel his hardon through his jeans pressing into my hip, and my legs went all tingly and my fingertips turned numb. All the blood drained from my brain down to my lady bits in a shot of desire that felt so good I moaned out loud. He growled a low instinctual sound from

~ 32 ~

deep within his bones in response. The vibration reverberated through my soul, making me sizzle in anticipation and lust.

In a rush, he lifted me off my feet and we spun onto the bed, tumbling in a mess of limbs. His tongue found mind and we had an entire conversation without words. Our bodies seemed to know their own ancient language, without the need of our brains or the alphabet.

"Ainsley." He whispered in my ear. "You're the best kisser."

Another compliment. More points. I was about ready to let him turn in all of those points for a prize when the door to the bathroom opened and Hailey came stumbling out.

"Get a room, you two." She teased.

"You're in our room." Blue countered back.

"So, I am." Hailey shrugged. "Todd's not back yet?"

"Nope."

She pouted.

"Ainsley, did you want to use the bathroom?" Blue asked me.

God, I loved the way he said my name. Like he's tasting it.

"Yea, I do, but I'm also really comfy right now." I wiggled into his arms a little closer and kissed his jaw. The stubble of his 3:00 am shadow was tickly against my lips. So, with one finger, I returned the tickle, drawing a line from his jaw down his throat. Ending in the little divot between his collarbones. I was rewarded by his shiver. Feeling triumphant, I pulled myself off the bed and moved into the bathroom.

After the best pee of my life, I thoroughly washed my hands for well over twenty seconds. I was grossed out by the color the water turned as the muck of the city washed from my hands down the drain. I avoided looking in the mirror, until after washing my face and every other bit of exposed skin I could with a fast sponge bath. A quick glance revealed a mess of hair that looked like it had just been in a bed making out with a really hot guy. I gave myself a wink and blew myself a kiss in the mirror. Proud of myself for getting out of my shell a little.

I pulled out the hair clips keeping the shorter layers of my hair out of my eyes, and did my best to give it a finger comb. Spying a travel sized toothpaste, I thieved a little onto my finger and gave myself a fast tooth scrub. I looked at myself in the mirror and adjusted my boobs before walking back out to continue my make-out session with the hot boy.

Todd was back and already under the covers in the far bed with Hails, lip locked. Blue was leaning back against our headboard, his legs stretched out long. He had removed his shoes and was now wearing sexy, black-rimmed, nerd glasses. A book in his hands.

He's a reader too! (Squeeee) My heart jumped. This new dreamy side to him revealed, I started imagining our white picket fence and 2.5 children.

"What are you reading?" I asked quietly as he removed his glasses and placed his book on the nightstand. His eyes, never once leaving mine.

"I can't remember. Come here."

My heart did somersaults as I walked towards the bed. He crooked his finger at me and I crawled onto his lap, straddling his legs. His hands ran down my ribs resting on my hips. His eyes caught up on my breast and I was grateful for my last-minute straightening and plumping the girls. He bent his head and his kisses ran along my cleavage and up to my collar bone. His tongue snaking up the side of my neck before settling in my mouth.

*Sparks*

"You taste different." He mumbled before taking a proper taste of my tongue. "You brushed your teeth." He kissed me again. "I need to brush mine too. Don't fall asleep while I'm gone." He flipped us so that I was now backside to the bed. With a kiss and a wickedly sexy smile, he disappeared into the bathroom.

Wow, he's hot.

~ 34 ~

I exhaled so loud Hails and Todd both stopped kissing to look over at me annoyed.

"Sorry." I squeaked and they threw the covers over their heads to continue making out.

Rolling over towards the night table, I picked up his book to read the cover. 'Enders Game' by Orson Scott Card. A classic Sci-Fi. I've read at least a dozen of the author's books. I flipped it open to see what part he was on and started reading, getting lost in the familiar story until the door to the bathroom opened again.

Blue smiled at me reading his book as he exited the bathroom. "Have you read it before?" he asked quietly.

"Yes."

"You like to read Sci-Fi?"

"I like to read everything." I smiled up at him.

His look became lustful as he plucked the book from my hand and placed it back on the nightstand. The bed creaked and I angled into his side as he sat down next to me. "Ainsley the reader. What else should I know about you."

"What do you want to know?"

"Everything."

But he didn't let me tell him anything, because he was already kissing me again.

Sliding under the covers our hands roamed along each other's bodies. Every touch sent sparks of electricity coursing through my veins. My fingers slid under his shirt and traveled over the hard muscles of his abs and pecks. I pulled up at his tee, hungry for the feel of his body against mine. "Off." I commanded in a whisper. Like some kind of contortionist, he stripped off his shirt in an instant, returning the weight of his body to mine before I even had the chance to miss it. He was in even better shape than I imagined. His abs...

Oh my God. (Drool)

Every muscle was defined and hard. I ran my fingertips over the dips and creases of his stomach and chest. Blown away that this Adonis of a man wanted me.

Slowly his lips trailed kisses down my neck and along the swell of my breast. His fingers barely skimmed over my nipples as his mouth continued south. He kissed me over my blouse and down to the button of my jeans, where his fingers stopped to play with the hem of my shirt. Slowly, he inched it up just enough to weave little figure eights on my stomach with his thumbs.

"Off?" He asked politely.

I was not as smooth. And after a small struggle, he helped me sit up slightly, as he slowly peeled my lacy, little top over my head.

"Holy fuck, you're gorgeous." He whispered, before he readjusted the blanket over our heads. Both his hands cupped my breast over my lacy black bra, as he lowered his head to my stomach. He kissed a line starting at my belly button, moving hot and slow up between my cleavage, leaving a small chaste kiss over each nipple.

I shuttered. I may have even blacked out for a moment. There was no longer blood going to my brain. He made me dizzy and we were only at second base.

The unmistakable sound of sex arose from the creaking bed springs next to us. "Are they?" I asked in a hushed whisper.

"Yeah, I think so." He chuckled a little "Don't let what they are doing pressure you beyond your comfort level, okay?" He whispered as he brushed a stray strand of hair off my face.

He was too good to be true. If this was some kind of reverse psychology, it was working. Our mouths and bodies subconsciously fell into sync with the rhythm of the bed springs, as we kissed, and fondled, and groped at one another in dry humping perfection.

Rolling on top of him, I took my turn exploring his chest and abs with my mouth. My tongue tracing the lines of his muscles, down to that sexy little crease next to his hip bone. Hooking my finger through his belt loop, I tugged down the corner of his jeans, just enough, to give me access to that little hollow besides his hip. He inhaled a sharp breath as I sucked just hard enough to leave a little purple mark. His fingers pulling my hair and digging into my shoulder in response.

"I left a little mark, right here." I said, sliding back up his body. My finger circled the spot, just inside his hip, over the hickey. "I hope when you see it tomorrow, it reminds you of tonight."

"Mmmm," he growled. "I don't need anything to remind me of tonight." His breath was warm against my ear as he nibbled my lobe and pulled my hips tight against his. Intensifying the feel of him long and hard pressed against the heat between my thighs. I rolled my hips into him; my body hungry for more. Starving for more.

His hands slid along the small of my back and he flipped me. His lips falling to the same spot on my body that I had just left the hickey on him. I moaned and arched into his tongue as a ripple of want flashed hot throughout my body. His fingers grabbed at my hips, pulling me closer to him, like he wanted to devour me.

I certainly wanted him to.

There were some very sexy sounds, and maybe a little cussing, as Blue left his mark on me too.

The sounds of sex from the bed next door ceased and was soon replaced by snoring. Our kisses slowed down too. Soon we were starting to drift off in one another's arms, waking every few minutes to kiss some more, then dozing off again to soft caresses.

# 4.

## January 1st

Ainsley:

"Ains." I was being shaken. "Ainsley, wake up." Hails urgently whispered.

I opened only one eye and took in Hailey's disheveled appearance as last night poured into my consciousness. There was Man snuggled up against my back, and one warm Man arm wrapped over my waist. I did not want to get up.

"Go away." I moaned.

"Ash called. Her guy needs his ID. He is leaving this morning too. And we need to get on the road if we want to beat traffic home."

"I don't like you or Ashley very much at the moment." I moaned as I ducked my head under the sheet.

"Too bad. Get up." Hailey pulled the blanket back off my head.

"Fine." I groaned as I slithered out of Blues arms trying not to wake him. I took a moment to appreciate the half-clad Man that I nearly had a one-night stand with. Perhaps I'll refer to him as my half-night stand. Even unconscious he was cute. I picked up my top from the floor and ran to the bathroom to pee and freshen up before leaving.

Ten minutes later and Ash and Hails were at the door ready to leave. Bending down, I gave Blue a soft kiss on the cheek. Not really wanting to wake him, but still wanting him to wake up.

"I have to leave." I whispered.

His eyes kinda half fluttered open and then closed again. A goofy closed mouth smile sliding across his face. "Bye" he said, waving and kissing the air as his head fell back to the pillow.

Wow. That lack luster goodbye killed so much of the magic from last night. I'm mentally thrown off balance, as the hope of being pulled back into his arms for a final amazing kiss evaporated.

Standing up quietly, I surveyed the room one last time, making sure I had everything.

ID. Card. Cash. Shoes…

I picked up my earrings lying next to Blue's book on the night stand and slipped them back in my ears. I didn't even remember taking them off last night. But all of the other memories from last night I do remember, as they flood back into my mind with a heated rush.

"Ains, let's go." Ash encouraged me, as I stared off into space.

I gave him one last kiss on the forehead, then we left.

# 5.

## Hungover and Alone

Cody:

I woke to an empty bed.

Sitting up with a start, I looked to the bathroom searching for a sign of her. But it was dark and empty. I scanned the room in a panic realizing she was gone. I searched the nightstand for a note with her number. I check the floor, then under the pillow. I stood up to search through the blankets, accidentally waking Todd in the bed next to me.

"You're not going to find her under the bed. The girls left early this morning." he said groggily.

"She didn't say goodbye?"

"She did. I think you waved and blew her a kiss, then fell back to sleep."

"Shit." I ran my hand through my tangled hair, dismayed.

"Did she leave her number somewhere?"

"I don't know?"

"Did you get Hailey's number?"

Todd stared at me with a dumb, blank look. "Who? Do you mean, Penis shoes?"

"Yeah."

"Nah."

"Do you know if Chris got Ashley's?"

"No idea Dude. He already left too."

I crashed back on the bed burying my face in the pillow with a groan of frustration. Ainsley the reader from Southern California. I hardly knew anything about her, yet the chemistry between us was so magnetic that the loss of her feels like the loss of a limb.

I hurt.

"There is Gatorade in the mini fridge and some Tylenol in the bathroom to help with the hangover." Todd offered.

"Thanks." I said, taking a deep breath and moving to the bathroom to piss and consume pain meds.

"Did you fuck her?" Todd asked just before I closed the door.

"No." I rolled my eyes, annoyed at him for being a dick.

"That sucks man. With all the sounds coming from over there, I thought you were getting some too."

"Actually, it was perfect exactly as it was." I said, shutting the door before he had a chance to say anything else.

I closed my eyes and exhaled as a knot of grief formed in the pit of my stomach.

Or perhaps it's alcohol poisoning? I felt sick over the idea of never seeing her smile again, or never hearing that laugh of hers again. After meeting Ainsley, I now believed in love at first sight. I had never felt an instant connection like that before. She had this magic air of wonder about her, just under the surface, that seems ready to explode. That light of hers, I wanted to be the one to catch it from the moment I overheard her talking with my buddy Nate in the gift shop. I could tell she was smart, and funny, and a rare kind of beautiful within moments. Knowing now that she reads sci-fi too, not typical of most girls I meet, makes me wonder what other secrets hide inside that beautiful head of hers. I wish I knew more about her.

I crave more Ainsley.

I think back to the way she was shy around the others, restrained. But she was confident with me. Like I alone held the key that could unlock her. She makes me feel... fuck, she makes me feel amazing and dizzy.

Or once again, perhaps that's alcohol poisoning.

Turning on the shower, I stripped off my jeans and was greeted by her little love mark, just to the left of my dick. All her little sounds and moans came flooding back to my mind in a rush of memory. I inhaled a sharp breath, tingles running up my spine, at the thought of her hands and lips on my skin. Finding light scratches along my shoulders, flashbacks bloom, of her nails along my back, as I returned the favor of the hickey.

Her teeth on my neck...,

Her lips...,

Her tongue...,

Fuck..., the way she kissed me.

My cock was at full attention.

I whacked off in the shower with memories of last night, and the imaginings of Ainsley, the reader from Southern California, in the shower with me. Wishing to hell that I had woken up enough to pull her back in bed and tattoo her number onto my arm.

***

Ainsley:

Traffic was nothing other than a cluster-fuck on our twelve-hour drive home. Seemed like everyone had the same idea of leaving early. Our biggest mistake was stopping at the outlets on our way home. Traffic caught up with us in the two hours we were shopping, and it was bumper to bumper, going no more than fifteen miles per hour, until we hit civilization again. But last night was 100% worth the cramp in my back from sitting so long in the car.

Once we finally parked, I stumbled from the parking lot on Jello legs, into the house, and fell into bed. I didn't even change my clothes. I woke up at 3:00 am dying of thirst and needing the bathroom. I decided I also really needed a shower. So, I grabbed my towel and jammies and started to prepare to go to bed.

Still half asleep, I only turned on the low lights in the bath as I brushed my teeth, then hopped in the shower. The hot water felt so good, I thought about just sleeping the rest of the night under the warm stream of water. But alas, that would be wasteful. So, I grabbed the shampoo and started cleaning off all the gross left over from Vegas.

Closing my eyes, I relived last night in order. From the moment I first caught those blue eyes looking at me from down the kissing line, to his head between my legs marking my hip. His hands on my ass pulling me against his tongue.

Fuck.

Looking down at myself, I found the little mark he left, and all the pent-up sexual energy came rushing back. Touching myself, I imagined my hand was Blue's hand. And I came hard, wishing I had remembered to leave him my phone number.

# Part Two

## Twenty-five Years Later

# 6.

## Cruise'n & Crush'n

Cody:

Do you ever think about what could have been? Since becoming single again, I have hunted down every one of my old girlfriends and love interests of the past, to see if maybe our timing is better now. Hoping that we have both grown and evolved, and might complement one another better. Wanting to give every opportunity a second chance.

But those were all a bust.

That is why I find myself standing in the boarding line for a singles cruise to Mexico. Five days and four nights of opportunity. Just in recent years, I have started traveling by myself. It was hard at first. Lonely not having anyone to share an exciting experience with. Then I joined a travel club and discovered this balance between group and solitary traveling. But this is my very first singles event where the goal is to meet someone. Or at least get laid. I'll take both if I can.

I scan the people around me who are my travel companions for the next few days. Not everyone here is a part of my group. There is a huge mix of people from all over the globe ready to enjoy a Mexican vacation. Families, young couples, old couples. Oh…, a bachelorette party. And it looks like the bachelor party across the room has already spotted them.

I smile as memories of my youth flood back to me. Stopping at highlights during my post grad life, my frat years, and high school. Picking out a few favorite memories from the different eras of my life. But there is one memory that I spend a little longer with. The one that got away. Ainsley the reader.

I was never able to find her. I was surprised to find just how popular her name was. Maybe it's a California thing? When my web search presented me with 40,000 listings for the name Ainsley, I shut the computer. I went back to Vegas for New Years the following year with my frat brothers. I waited in front of the Paris hotel, just like we had planned at midnight, just in case. But if she was there, I never found her.

Not even my late wife of eighteen years and I had the kind of chemistry I felt with her that night. Which makes sense I suppose, considering we only got married because I knocked her up on the fourth date. But we were good together, and had fun together, and she was an amazing mother to our son, Austin. Perhaps, I have given Ainsley's memory so much weight because it ended unfinished. Maybe it was the magic of Las Vegas, or because it was New Years and we were both drunk. I've tried convincing myself that I have built the memory of her kiss up to be greater than it was; creating an impossible standard. But I don't think so. After a few hours of therapy, I've come to accept that our night together was just as it was meant to be. Not all love stories have to end in 'happily ever after'. But that doesn't stop me from daydreaming about bumping into her one day. Picking back up right where we left off.

Then I see her. I know it's not really Ainsley the reader. It's just my mind constructing her potential in a woman similar in height, build, and coloring. There is some scientific name for the phenomenon, but I don't remember it. I watch her walk across the lobby pulling her suitcase behind her because she is pretty. Not because I hope she is a ghost from my past.

She seems to be traveling alone too, and hope flairs in my chest. She turns around and smiles at the worker who takes her boarding souvenir photo and a flash of déjà vu hits me hard when she smiles.

I feel it right in my chest.

Maybe it is her, flashes through my mind. But I don't allow myself to dwell on the idea as I continue watching her.

"Next"

I shuffle my bag forward and check in. Distracted. Thoughts of Ainsley the reader, slipping from my mind as I present my ticket and passport. I received my boarding pass and a rainbow of wrist bands announcing my participation in the singles group, my open bar band, and cruise ID. I then make my way across the lobby. Skipping the souvenir boarding photo, I join the slow shuffling line onto the gang plank and up to the ship.

***

Opening the door to my tin can room, I dump my bag on the bed and move to the balcony. I take in the view of the San Pedro Harbor, looking south to Long Beach, and beyond. It's a beautiful day, so after unpacking and freshening up, I head up to the pool level to get a drink. A Mariachi band plays at one end, and the cruise director organizes a trivia game at the other. I find a spot right in the middle, where I have a great view of the comings and goings, and people watch for a few moments before checking in one last time with my kid.

> Cody: "Sipping my first beer on the pool deck. Don't forget to walk, feed, and water the dog twice a day or she will mess in the closet."

> Cody: "Don't throw any raging parties. Love you."

> Austin: "If I don't feed and water the dog, she won't be able to leave a mess in the closet."

> Cody: "Smart ass"

> Austin: "My ass is one of my best features"

I laugh out loud. Austin came out to me when he was fifteen years old. But I've known since he was about seven that he was gay. I could not love him more or imagine him any other way. He took my wife's death extremely hard. Until then, he thought she was the only one who knew his secret. Now, he is so far out of the closet it's hard to remember the time before. Austin likes to consider himself 'Flaming'. He and Vanessa had so much in common, their love of old movies and musical theater especially. I must be honest; I was grateful once Austin was old enough to take my place as my wife's date to some of those shows. But after her death, I kicked myself for not making their party of two, our party of three more often.

> Cody: "I love you kid. I'll check my email twice a day if you need me."

Austin: "Don't. I won't. And I promise that Fluffs will still be alive and your closet will be urine free when you get home."

Cody: "Fluffs and I appreciate it."

Cody: "Thanks again for ditching your bachelor pad to house sit for me."

Cody: "Love you."

Austin: "Stop texting me and go find my new Mommy!"

I was laughing out loud again.

Austin is the one who suggested the singles cruise to me. He said, I seem lonely since he has been off at college. And he is right. After Nessa died, raising Austin consumed me. Now that he has been out of the house for two years, the void that his laughter and light have left, has been depressing. That is what got me traveling. It was easier when I was not at home, to forget that I was alone.

Looking up, I notice another blue singles wristband on an older gentleman who looks to be in his eighties. I both admired him and prayed I would never become him. Alone in the twilight of life. But who knows, maybe he has some little blue pills to match that wrist band, and is just here for the horny old ladies. He looks like a ladies' man, I decide the more I study him, constructing a pretend history for the man.

Another blue wristband steals my attention from my game of pretend identities. This face, I recognize.

Brent.

One of my new travel buddies and closest friends. We met on my first group trip to Australia, nearly two years ago. Brent is from Canada and now lives in Chicago. He does something with hedge funds in the Cayman Islands. Or he did, until he sold out to his partner ten years ago, after a heart attack changed his viewpoint on his priorities. It's funny how the threat of death has the power to bring you back to life. When I mentioned to him that Austin had talked me into booking a singles cruise, he jumped at the opportunity and booked the trip too.

I stand to catch his attention, calling his name across the ship. "Brent!" I wave, as he smiles and walks over to join me. Clapping me on the back in his version of a Bro hug. "When did you get in?" I ask as he takes the seat across from me.

"Just this morning, Mate. The time change worked in my favor and I was able to catch an early morning flight in and shuttle directly to the ship. I boarded right at noon." he says, before taking a swig of his beer. "How 'bout you?"

"I've only been on board for about half an hour. What's good so far?" I ask.

"The Cerveza is cold, the girls are pretty, the weather is two hundred percent better than back home. So, I would say everything." he grins.

"Have you checked the itinerary yet?"

He nods, "There's a speed dating meet 'n' greet at 9:00 pm tonight."

"Have you ever done one of these singles cruises before? How awkward should I be prepared for this to be? How much liquid encouragement do you think we may need before speed dating tonight?"

"Ha! It's my first too, Mate." He says slapping his knee. "There is a neat pub style bar off the Baja deck. Want to meet there at 8:45 pm for a few shots of whiskey courage, then hit the party?"

I smile when he calls me 'Mate', a habit he held onto from Australia. "Sounds like a good plan." I agree

"Oh! look Shirley, more blue wristbands." We hear. Looking up to greet a group of elderly ladies in red hats and purple dresses, I smile in polite greeting. I can just imagine the older gentleman from earlier with a pair on each arm later tonight.

"Ladies." Brent tips his imaginary hat at them, and they giggle like school girls.

"Hope to see you handsome young men tonight at the meet 'n' greet." one of the ladies says.

"Wouldn't miss it." Brent replies, as they walk off towards the other end of the ship.

"Brent, please tell me you've seen a few blue wrist bands under the age of seventy?"

"Oh yeah, I've seen a few lookers."

"Thank goodness."

"You know Cody, there is a lot to be said for experience." He winks.

Brent has about five years on me, but those ladies are still old enough to be his mother. "Brent, you know I'm not one to shy away from trying new things, but the Mrs. Robinson fantasy has never really been one of mine."

"Suit yourself." he shrugged, carrying on about the benefits of experience. But I was only half listening as Ainsley the reader's doppelganger catches my eye. She is wearing a little yellow sundress with white flowers. The breeze from off the ocean ruffles the skirt around her thighs. I lose track of what Brent is talking about, as my attention focuses in on her long bronze legs.

"I'm guessing she is more your style?" Brent's words permeate my thoughts.

"One hundred percent." I reply without looking back at him. "She looks like a girl I knew a lifetime ago in Vegas."

I see a flash of blue on her wrist and my heart soars. She walks over to the other end of the ship and joins a woman lounging on one of the chaises. Her friend hands her one of two fancy drinks with pineapples and strawberries kebabbed on the straw, and I watch as she takes a sip before an animated conversation between the two women begins. I wish we were close enough that I could hear her voice. I wonder if I would recognize the sound of her. I swear her moan is etched

~ 51 ~

into my permanent memory. I watch her laugh at something her friend says and strain to catch the sound over the band. I know I would recognize her laugh if I could hear it.

"Wanna go over and see if it's her?" Brent asks me.

"No, not yet." I say taking a slow swig of my beer. I wasn't sure I was ready to let my dream of her being Ainsley the reader die just yet. My mind feels a bit too discombobulated at the moment, to hold a coherent conversation anyway. I don't think I would know what to say to her if it really was her.

'Hey, that night in Vegas was one of the best memories of my life, Can I have your number?'

Would she even remember me?

"Then, may I suggest you stop staring like some stalker. Although her friend is pretty cute too." Brent nudges my arm.

I finally take an evaluating look at her companion and can appreciate what Brent sees. She is very pretty, with lots of blond hair and big boobs. She reminds me of Charlize Theron a little.

"You can have the brunette, and I'll go for Blondie over there. Come on, let's go see if they want to team up for the trivia game." Brent suggests. Never one to let an opportunity slip by him.

Still staring at them, I try to decide if half a beer is going to give me enough bravado to introduce myself to a complete stranger. Or re-introduce myself to Ainsley, the one who got away, when her eyes lock on mine and she gives me a little smile. My heartbeat quickens with that smile, and it gives me all the confidence I need.

"Okay." I say, taking another swig from my bottle and scooting my chair back to stand.

"Brilliant!" Brent stands too, collecting his Corona as we start to walk across to the ladies. But we only make it about three steps before three other men, also with stupid blue wristbands, take our intended place next to them. Chatting them up, just as we had planned.

"Damn, looks like we were too slow this time." Brent says, as we both look at each other, then back at our little table which still sits vacant.

"Want to go play the trivia game anyway?"

"Yeah, let's go."

We pass by, and I smile when I catch her attention. It may be my imagination, but I think I see a little light of recognition in her eyes too.

Maybe.

# 7.

## Meditating on Making-out

Ainsley:

"The speed-dating event starts in an hour. Do you think we should head back to our rooms soon to start getting ready?"

"Yeah, good idea. Let me just finish the last of my lava flow real fast." Sarah says, grabbing her drink and slurping down the final third in one long suck from her straw.

"I'm nervous. What are you going to wear tonight?" She asks me as we walk back to our rooms to prepare for our first singles event of the cruise.

"I planned on my floral cocktail dress for tonight."

"The magenta and orange one?"

"That's the one." I nod.

"I love that dress on you. The colors bring out your tan."

"Thanks." I smiled at her. My bestie Sarah has three inches on me, given by the grace of God. And another three inches from the nock-off Mui Muis she is wearing.

"Hair up or down?" she asks.

"Down I think."

"So, more casual tonight?" she questions.

"Ummm, maybe? I guess? I've never been to a singles event like this before either, you know." I smirk at her. "I suppose I was thinking of giving a visual of who I am with my outfit tonight. I love nature, thus the floral dress. And I'm a barefoot, hair down kind of girl, versus ball gowns and diamonds. I'm hoping to attract someone with the same interest and relaxed energy."

"Oh, that's so clever. Men are very visual creatures. Why didn't you reveal this plan to me while we were packing?"

"Oy, sorry, Sarah." I laugh. "Well, what are your options for tonight?"

"I brought my light purple cocktail dress, and I have a flirty black skirt, and silk ivory blouse."

"Oh, wear the purple dress. That one is so pretty against your blond hair. And the color is fun. Black and white doesn't suit your personality anymore."

"Thank goodness for that." She nods. "But I am a girl who likes diamonds, so I'm going to bling it up a little bit."

"As you should." I agree.

We get to our rooms, deciding to arrive at the speed-dating event a little early to make sure we can grab tables close to one another.

As I move to the tiny bathroom to wash my face, I think about what I told Sarah. How I hope to meet someone who enjoys the same things that I do. Is that silly of me? To hope to find a real connection on a four-day, hook-up cruise? Maybe it is silly. But it's what I've been meditating on since Sarah presented this idea to me a few months ago. Ever since, I've been daydreaming about meeting someone who will want to go for hikes and who will enjoy exploring nature with me. Someone to go to music festivals with, and ride roller coasters with. Someone to snuggle up next to on the sofa and watch old movies with. Someone to do adult things with..., I release a long-winded sigh.

Man, I'm lonely. I miss that zing that a romantic relationship provides. I really miss it now that I'm in my early forties. My over active libido is proof that what they say about a woman's hormones when she hits forty is 'Hella' true. I eat romance novels these days. And I wouldn't mind trying out some of the positions I've read about with a real human male instead of just my vibrator and imagination. But I have never been the vacation fling type. I usually need some kind mental or energetic connection before I am ready to move things to the naked level.

I feel my cheeks turn pink, as my memory flashes back to my half-night stand, on New Years in Vegas, so many years ago.

Blue. I exhale a sigh.

That was a chemical connection from the moment we locked eyes. I want more of that in my life again too.

I close my eyes for a moment, remembering his kiss, and chills ripple down my spine from just the reliving of it in my mind.

Mmmm, I need to spend time meditating more of that kind of mind blowing chemistry into my life; I decide, as I apply my moisturizer and make up. I dream about my 'Dream Man' with the blue eyes, as I zip up my dress and put on my shoes. I'm excited and optimistic when Sarah raps her knuckles against my door, letting me know it's time to leave.

"Are you ready for this?" she asked me.

"Sure am. Let's go!"

# 8.

## Infused with Confidence.

Cody:

I'm not ready for this.

I get to the pub a little before 8:45 pm. Arriving before Brent, I grab a seat at the bar and order three shots of Jameson. I hit one while I waited.

I don't have to wait long.

"Looking good Mate." Brent slaps my back, then grabs his shot to cheer me, before sitting down.

"You're one behind." I warn him. So, he orders another as we let the booze infiltrate our veins.

"You ready to do this?"

"Nope. But, it's now or never." I reply, stretching as I stand up. I enjoy the buzz that zips to my brain with the change in elevation, thanks to the two shots of Jameson.

"Ha, I'm stoked. What are you nervous about anyways? You've dated since...." He didn't finish. Well, he did finish I guess, considering he stopped talking.

That was all he really needed to say.

"I know, it's not that. I'm nervous that the woman from the deck this afternoon is the same girl I once knew in Vegas. I'm also nervous that she's not."

Brent gives me this quirky half smile, like he is trying to figure out what I mean. "Good night, was it?"

I answered him with my eyes, and with my eyebrows, and with a long exhale that I didn't mean to have escaped my mouth. "She has been my number one naughty fantasy for the past twenty-five years."

"Fuck Mate."

"Right?"

"Well, let's go see if it's her. And if it's not, maybe this new woman is even better."

"Doubtful, I don't think any woman is capable of living up to that memory."

"Dude," he says, pulling away from me. "Don't be like that."

I slap my hands down on the bar. "Fuck, you're right." I shake my head. I shake out my hands, wiggle each foot, casting off the bad mojo flowing through my veins. I give my whole body a little shake and imagine bad mood dust falling from my skin, to the floor.

Brent laughs, "Better?"

I nod, "Yup, let's go."

# 9.

## Three Minutes of Bliss

Cody:

The event was in a little cocktail lounge that held two dueling pianos. Small round tables for two were scattered all around the room. Most of them were already filled with single women, while the men waited awkwardly around the bar. Two cruise staff members greeted us with champagne as we checked in.

"Welcome, let's get you both name tags. We are about to begin." the little brunette said. "We just need first names. And there is a spot, 'here', if you would like to include where you are from. It's a good ice breaker." she encouraged. Brent and I picked up pens and completed our badges; slapping them onto our chest. We both declined the Champagne and went to the bar to order something more beer-like.

I scan the room, instantly finding Ainsley, or her twin, at a table near one of the pianos. She is in the midst of a conversation with her blond friend from the pool deck, who's seated at the next table over. Unfortunately, her hair is covering her name tag.

Damn.

I try not to be stalkerish and continue scanning the room. Chances are, this is not Ainsley the reader, and we will not fall instantly in love. So, it is best that I stop putting all my eggs in one basket. A basket that is nothing more than a pipe dream. There are a number of beautiful women that I could easily imagine wanting to get to know.

Yet, my eyes keep circling back to Ainsley. Or whomever this look alike is.

"Welcome everyone! I am Sven, the coordinator for the singles activities this week," A tall man with bright, blond hair said, his Scandinavian accent filling the room. "If you have any questions or concerns, please allow me, or either of the ladies up at the front, to be of assistance. Now, who is ready for a little speed dating?" A few cheers went up, but mostly it was just awkward silence.

"That was horrible everyone." Sven laughs. "Let's try this again. I said, who is ready for some speed dating?" The crowd was three times as loud, with no one wanting to have to do one of those cheering battles if we didn't have to.

"That's better." Sven nods. "Now, all of you gentlemen have numbers on your name tags. They match with a table number and your first date. Go find your seats." I am number nine. She is number sixteen. I have seven opportunities to warm up and figure out what I am going to say. "There are twenty tables tonight, so only three minutes each. Make it fast, make it memorable!" Sven says to the crowd.

I find table number nine and I'm greeted by a pair of green eyes wearing a green dress to match. Tiffany from North Dakota. Newly divorced and newly relocated to San Diego. I place her in the 'rebound' phase of dating. Then the bell dings and Sven's voice fills the room once again.

"That's all folks. Three minutes. Time to say goodbye. Men, please move to the next table. If you were at table one, move to table two. Table two, moves to three, and so on. If you were at table twenty, please move around to table number one." The scooting of chairs and shuffling of bodies replaces Sven's heavily accented voice as we all shift over.

Table ten is Ruby. I like Ruby. She is a hair stylist from L.A. She is vibrant and funny and the three minutes pass by quickly before we have to say goodbye, and I move to table eleven.

Table eleven is Beth. Beth is quiet, and shy, and probably needs something stronger than the bottle of water sitting in front of her. It's like pulling teeth trying to get any emotion out of her. She has some walls built up, and could probably use a hug and a therapist, more than a singles cruise right now. But the good news about table eleven is that I have a great view of Ainsley's twin right behind Beth. I do my best to be inconspicuous, sneaking glances over Beth's shoulder. Trying to sneak a peek at that name tag again. It ends in a 'Y'.

That's all I can see due to the back of her current date, who is currently blocking the rest of her.

Ding. The bell goes off.

"It was a pleasure to meet you, Beth." I say, standing to move on to table number twelve. Glancing over to table sixteen, I'm able to see her name tag clearly for the first time.

Her name tag says Ainsley.

My heart immediately falls into my stomach and I feel like I want to throw up. Not the reaction I expected out of myself.

"You okay?" comes a lilt voice to my side. I look down at my next date. It's Shirley from the pool deck earlier in the day. Red hat and purple dress replaced by a cream dress suit and navy scarf.

Taking a deep breath, I take the seat across from her and smile. "I'm fine. Just saw a ghost from my past."

"Thank goodness! I was afraid that look was for me!" she laughs and I immediately feel better at the warmth in her voice. "Now, tell me your ghost story." she prompts.

"Not much to tell, a missed opportunity twenty-five years ago."

"And you think she is here tonight?"

"Right behind you."

Shirley picks up her handbag and pulls out a compact mirror. Flipping it open she peeks behind her like a proper spy. "She's pretty."

"She is." I smile.

"Are you sure it's her?"

"Yeah, it's her."

"Oh, this is so exciting!" Shirley claps. "What are you going to say to her?"

"I have no idea. Suggestions?"

"Well, try not to look like you're about to throw up on her would be my first tip."

I laugh out loud. "That's excellent advice."

"Do you think I should bring up the past, or get to know her first?"

"Don't you think she'll remember you? A handsome man like yourself wouldn't be easy to forget."

"I don't really know. It was one night of kissing in Vegas, twenty-five years ago." I shrug my shoulders. Unsure if this memory means as much to her as it does to me.

"She must be a horrible kisser to make you go green in the gills the way you did when you saw her."

"No, the exact opposite. Those are the best lips I've ever kissed."

"Wow." Shirly fans herself.

Bing! Goes the bell.

"I have confidence the right words will cross your lips at the right time. Good luck, Cody." She says, as I graciously bow my goodbye and move on to table thirteen.

Table thirteen is Shirley's friend Mable. Before I even sit down, she knows my story. Eavesdropping perhaps? Mable is a hoot, and full of both good, and bad advice. And our time together zips by quickly.

Tables fourteen and fifteen were both lovely young women, and I'm pretty sure I held an intelligent conversation. But my mind was focused on table number sixteen.

Bing!

I take a deep breath through my nose, and release it slowly through my mouth. I'm not usually the nervous type when it comes to women, but this is different. I have had recurring dreams about this woman over the past twenty-five years. I don't want to fuck this up.

Again.

Calmer, I sit down across from Ainsley the reader.

Not her doppelganger. Not her twin. The real Ainsley.

"Hi."

It is as all I can manage to say, as I look into those soft brown eyes of hers. I am just as drawn to her now as when I was twenty-one. The magnetism I felt all those years ago is still here, and just as strong.

"Hi." she replies slowly. Like she needs to think about it. Like she is trying to place me.

"My name's Cody." I smile.

"Ainsley." She replies slowly. The wheels in her brain are working so hard, I can practically see them spinning. "Do I, ...know you?" she asks with a tilt of her head.

"We knew each other once." I look into her eyes and whisper. "Paris at midnight. New Year's Eve, twenty-five years ago."

Sucking in a sharp breath, her finger tips move up to touch her lips, and I know she remembers.

"Blue." she whispers, releasing the gulp of air she had taken. "You're the really great kisser." She says, her smile slowly reaching up the sides of her face and her cheeks turning pink with memory of those kisses. Her smile and that beautiful blush, light up her face and the little bit of anxiety and trepidation inside of me evaporates.

"That is how I have always remembered you too. I have never kissed lips like yours before. Or after." I say taking her hand in mine from across the table. Our fingers entwine like the most natural thing. The chemistry is still here. I can feel it running up my arm and filling me with the need to taste her lips again.

"I wish you had left me your number. I would have called you."

"I wish I had left you my number too," she says. "That night is one of my favorite memories. I used to touch myself to thoughts of you."

Fuck!

My heartbeat quickens and my dick is wide awake. My penis brain is now an active contributing member of this conversation.

I suck in a lust filled breath at her words, "Dear God, Ainsley. I think I'm done speed dating." I say with a slow grin and a desire filled exhale. "Do you want to get out of here and talk for more than three minutes?" I whisper.

"Yes." comes her immediate reply. "But, can we do that? Just leave in the middle?"

"The way I see it, the crew should consider it a match and be happy for us."

"Okay." She smiles a little nervously as we both stand up to leave.

"Sarah," she leans over to her friend, "I'll see you tomorrow. I ran into an old friend and we are going to go catch up."

"Catch up naked?" Sarah whispers loud enough for anyone within a six-foot radius to hear.

"Probably." Ainsley whispers back more discreetly. My cock grows a little more, as a heated hope spreads throughout my chest, and down to my groin.

Walking passed the check in, I let Sven know that this was the most successful speed dating event I had ever been to, and that he should have everyone skip over table sixteen. Then I shoot Brent a peace sign as we walk out the door.

# 10.

## Hormones in Control

Ainsley:

OMG! If I could breathe, I would be hyperventilating right now. But seeing my long-lost day dream from the past has me breathless. Not only breathless, but speechless too. After my tremendously smooth announcement that I only remembered him as the really great kisser from Vegas. Followed by blurting out that I used to touch myself to thoughts of him; I mentally glued my trap shut.

God!

I must have turned ten shades of red when those little words fell out of my mouth. I can still feel the heat of the blush at the tips of my ears. But then again, considering that Blue is now holding my hand, as he leads us outside to a romantic spot where we can re-equant ourselves; maybe my loose lips are not such a bad thing after all.

I don't even know this man, yet all I want, with the full core of my being, is to be kissing him right now. Just like back in Vegas. We didn't know each other then, either. Yet..., I have never felt closer to someone as quickly as I did him, that night, all those years ago. I feel close in that same way now, as my hand tingles in the grip of his palm. It's like our souls recognize each other from another life. As if, we already know we are good together.

Really fucking good.

But that is probably just me being a new-age, hippy, romantic.

Yet, something in my heart is fluttering. And every thought in my head is going ten-billion miles a minute.

What if he starts talking and he sucks?

What if I start talking and I suck?

Maybe we should just pick up where we left off? Lips and bodies entwined. That didn't suck at all. I shiver at the thought of his lips kissing down my stomach and my VJJ heats up so fast I have to clench my butt cheeks together to keep myself from pouncing on him. I take a deep breath as shivers course down my spine.

He wraps his arm around me, pulling me into his side for warmth as we walk through the portal doors, against the gush of cold wind. Giving my shivers the perfect alibi.

"Watch your step." He warns me, as he lets me go first to step over the lip of the door.

Points for being considerate.

Which reminds my blood starved brain of all the points he racked up twenty-five years ago. How sweet and gentlemanly he was back then. Not pressuring me into sex even though Hailey, and the guy she was with, were shagging in the next bed over. He is being kind and thoughtful now. And I should be wanting to talk to him, and get to know him better now that we have escaped our three-minute time clock. But all I want to do is try out a few of my slutty daydreams with him back in my cabin.

This is so totally weird. So odd for me to be so lust crazed and 'Man' like. But for fucks sakes, that night with him in Vegas has been my go-to, "what if", day dream since meeting him. All the ways I thought about what could have come next. Right now, I want this man for sex. We can figure out if we are compatible tomorrow.

# 11.

## Manifesting Day Dreams

Cody:

Ainsley's hand in mine, we round the corner and head for the port side door and the empty walkway outside. The night air is cool, and there is a strong breeze, leaving this portion of the ship completely deserted except for us. Finding a small protective alcove, we nestle in. Without thinking, we simply fall into each other's arms.

"I can't believe it's really you, Ainsley the reader from Southern California." I whisper, holding her face in the palms of my hands. Studying her to make sure she is real. My fingers caress the side of her cheek and her jaw, amazed to be touching her.

"You're like a fucking dream made manifest." I tell her, my heart and mind vibrating a million miles a minute. She makes this little whimper sound and bites the corner of her lower lip.

God, I love it when she bites that plump lip of hers.

Her eyes meet mine and she releases her lip and smiles. That smile lights up her face and my entire fuck'n world right along with it.

As my lips inch towards hers, her fingers grip onto my shirt, pulling me closer, and her head tilts up to mine in welcoming response. That first touch of our lips…, Fuck.

It is all kinds of magic. Like no time has passed at all.

My hands move into her hair and my tongue slides between her lips. She tasted like berry wine and I can feel myself getting drunk on her. Then she makes this little moaning sound and I nearly come undone as I am mentally transported back to Vegas and all the amazing sounds that came from her lips back then, flood into my mind. Followed by all the lusty daydreams I have imagined since.

Ainsley, soft and warm in my arms, here in real life, is so much better.

I would have expected that all of the hours I've spent lusting after her. Trying to manifest her back into my life would have made the memory better than reality. But that thought has just been busted, because this is more. Her kiss is better than my memories. Better than my daydreams. Her lips part perfectly as I kiss her, slowly tasting her and feeling the tip of her tongue as she tastes me too. A tingle buzzes in my chest and in my brain, as if my heart is creating a new neuron path specifically for Ainsley.

"I love the way you cuss metaphysics to me." She exhales before biting my lower lip, sucking it into her mouth then letting her tongue wander in to tango with mine.

She makes my knees weak. I think I'm in love. I'm at least in lust. I want to be in love with her. Because right now, I can't imagine ever wanting to be with anyone but Ainsley. Maybe it's her pheromones, or some weird cosmic soul connection. Maybe it's the fact that she says really sexy things like,

'I touch myself to your memory.'

Which may be the most amazing thing a woman has ever said to me. What is for sure, is this magnetism between us. This is what fairytales are made from.

"Even after all these years, you're still the best kisser in my life. If I had some cheap plastic beads, I would string them over your head." she says, kissing a line along my jaw, her hands running down my shoulders and arms, which I am admittedly flexing for her.

"I still have the blue one you gave me."

"No shit, really?" She laughs. Oh, her laugh is even more wonderful too. It makes my heart smile.

"How could I ever part with the only reminder I had of these lips." I kiss her bottom lip, full and soft. Then her top lip. My tongue sliding over the peaks and divot before slipping inside her mouth and running against the edge of her teeth, meeting her tongue. She shivers and I pull her closer, just as she digs her nails into my shoulders and all the blood drains from my brain.

I want this woman so badly I'm insane with it. My hands roam down her waist and ass. Down her thigh, pulling one leg up around mine. The need to be closer to her, takes over my good senses. My groin grinds against her all on its own, now that my dick has overridden my brain. I hold her tight to me, trying my best to simply absorb her into my body. She exhales a "Fuck Yes." And I'm completely lost in euphoria as every nerve in my body lights up. I feel primal in my need for her, as a deep guttural sound emanates from under my ribcage.

Shit, did I just growl? She is making me wild.

"Want to come back to my room and pretend it's New Years Eve?" she asks between kisses.

"Yes. More than anything." I groan, deep and growly into her ear. Biting her flesh softly between my teeth. When did I become a carnivorous bear? I want to devour her. I was ready to take her right then and there, but I'm pretty sure we would get thrown into cruise ship jail for indecency for that.

Instead, we kiss in our little dark corner for a few minutes longer before moving to the elevators.

"Where are you staying?" I ask her as we wait for the lift.

"I'm Aloha 9016. You?"

I smile at the coincidence. "Aloha 9014"

"So, we don't need to worry about being too loud for the neighbors." She winks.

Fuck, I do love her.

I bite her shoulder. That little spot where it turns into her neck; and she jumped back against me with a sigh. Settling her back against my chest, my arms wrap around her waist while we wait for the doors to open, then we move back into the corner as the rest of the people fill in.

The elevator is crowded so we restrain from making out. Even though the fantasy of pinning her to the wall of an elevator is one I often fantasize about. But my lips do not miss her skin for long. Once we get down the empty hall, my lips find her fingers and I trail kisses up her arm and over her shoulder as she unlocks her door. My mouth is hot against her neck as we stumble inside. Her hands are pulling at the buttons of my shirt, and my hands are already under her dress and around her ass, as the door to her room slams shut.

Dear Lord, she has a fucking amazing ass.

I think, as I give both her cheeks a little squeeze. She makes one of her sounds and I pull her pelvis against my erection; the cave man in me coming out of his cave. Lifting her legs around my waist I carry her towards the bed. Absolutely blinded by my need, I stumble against the wall of the narrow hallway, my feet tripping up on the luggage caddy. I feel us going down, so I shift my weight, so that I take the fall with Ainsley landing with her legs perfectly straddled across my hips.

We both sit laughing for an instant. But her laugh is just as sexy as the rest of her, as she straddles my waist unbuttoning my shirt, and my brain goes dizzy for the twentieth time tonight. I'm not laughing any more. My hands run up her back and into her hair, pulling her lips down to mine, so that I can plunder her mouth as my fingers slide down the zipper of her dress. As the last button pops from my shirt, she pulls it back off my shoulders helping me strip. With one hand I reach behind my head and yank off my undershirt too. Her finger tips tickle down my chest and over my abs, her eyes following their descent over my body.

I love the way she looks at me.

My fingertips follow her lead as my hands slowly caress the shape of her breast, down her waist and over her hips. My hands trail down along her thighs to her knees and then back up under the skirt of her dress, and around her sweet little ass again. I slide my fingers up her ribs, pulling the dress up and over her head. My lips kiss the soft skin of her stomach, and cleavage, up to her collarbone and neck. Following the progression of her dress and the new skin I had been given access to.

My fingers work to remove her bra as my tongue invades her mouth. Her pelvis rolls against me in the most beautiful, mind shattering fashion, just as the snap releases from her bra.

Groans and growls echo somewhere in the back of my mind as the bra releases her breast into the palms of my hands. God, the perfect weight of them. The way the peak of her nipples lay perfectly in line between my cupped palm and thumb.

She is fucking beautiful.

Her skin is still that gorgeous honey color I remember. Soft and smooth. Her breast and hips show light signs of motherhood now. But those clues to who she is, just spark the desire to know more than just the way she tastes. And a new wave of fucking, crazy emotions flare in my soul.

She has an entire life that I know nothing about. She is already so much to me, yet there is so, so much more. At this moment, I want all of her. I fill my hands with her.

Needy.

Possessive.

I Wish I had eight hands instead of only two, so that I can hold her more completely.

Running my fingers up her hips, over her stomach and breast, my lips kiss every inch of exposed skin that I can reach. Her fingers start unbuckling my belt and the desire to be inside of her makes me shudder, as her hands skim over the bulge in my pants.

"I've never wanted anyone the way I want you." I growl pulling her nipple into my mouth, enjoying the way it tightens under the pressure of my tongue. Enjoying the sharp bite of her nails on my thigh as she arches her chest against me, making one of her little gasping sounds.

"Twenty-five years is a lot of foreplay." she says in a moany, rushed exhale.

I laugh. "Yes. I say it's enough." And I scoop her up, laying her back against the bed as I strip out of my pants and grab a condom, before kissing my way up her legs.

This is my first experience with her legs. Twenty-five years ago, her jeans never came off. If they had, I would not have fallen asleep like I did back then. Her legs are long, lean, and toned. She is in amazing shape and I guess that she might be a runner. I study the smooth caramel honey color of her skin as my tongue licks slowly up her calf. She's warm against my tongue and makes the most delicious little moaning sounds. She giggles, and rewards me with a few sharp inhales, as I crawl between her thighs, lightly tickling and nibling the delicate flesh inside her legs. My mouth kisses the most feminine soft panties I have ever had the pleasure of removing and I can smell her.

Fuck, it is definitely the pheromones. I'm ready to drown between her thighs if she will let me.

My fingers pull down at the pretty little swath of fabric. My eyes following it passed her gorgeous thighs and over her knees. Memorizing as much of this as I can for nasty X-rated daydreams later. Slipping the little thong past her calf and ankle, I fling her panties over the corner of the TV. They dangle there proudly, like a flag claiming victory over a newly found territory.

Sitting back, I take in her glorious naked form. From her toes to her smile, I am still in awe that this is real. That she is really here with me.

Here with me Naked! I am a lucky man.

Crawling over her thighs, I settle my mouth over that delicate spot of flesh just inside her hip, where we each left hickeys so many years ago. I let my tongue do a few roles, then I suck. Hearing her gasp and feeling her move her pelvis against my mouth, makes the already incessant need to be inside of her overwhelming. My fingers move to the V between her legs and I tickle open the folds, letting my two fingers wander inside. Her hips arch into my fingers as they slide inside her silky, hot, wonderland and I suck a little harder. She tugs my hair towards her sex and my mouth gladly moves to the Garden of Eden between her legs as I take a slow long taste of her pussy. I shudder and see heaven as I swirl little circles around her clit, then suck on that little pearl of honey.

Her gasp of pleasure has me so rock hard it hurts. I slip my wet fingers in my mouth to taste the warm nectar of her inner-being and she is better than the best whiskey. Better than the strongest drug.

I shudder, dragging my kisses up her body. My tongue strolled over her stomach. Dipping down into the canyon of her very cute little navel, before kissing up the gentle curve of her breast. My tongue rolls slow circles around her nipple before sucking it in my mouth; just as I had to her hip and her clit.

"Fuck!" she cries out.

"Was that a good 'Fuck' or a too hard 'Fuck'?" I mumble against the curve of her cleavage.

"Fucking amazing. Please do it again." she pants.

Smiling, I kiss her other breast, slowly teasing her with soft licks before giving her the pressure she's been waiting for. Her reaction is amazing, and knowing that I'm pleasing her, pleases me. Moving up her body, I kiss her collarbone and neck before settling upon her lips; And our bodies just fit. My cock presses against the folds of her pussy and we start to move to our own pulsing rhythm as we grind against each other in naked, dry humping, perfection.

"I want you." She whispers in a rush, her breath hot against my ear.

"I want you too." I mumble only semi coherently.

"I want you inside of me."

BING! The bell goes off in my mind. We mold together perfectly as the head of my dick slowly pushes inside of her.

Jesus fucking Christ, the sound she makes....

I have never heard a sound more phenomenal. I have never felt anything as astounding as Ainsley feels. Her body absorbs each inch of me as I slowly fill her completely. Holding still a moment, as my tip kisses the depth of her well, before slowly pulling back out and in again. Her nails dig into my shoulder with a painful bite that makes me wish she would dig a little harder. Scratching down my back, she moves and grinds under me, meeting my thrust with ones of her own. Her hard nipples rubbing over my pecs as she arches her back and her entire body rolls into me, deepening the penetration to the end of her.

I never thought you could make love to someone you don't really know. I always thought that was just considered fucking. But my perspective has shifted. Because what we are doing is making love. I am loving every inch of her body. I am loving every sound she makes, every word that comes out of her sailor's mouth. I am loving the way she moves with me seamlessly. I love the way her nails dig into me, pulling me closer, deeper. I love that she wants and needs me with the same amount of gusto that I feel for her.

I feel her body tighten around me, I can see it in her eyes, the way her head falls back against the pillow, that she is close. My fingers glide back and forth over her clit and she yells the most amazing obscenities as she shutters' and cums around me. I lose myself in her in that moment, cumming to the feel of her orgasm, and the way her muscles clench and spasm around my cock.

# 12.

## Q & A

Ainsley:

We lay in my bed panting. His fingers tracing the shape of my body. His lips kissing my skin. Even after we are finished, he is still loving on me. I have never felt like this before.

Wait. Yes, I have.

Twenty-five years ago, in Vegas. He made me feel like the only girl alive back then too. Just like now. But it's not just that. There is still this kinetic magnetism between us that has every cell in my body doing back flips. I have never felt instant attraction with anyone like I do with him.

I'm not that surprised that the best kiss of my life would also turn into the best sex of my life. And that was only our first try. I sure hope we have more in common than just the physical, because I don't want this to end. Maybe ever. I have never felt more content, more cherished and beautiful. I hope I make him feel this good too. Part of me is afraid to talk and ruin this perfect moment, but the words fall out of my mouth anyhow.

"That was the best sex I've ever had."

"Fuck, me too. And it was only our first try." he says exactly what I had been thinking. Hope flairs in my heart, that we may possibly be as in sync mentally as we are physically. God, I hope we are even half as much. 'Cuz physically…,

Wowza!

I lean up to him and kiss his jaw. "Cody." I try out his name. I like it better now than I used to. Over the years, I would sometimes get lost in daydreams of 'what if.' I knew so little about him that every little bit has become better.

He does his sexy growl thing in response, "That's the first time I've heard you say my name. I really like the way it sounds coming from your mouth." Goodness, I love his sexy growl thing.

"I didn't know your name for a long time. I nicknamed you 'Blue' because of your eyes."

"You can call me Blue. I kinda like that you have a nickname for me. You were always 'Ainsley the reader' to me." he smiles. "Do you still like to read everything?"

"I do." I beam. Amazed that he remembers that little tidbit about me. "I read at least five novels a month. So long as they are different genres, I will sometimes read them at the same time. Do you still have those sexy nerd glasses and like to read Sci-fi?" I grin up at him.

"Yes, to both. Although, I have a new prescription and I've expanded a bit beyond Sci-fi over the years." He smiles down at me, tracing my lower lip. "Are you still living in California?"

"Mmmhmm. North San Diego County. Are you still in Arizona?" I whisper, feeling fuzzy in the brain.

"No. I'm originally from Taos, New Mexico. I moved back a few years after graduating." He tells me, before delivering a soft kiss on my bottom lip.

"What did you study?" I whisper as my eyelashes flutter back open.

"Business. But I ended up getting into Real Estate. What do you do?" he asks, nibbling my ear lobe.

"I'm a wedding photographer. I usually shoot… hmmm that feels nice…. out in the wineries… in Temecula." I respond only half focused on the conversation.

"That sounds like a fun job. Have you ever been to Taos? We have some amazing scenery."

"Not yet." I hum.

"We may have to remedy that." he says with a twinkle in his eye as he leans down, kissing me slowly and sweetly.

My heart does this fluttery thing at the idea that he would want me to visit him in Taos. This little Q&A's fun. A little backwards in the scheme of things, but somehow it means more now. The fact that he still wants to get to know who I am as a person, even though he has already had the milk for free so to speak, has me building up hope that my long-time daydream might add up to something more than a hot vacation lay.

I think back to my old sorority sisters Ashley and Hailey. They would be so proud of prudish, little Ainsley for finally following through with my Vegas one night stand. I giggle to myself at the thought.

God, twenty-five years. He has lived an entire life during that time.

"Family?" I ask him, as my fingers draw little circles over his chest.

"I have a son. His name is Austin. He is twenty years old and is currently studying theater at UNM. He is my everything."

I could hear his smile through his words at just the mention of his son, and it made me smile too. "My wife, his mother, died when he was fifteen. So, it's just been us."

My smile shatters and my heart brakes for him as the familiar pain of loss floods my senses. "I'm so sorry Blue." I say as I rest my head against his heart, listening to the life beating inside of him.

He kisses the crown of my head sweetly. "How about you?" He asks.

"My husband died five years ago too." Comes tumbling out of my mouth. I didn't mean to say it. It wasn't the answer to the question he was asking. But the pain is still here, flowing through my veins. He holds my face, looking me in the eyes. Neither of us speaking. Just staring, studying each other until we fall back into a sweet slow kiss that makes me forget all of my heart ache.

"How did it happen?" he asked quietly.

"Car accident on his way home from work. Alice had just turned eighteen and Bodhi was sixteen when Brian died." I told him as a lump formed in my throat.

"Vanessa was sudden too. Brain aneurysm." He says in a ghost of his usual voice. "I'm so sorry, Ainsley. I would never wish this for your history."

"Nor me for you either. But at least our crappy past has led us here." I smile up at him, pushing back the painful past in exchange for the sexy present.

"The present moment is definitely my favorite." he says kissing me again, his hands roaming over my body; an excellent distraction.

We kiss and fondle and even make love again before sunrise. All of my daydreams of him from years past are only a shadow compared to the reality of him.

# 13.

## A Sweeter Way to Greet the Day

Ainsley:

I wake to gentle kisses along my shoulder and Blue's fingertips gently running along the curve of my breast. I stretch with a sigh and settle into the warm man lying before me.

"This is a nice way to wake up." I purr into his chest.

"Mmm. The best." he growls.

"Much better than having Hailey shake me awake to leave at the crack of dawn."

He laughs at the memory. "A hell of a lot better than waking up to an empty pillow."

"Shall I put my number in your cell now?" I tease.

"Yes! I'm not letting you get away again." he says, nuzzling my neck and pulling me closer to him.

"Do you have anything planned for Catalina today? Maybe we can enjoy the day together?" he asks, and my heart sparks over the fact that he is thinking of me when planning his day.

"Nothing is booked yet. I've been to Catalina a few times and Sarah and I were thinking of renting a golf cart and maybe going kayaking or ziplining."

"Is that your friend whom you were sitting next to at the speed dating event?"

"Yes. Are you here with any friends?"

"My friend Brent and I met up for the cruise. We met while traveling together nearly two years ago. He lives in Chicago."

"Maybe we can get a foursome together for today?" I suggest.

"I like that idea." he smiles. "Brent and I spotted you and your friend yesterday on the pool deck. I feel pretty confident that he would be stoked about an afternoon tagging along with her."

"Sarah is pretty spectacular."

"Brent certainly seemed to like her.  But I like you." he adds with a seductive smile.

There he goes again, making me feel like the only woman on earth.

I love it.

His head bends to take my breast into his mouth, and all thoughts of our itinerary leave my mind as his tongue does amazing things to my nipples. Then he moves south and all thoughts obliterate from my mind completely.

# 14.

## Catalina Kisses

Ainsley:

Ninety minutes later, and the four of us were all ready for a day of fun on sunny Catalina Island, off the coast of California. Sarah and Brent hit it off right away, and our little foursome hops in the golf cart ready to explore the island. Blue drives and I sit shotgun, while Sarah and Brent get to know one another in the back seat. Sarah and Brent seem absolutely smitten with each other within minutes. They melt into their own little world for the next two hours, leaving Blue and I to entertain ourselves in the front seat.

As we drive along the hilly streets, we take turns pointing out our dream homes, imagining what could be if we were only to win the lottery. Blue and I seem to have similar taste, and it makes me want to get to know him even more.

"What kind of real estate do you practice?" I ask.

"My dad and I started flipping houses after I moved back to Taos. He's a General Contractor and I've picked up a bit of knowledge from him over the years. Then I found this old camp ground and renovated it with tiny houses. I started renting them out as vacation rentals and fell into property management that way. I have a team that takes care of ninety percent of it now. I just over see some of the big deals and work the campground these days.

"Wow." I was impressed. He ran his own business and raised a child while dealing with the grief of the death of a spouse. And he seems perfectly normal. He obviously isn't a workaholic, since he is on vacation now, midweek. And the little bit I've gleaned so far, it seems like he travels often. He is obviously much smarter than the hot, frat boy I used to imagine him to be.

I like smart. I need smart.

He seems really well adjusted and comfortable with life as he goes on about the camp ground that he and his father created, and how they drew up and constructed all the tiny lodgings. I like the way it brings him joy. How his eyes twinkle, as he talks about working with the natural materials of the land.

"How about you? What is life like as a wedding photographer?" he asks.

"It's mostly a lot of fun. That is how Sarah and I became close friends. She is a wedding coordinator. Her divorce just finalized last month. This cruise is kinda like her 'coming out'."

"Is this your first singles cruise?" he asks.

"Yes. So far, I would say it's been a success." He gives me one of his hundred-watt smiles in return. "Have you been on a singles cruise before?" I ask him back.

"No. This was my son's idea. I am going to have to call him and thank him." he says, squeezing my hand.

***

The four of us arrive at the Eco Zip Line tour a little before our last-minute reservations at eleven. I was excited and Sarah was nervous. But Brent was taking care of her nerves, encouraging her sweetly.

"Have you ever been zip lining before?" Blue asks me.

"I have, through the jungle in St. Lucia and once in Cancun."

"You've been to some fun places. Do you travel often?"

"Not as much as I would like. I work a lot of weekends, so smaller three-to-four-day trips midweek have been my go-to. Although, I did spend ten days in Ireland last year. Most of my traveling abroad I did in my early twenties after graduation."

"Where's your favorite place?"

"I don't know, I haven't been everywhere yet." I tease "But, I was really impressed with Switzerland. The Swiss really have their shit together." he laughs at my comment. I love his laugh, deep and true.

"How about you? Do you get to travel much?"

"After Austin left for college, I started traveling more. I want to make sure I live life to the fullest while I'm here on the planet and my body is still fully capable, you know?" He gave this cute little shrug. "I've been to Australia and Montreal. Spent a week camping in Zion and a few short trips to Chicago and upstate New York. I'm trying to plan a trip of some kind every other month."

"Wow, that's my goal too." I say feeling a little in awe of the coincidence. "I've always wanted to go to Australia. It's in my top ten. You said that's how you and Brent met?"

"Yup, it was a hosted bus tour through Fromers. Two weeks on a bus with fifty other people from all over the world. It was a blast, and I made some great lasting friendships."

"That sounds like fun. Do you have any new vacations planned?"

"I might have to plan a trip to North San Diego California soon." he smiled, letting his gaze drop down to my breast then down over my legs, making my cheeks burn. "What other locations are in your top ten?" He asked in a voice that was much deeper and sexier than his question warranted.

"Oh, there are soooo many. Puerto Rico, Iceland, Machu Picchu, The Panama Canal, Tahiti, Prague, The Philippines, New Mexico..." I add slowly, daydreaming of all the places left on earth for me to discover. Maybe with him.

"Let's make sure that the last one happens. And maybe we can knock off a few of the others together too?"

Butterflies.

There he goes, saying what I'm thinking again. I'm glad he is brave enough to say it. Because it makes me feel amazing. He makes me feel amazing. I can feel my smile reach my ears. I probably look goofy just staring up at him as I

~ 83 ~

am, but my heart is beating too erratically for me to answer. So, I kissed him instead.

"Party of four for Brent!" is called out from the main office, keeping our kiss from escalating from G to PG. "I would love to travel with you." I say quietly, still wrapped in his arms. Neither one of us is ready to step away yet.

"Come on you two sex crazed beasts!" Brent slaps Blue on the butt as he and Sarah pass us to go get suited up.

"Are you ready to go fly through the trees?" Blue asks me, pulling a stray hair from my forehead.

"I'm always ready to fly through trees." I smile and he kisses my nose, releasing me.

*****

We join our friends and start donning the gear for our ride alongside them.

"Who's my first victim?!" Tony the zip line guy hollers.

No one speaks up.

"I'll go." I pipe in.

Hooking me up to the carabiner, Tony gives me some last-minute tips on positioning myself and how to slow down and speed up. And with a push I am off. The feel of the wind through my hair, and the adrenaline rush of flying between the trees and canyons is fantastic. I land on the first platform feeling exhilarated, as I wait for the others.

Blue is next."That was fucking fantastic!" he smiles, landing with a heavy thunk, and skidding to a halt. He walks over to me, wraps his arms around my waist, and kisses me with all of that adrenaline.

"It was surprisingly sexy the way you jumped up and volunteered to be first. I like that. I like you Ainsley. A lot." And he kissed me again until we heard Sarah screaming,

"Oh no, dear God." As she came in for a fast landing.

Blue steps back and braces himself to help Sarah land. She trips and stumbles gracelessly, but he grabs her and keeps her upright on her own two feet.

"You okay, was that fun?" he asks, trying to decipher the look on her face.

"I think once my stomach returns to its rightful place, I'll be fine." She says a little shakily. "Thank you. You may return to making out with Ainsley if you like." He gives me a wicked grin that says he wants to be doing a lot more than making out with me right now, and I feel my blush return. Brent lands with a whoop a moment later, followed by Tony.

"How was everyone's first ride?" Tony asks. "Everyone having fun? No one puked right?"

"That was a blast!" Brent comments.

"Are you all ready to go again?" Platform two, right this way.

"Do you want to go first this time?" I ask Blue.

"Nah, I enjoyed watching you swing through the air from behind."

"Pervert." I tease. He grins back at me and kisses the crown of my head.

"Ainsley, are you my brave one again?" Tony asks me.

"I'm ready." And off the platform I jump. "Geronimo!"

Two hours later, and Tony is bussing us all back to the main office and back to our golf cart.

"I'm famished." Brent pipes in. "Hey Tony, where's a great place to get a bite and some cold drinks?"

"Well, the Descanso Beach Club is within walking distance. Or if you're headed back into town, El Galleon is always a hit."

"Walking distance sounds like food faster. I say we go to the first place." Sarah suggests.

"Isn't the Descanso Beach club, where we can rent kayaks?" I ask Tony.

"Sure is. You can rent them by the hour."

"That sounds fun. Maybe after lunch?" Sarah suggests.

"I'm down." "Me too." The guy's pipe in.

With the rest of our afternoon planned, we find a lovely little table under the shade of some palms and enjoy fresh fruit, salads, and fish caught that morning.

***

Down by the water we met up with Carlos, the kayak guy, who sets us up with two doubles. Blue and I in one, Brent and Sarah in the other. Slipping off my shorts and tank top (My bathing suit underneath) I catch Blue staring, and a blush rises to my cheeks. I love how he makes me feel desired, so I wiggle my butt at him for fun. I don't hear him until I'm halfway in the air.

Blue scoops me up in his arms and plants a big ol' kiss on my cheek. Then he places me gently in the kayak.

"Maybe we can find a deserted little cove and you can do that butt wiggle thing again."

~ 86 ~

"You wish." I tease. "You can have the butt wiggle after you take me out dancing tonight."

"Sold." he smiles. "Hey Brent, dinner then dancing tonight, you two in?" Blue yells over to our friends, who are currently putting on their life vest.

"Yeah, sounds good, Mate."

"Lovely." replies Sarah, and the two of them share a look that would have me betting that Blue and I won't be the only match this week.

"They make a cute couple." Blue whispers in my ear.

"Exactly what I was thinking." I smile back. He does that a lot. Says what I'm thinking.

Carlos pushes us off and Blue and I paddle along the shore headed up the coast, with Brent and Sarah close behind. The water is so clear out here. Just twenty-six miles off the Southern California coast and it feels like another world. You can see all of the fish swimming between the seaweed for yards under the water.

Suddenly, a wave splashes us from behind, interrupting me as I am pointing out the little fish.

"Hey you two. Sarah and I are going to head over to that little alcove along the shore. You can go on ahead and pick us up on your way back." Brent yells over at us. I look over to Sarah and she has this dreamy look in her eyes. I have a pretty good idea, that we are purposely not being invited.

"Shall I give a warning on our way back?" Blue teases.

"Might as well."

"Okay, have fun kids." We continue to paddle farther north as they head inland.

"Brent stole my idea. Now we will have to find an even better hideaway." Blue says.

We paddle for another ten minutes and then our little Shangri-la revealed itself. A tiny protected bay, surrounded by palms and bright pink bougainvillea.

"Here?" he asks.

"Definitely here."

Angling towards the shore, it's a struggle fighting against the current. By the time the kayak pulls onto the sand I'm sweating.

"Wanna go for a swim?" I suggest, needing a little cool off.

"I can't think of a prettier location for one." He agrees.

I wade halfway out into the little lagoon, then kick and swim to the middle, sending up a big splash in Blue's face.

"Oh ho, ho… This is war!" He says, chasing after me with fun in his eyes. I squeal and swim farther away, kicking up another wave. But I have to slow down to keep from drowning, as I fall into a fit of laughter at his expletives from the second wave.

Then he catches me.

His hands around my waist, he picks me up and tosses me back in the water. I come up for air laughing and loving that he likes to play and is still a child at heart. Then he dunks me again. So, I lunge for his back and we go down together in a fit of giggles.

We come back up lip locked, holding onto each other for dear life. If I could just absorb him I would. His hands pull against my thighs lifting me so that I can easily wrap my legs around his waist. I can feel his hard dick between my legs, and I want him so badly that I consider ditching my 'No Beach Sex' rule. He would be worth sand in my unmentionables.

Then a motor boat goes by, so we cool our engines slightly as he releases my lips but not my legs.

"I really like your bathing suit." He says playing with the strap.

"I really like you shirtless." I whisper back, my fingertips running down his chest. He is still in amazing shape considering he is twenty-five years older. Not gym obsessed ripped, but nice. Firm in all the right places. It's obvious that he is active on a regular basis, not just on vacation.

"I like you shirtless too." He grinned like a teenage boy.

"Is sex all you think about?" I roll my eyes in mock annoyance.

"No." he says indignantly. "I wonder what your favorite color is. And what kind of music you like. I think about when I can fit in a visit to San Diego, and marrying you in that little chapel on board the ship."

My cheeks catch fire. Holy fuck!

"Too far?" He smirks. "I mean, I have known you for twenty-five years. It's about time. Everyone thinks so." He could not hide his teasing smile.

"Oh yeah, who is everyone?" I test, my cheeks still fire-engine red.

"Sven for sure. You should have seen the thumbs up he gave me when we left the speed dating event early last night."

"You don't say." I grin up at him.

"Brent and Sarah are rooting for us."

"I'm pretty sure Brent and Sarah are too busy rooting around each other to be thinking about us right now."

"Ha!" Blue burst into laughter. God, I love his laugh. "You're funny." He says.

"Thank you." My blush grew.

"So, are you going to answer my question?" He whispers against my lips, as his fingers run up my neck and into my hair, causing a fire to go shooting through me. Maybe in fear of just what question he wants an answer to, and maybe in lust over the way his eyes seem to melt my skin.

"What question was that?" I ask breathlessly.

"What's your favorite color? Obviously." he smiles and then his tongue is in my mouth, and I swear I hear church bells ringing.

"Blue." I whisper between kisses. "Like your eyes. What's your favorite color?" I ask him as his teeth nibble my neck.

"I don't know what it's called." He mumbles as he licks a hot line of sexy down my throat. "It's the color your skin turns when you blush." He kisses my chest and I can feel my skin flush.

"Yes, that's it." He groans, kissing me over my beating heart.

"What about answering my other questions." he adds, as the pads of his thumbs trace the outline of my nipples and fire races from them to my lady bits.

"I like top 100 and country, with a little 90's rap mixed in." I answer distractedly.

"Perfect," he responds. Kissing me slowly. So slowly.

"You?" I ask, in a kind of moan in-between kisses.

"Same."

And we kiss some more, lost in the moment. His tongue is the best tongue that has ever been in my mouth. His lips are the best things that have ever touched my skin. His mouth is currently inching closer and closer to my breast, and I'm afraid of losing consciousness, he feels so damn good.

"Favorite cereal?" I ask, trying to stay in control of the moment.

"Hmmm," he thinks. "That's tough. I like to mix cereals. But if I had to choose one, probably cinnamon toast crunch." He smiles like a little boy and my heart flutters.

"Me too!" I say excitedly. I don't know why I should feel like his breakfast cereal habits should hold such undeniable proof that he is perfect.

But it does.

"Chunky or Smooth Peanut butter?" he asks me next. The tenor of his voice is an onomatopoeia for the word 'Smooth' itself. His voice is so sexy. I can feel the vibration of it run down my spinal cord, like the effervescent bubbles in champagne all along my spine. Can you be addicted to a sound? Because the shivers he gives me with just his vibrato…, Sweet Mother, I don't think I can live without this now that I've experienced it.

Experienced him.

"Smooth." I mouth, unable to make a sound.

"Correct."

"I didn't know there was a right or wrong answer." I laugh.

"Smooth is more versatile." he answers matter of factually, then winks.

"You're very wise."

"True." He says like a smart ass, making me giggle.

I enjoy our banter back and forth. He makes me laugh in between all the feels. And I love that he is trying to get to know more than just the physical parts of me. It hasn't even been twenty-four hours and I'm already starting to fall hard for him. There are so many emotions tumbling around inside of me. All of them are good.

***

Time seems to fly. Or maybe it's been standing still. All I know is that the sun has shifted in the sky enough that we probably need to start heading back soon. As if he was reading my mind, again, Blue spoke.

"It would be a shame to miss the boat and be stuck on this island with you. Deserted, alone, naked. Nothing but each other to keep us warm."

I grin at his tease. "Missing the boat sounds like it should be Plan 'A' when you say it like that." Sand be damned, I am ready to let this man have his way with me. I bite my lip to keep from risking public indecency.

"Fuck Ainsley, I love it when you bite that lip of yours." he hisses through his teeth. As if he is holding himself back too. "It means there is more. More of you for me to discover." He whispers, his voice deep and slow. His lips fall on mine and he steals my bottom lip from between my teeth and bites and sucks it himself.

I melt.

He can have all of the hidden pieces of me.

Another motor boat goes by, and we take a moment to check the time. Responsible adults that we are.

"We really should head back if we don't want to miss the boat." he says, sounding a bit let down.

"Okay. Let's go snag the other love birds. They certainly seemed to hit it off, didn't they?"

"Makes sense that the people we like would like each other too. I say it is just more proof that we are meant to be." Wow. He thinks we are meant to be. There are those damn butterflies again. "You know, how like energy draws like energy." He continues as he swims back to shore giving a boyish grin over his shoulder. "I was drawn to you all those years ago in Vegas, and again on the cruise. I'm not sure what this energy between us is, but I really like it. Hell, I fucking love it." His smile fills his entire face. "I really like you Ainsley."

"I really like you too." I smile like an idiot.

He stops and turns back to wait for me, hand outstretched. "It's funny, I feel like we are doing this whole thing backwards. Starting at the physical end as we did. Not that I'm complaining." He winks. "But the more I get to know about who you are and what you enjoy, the more I like who you are as a person. I think if we give it a chance...," He trails off with a hopeful, puppy dog look, in his eyes. My fingers entwine with his and he lifts the back of my hand to his lips and gives it a sweet kiss. My skin flushes and my heart beat starts to race. I am both terrified of what he is about to say and praying that he says it. Because it is exactly what I am feeling.

But the pause is soooo long. With each millisecond, my heart thuds harder in my chest, the need to finish his thought overwhelming me.

"I would like to give it a chance with you too." I smile up at him from under my lashes, hoping to release some of this tension in my chest. "The tiny bit I've learned about you makes all this physical attraction between us even better. Just imagine if we...," I can't finish the thought due to the way his blue eyes are burning into my soul. So, I stopped the sentence short, just as he had.

"...If we fall in love." He finishes. His fingers tracing the curve of my jaw.

Sweet mother of baby Jesus!

I could fall in love with him so easily. I want to fall in love with him. This is terrifying, to feel so much, so fast. I slowly nod my head, "Yes."

"I think I may already be falling for you, and it's kind of terrifying; but I don't know any other way to describe this feeling. It's electric. You make my skin buzz, Ainsley."

Fuck. Every cell in my body is on fire. The little chapel on the ship just might be in our future after all.

"You make it hard not to jump you, when you say pretty words like that." I whisper as his fingers scratch down my back. Wrapping my arms around his neck, pulling myself up to his lips. The flutter in my chest turns into a flaming tingle, as hot spikes of desire race along my skin. The physical is already so amazing, I can't imagine surviving a night with him with the added emotion of love in the mix. But I want to try.

So badly.

He kisses me again. Hard and deep. "These lips," He exhales as he slowly pulls back, resting his forehead on top of mine with a shudder. "It's so hard not to kiss you constantly." Grabbing my hand, he pulls me back to the sand near our life vests.

"Come on, we should head back. I've been imagining spinning you around the dance floor tonight, and that butt wiggle you promised me." he crinkles his eyebrows suggestively a few times.

"I suppose that's a good reason to leave paradise." I say wistfully, as we put our life jackets back on and pushed off from shore, leaving our little Shangri-la behind.

**15.**

## Our Own Gangsta's Paradise

Cody:

We agreed to meet up at the bar before dinner at 7:45 pm. Her favorite color is the blue of my eyes. It would just so happen, that I own a dress shirt to match them. It's something of a dark teal, and along with my black pants and clean-shaven face, I look pretty good for a middle-aged widower. I check the clock on my phone, 7:31 pm, just as the room phone buzzes. It confuses me for a moment and I try to answer the land line on my cell. Thank God no one witnessed me do that. I can just imagine Austin calling me a Boomer for it.

"Hello?" I finally answered the room phone.

"Hey Mate," Brent's voice came across the line. "Sarah just rang. She and Ainsley are going to finish getting ready together and said they would meet us at the bar. I'm ready, if you want to head over now?"

"Sure."

We open the doors to our rooms at the same time. Brent is on the other side of me in room 9012. I assume Sarah is probably on the other end of Ainsley in 9018. The four of us all in a little row. It really does feel like the universe is trying to throw this in my face. Like, here you are, right where you are supposed to be. Don't 'F' it up this time and miss another twenty-five years with her.

"So, did you and Sarah have fun today?" I ask, elbowing Brent in the arm as we walk down the hallway.

"Sarah is amazing!" Brent smiles over at me. "She is so full of life, and the excitement to try new things. Not to mention, that she is the most gorgeous woman I have ever seen. But I swear, she's even more beautiful on the inside. I'm pretty sure I'm going to marry her." he nods. And I see something in his eyes that tell me so much more. He looks, like I feel. A man with a goal.

"I'm happy you found her, Mate." I say, and he smiles in thanks.

"So, what is the story with you and Ainsley? Do you still like her as much as you did back in Vegas?"I realize that since ditching Brent in the middle of speed dating last night, I had not given him any kind of an update.

"Oh yeah, and she is even better in real life than I imagined."

"We may be cutting off these blue wrist bands before the end of the cruise with these two women at our sides." Brent says jokingly. But I am pretty sure he means it.

I certainly am not feeling very single any more.

***

Arriving at the piano bar, Brent and I ordered two beers and two Pina Coladas for the girls. We are in the middle of comparing highlights from our day, when Brent's eyes leave mine and his gaze bugs out at the door.

"Fuck, Mate. We're dating supermodels." He whispers with a crooked smile, slapping me on the arm to encourage me to look his way. She stole my breath. Ainsley wore a flowy red cocktail dress that tied at the base of her neck. Her hair piled up in some kind of messy knot, tumbled down her back in big loose curls. Long crystals drip from her ears, and her skin is glowing from all the sun we were exposed to today. She is simply radiant. I stand there staring, beer held in my mouth, forgetting to swallow.

"Hey there handsome." Sarah calls out to Brent, as the women approach us, and I finally regain my composure.

"Wow, you look fantastic." I say, pulling Ainsley into my arms for a kiss.

"So do you. I love this color on you." She says, complimenting my shirt, while running her fingers down my pecs.

Score.

"Are those fancy drinks for us?" Sarah asks, pointing to the Pina Coladas sweating on the counter.

"Sure are." Brent replies. Licking his lips as he watches his date seductively suck her straw into her mouth.

"They are seriously indecent." Ainsley whispers jokingly into my ear. Just what I was thinking, and I laughed out loud. She does that a lot. Says what I'm thinking. I'm almost afraid to mention all the similarities between us; for fear she'll think I'm faking it.

"Hungry?" she questions as my stomach loudly growls.

"Famished." I nod. Ready to leave the bar and head for the restaurant.

Arm in arm, the four of us join the check-in line for dinner. The food is excellent and the conversation flows smoothly with many bouts of laughter. Brent and I share anecdotes from our vacation in Australia and the girls share wedding horror stories. After dinner we all watch the theater show, which is phenomenal. It is a mash up of many different famous Broadway songs. Most of which I know thanks to Austin.

"What's next ladies?" Brent asks, as we move through the crowds exiting the theater.

"Dancing!" Sarah proclaims, taking Brent by the hand and leading him towards the night club.

Brent and I offer to get water for everyone, while the girls head out to the dance floor. As soon as we turn our backs to order, the blue wrist bands start swooping in on Ainsley and Sarah. The two women really do look like supermodels. Sarah with her classic tall, blond, bombshell looks. And Ainsley, more exotic and mysterious with her warm, tan skin, and soft, brown hair. She has this natural rhythm to her movements that is hypnotizing.

"The sharks are swooping in, we better hurry." I nudge Brent.

"Even without those wrist bands, I bet we will constantly be fighting off hopefuls. I mean, just look at her. How did her ex ever let her get away." He shook his head in amazement as he stared at Sarah moving on the dance floor.

The man has tunnel vision for Sarah. He is completely smitten. It's fun to watch him, knowing I am probably walking around with the same puppy dog, lovesick, look on my face for Ainsley.

Collecting our drinks, we find a small bistro table and reserve it with our jackets. We head out to the dancefloor to shoo away the competition and have some fun swinging our women round. As we join them, I can see Ainsley politely sending a potential suitor packing as she points in my direction. To say it makes my heart leap would be an understatement.

Now, I am a tall white guy, and my dancing skills leave a lot to be desired. I have mastered the white boy shuffle and the cabbage patch. That is the extent of my dancing repertoire. But once Ainsley is in my arms, her rhythm seems to become my rhythm and suddenly, I have moves.

She may be a sorceress, because this night feels like magic. Everything I have ever experienced with her feels like magic.

My hands roam the exposed skin on her back. My fingers sliding up to play with the tie at the base of her neck. My imagination kicks into overdrive as I visualize pulling that silky piece of fabric and letting her dress fall to the floor. I wonder what color her underwear is? I don't think she is wearing a bra, maybe a strapless? My fingers trail down her back in hunt of some clues.

Strapless.

Thong underwear, I guess.

I wonder if they are red to match her dress. I can feel my dick starting to grow, so I take a deep breath to compose myself. She makes me feel wild and out of control. I breathe in the scent of her hair, (coconut), and the smell of the ocean and sun, still on her skin. The pheromones, or whatever magic potion she exudes, overwhelms my senses and I lose myself kissing her neck, just below her ear. My dick grows bigger as I pull her tight against me.

"You look absolutely gorgeous tonight and you smell amazing." I say into her ear as my fingers untangle a lock of hair from her dangly earrings. "It's been a struggle all night, to keep from pulling apart that little bow at the back of your neck. My mind keeps imagining dark corners with your skirt around your waist." She shivers in my arms and I pull her closer. I love that my words give her the chills.

I absolutely adore it. Maybe even more than making her blush.

"What other naughty things do you imagine?" she asks, in a siren voice.

"I wouldn't mind that butt wiggle you promised me."

She laughs out loud, and the sound is better than the music playing. "A few more songs and you can take me back to your room and I'll be your sex toy." she whispers into my ear.

Fuck. I growl, some kind of neanderthal-like sound.

The naughty things she says makes me dizzy.

"Maybe just one more song." she adds in a breathless voice.

"Good God woman, if you don't turn off that Siren thing you've got going on I may devour you right here on the dance floor." I say in a deep shaky voice that is both a warning and a plea. My mouth falling upon hers, our kiss takes me to images of my flesh on her flesh.

As if the DJ knew of my intentions, the song seamlessly blends into a slow romantic number, and the disco ball spins on. Looking into her eyes, she gives me the butterflies. The disco ball illuminates her skin, making it glow and sparkle like an angel. Our lips meet in another one of our perfect kisses. Her mouth is soft and warm against mine. Welcoming and Giving. I wasn't sure if I would make it through the song, as her fingers pulled at the back of my head and her tongue slid in my mouth.

We sway back and forth until the song is over and the next song's tempo picks up to a sultry Latin number that has

Ainsley moving her hips back and forth to the beat. The way she moves, Fuck. My knees may give out on me. We dance the next two songs without me dragging her back to my room because the foreplay of her body against mine is too divine to stop. Then Coolio comes on with a little Gangsta's Paradise and her eyes light up, as she starts rapping every word. I feel this warm rush of wonderful spread through my chest as I join her, word for word, belting out each verse. I may seriously need to look into booking the chapel.

After Coolio and the Gang exit the sound waves, we make our way back to the bistro table Brent and I reserved for a cool down and a drink.

"That was fun!" she yells over the noise. "I can't believe you know all the words to Gangsta's Paradise." She smiles up at me.

"You know them too." I smile back. "When I was a kid, I snuck in to see that movie, Dangerous Minds. I was convinced I wanted to become a teacher for inner city youth for about three months."

She laughs hitting my arm in playful shock. "Would you believe I have the same story? I think we told our parents we were going to see Toy Story instead." her smile lit her eyes.

"What were you like as a child?" I ask, curious for as much knowledge as I could glean.

"I was quiet. Sheltered." She shrugs. "I grew up in a small farming town where everyone knew everyone else. But I found it hard to fit in. I was just kinda part of the background."

"I find that hard to believe."

"Believe it. Nothing more than a wallflower over here.

I thought back to the Ainsley I knew from twenty-five years ago. She was quieter back then. I remember the absolute fear in her eyes when her friend announced that the three of them would be the judges of the kissing contest. I knew back then she wasn't like her two companions. Yet, she nodded along anyway. That was one of the things I liked about her, she was brave enough to put her nerves aside. Brave enough to be the first to jump off the zipline platform too.

"How about you? Were you Homecoming King or a band nerd?" she asks.

"Neither. I played baseball and was captain of the debate team. But I hated speaking in public. I was always terrified."

"So why did you do it?"

"To overcome my fear."

"Did it work?"

"Not really, I still hate speaking in public. But I know I am capable of it, and that is half the battle."

"Blue?" she whispers, placing her hand softly on my thigh.

"Yeah?"

"I think I'm ready for you to take me back to your room and pull this dress off of me now."

I really love the words that come out of her mouth. I growl as I lift her hand up to my lips, kissing the pulse in her wrist slowly, before taking her hand in mine as we leave the club. We don't say goodbye. I'm not even sure if Brent and Sarah are still here. But we are gone.

***

Running down the two flights of stairs to our rooms, she holds her heels in her hands laughing as I tickle her waist every few steps. We arrive in front of room 9014 together out of breath. I catch her against the door, wrapping my arms around her, and pulling her tight against me. I can feel every curve of her body through her silky dress. Reaching behind her back I slip the key card over the lock and push the door open. Both of us fell through the opening, into the dark entry hall, the weight of our bodies shutting the door with a slam.

My hands roam over the curves of her body greedily. I am hungry for all the places that I couldn't grope in public.

Starving.

My palms slide over her breast, cupping them, and feeling their weight in my hands. The silky fabric pinches between my fingers. And she gasps in response to my touch. Moving around to her shoulders, I give a small pull on the tie at the back of her neck. But the damn thing doesn't budge.

"Pull harder." She whispers in a rush of desire, warm against my neck. While her fingers unbutton my shirt.

I do. I pull hard, releasing the knot in the soft fabric. The need tightening in my balls.

The red satin fabric falls, revealing even more satin. Her bustier is black with little red roses all over it. "So pretty." I say, before kissing a hot line of want between her cleavage. My fingers pull down the zipper at her back, and I start to work the facets of her bra. But it is nearly impossible for me to focus on the task at hand as she starts pulling down my pants. Her fingers sliding up and down my shaft make fireworks spark behind my eyes. Kneeling, she takes my cock into her mouth and I have to grip the wall to keep myself upright. Her warm, wet lips feel so damn good. Her fingers circle the base of my cock and she slides them up and down, along with her mouth. She has me so hard for her that I can barely see. Her tongue flicks the rim of my tip and that is it.

I need her NOW

Pulling her up my body, I yank the rest of her dress down over her hips. She stands there in front of me in just her matching, pretty, under things like a goddess. I stand in front of her feeling like a tiger, ready to pounce.

But..., my pants are caught in my shoes around my ankles.

"Let me watch you take it off." I command/ask as I step out of my shoes and work my pants from around my legs. She obliges. But first, she turns around so that I am looking at her behind. Her panties are Cheekys and her butt is plump and amazing as she wiggles it for me, just like she had promised. I can feel my ears burn. Like a cartoon, whose brain is smoking because the hot lady rabbit just crossed the street. She slowly unhooks her bra and tosses it onto the floor.

Side boob. (Drool)

Bending over she wiggles again as she pulls her black rose print Cheeky's over her rump and down her thighs. By the time her hands hit her ankles my cock is pressed against her ass and my hands are on her hips.

"Bed, hands, and knees. Please." I demand/ask as I roll my hips against her in practice of what I want to be doing inside of her.

My hands follow the shape of her form as she stands up and moves into position on the bed. Her legs spread and ready, I have the most amazing view of her red and swollen, glistening, wet, and ready for me. Grabbing her thighs, I bend between her legs. My tongue instinctively finds her clit and tastes it. Playing with it in little circles until she is cussing at me to "Fucking stick my dick inside her."

Sweet Mother of all that is good, I want to die listening to her talk dirty to me.

"Say it again." I politely demand.

"I want you to stick your massive hard cock in my wet pussy." She says in a panting rush.

Fuck! I'm in love.

Running my cock back and forth over her, I watch as the head of my dick slowly disappears inside of her. Warm, wet, and tight. I slowly push deep inside, then pull her hips against mine as I thrust hard, filling her completely.

Oh, the sound she makes.

It vibrates in my chest. Her moans make me harder. Her gasps of pleasure give me stamina. But when she cries out my name, while racked with spasms of release, I can't hold on any longer, and I crumble and disintegrate into bliss.

***

"Where did you learn to talk dirty like that?" I say into the back of her neck as we spoon post coital.

"I read a lot of trashy romance novels." She smiles, turning her head to look at me.

"Promise me you will never ever stop reading those." I kiss the side of her forehead.

"Do you like when I talk dirty?" she asks. I growl and bite the edge of her lower lip in response. Because I adore her dirty talk.

"Mmmmm," She hums against my lips. "I like when you bite me like that. It means there's more." She says in a husky whisper, repeating back my notion from earlier in the day.

So, I give her more. I give her everything I have, all night long.

# 16.

## Walk of Shame

Ainsley:

Day three is an at sea day as we sail south towards Ensenada. There is no need to get out of bed. No need to put on clothing.

I am so happy and content right now. Blue lays warm along my back. His arm wraps around my waist, his hand cupping my breast in sleep. I can feel my nipple tighten under the warmth of his fingers, as I think about the things we did last night. A little electric buzz runs down my spine and I can feel myself moisten from the memory.

I also feel the need to pee.

Doing my best not to wake him, I slide from his arms and move quietly to the bathroom, closing the door before turning on the light. I am slightly sore all over and wonder how much is from ziplining and kayaking vs. fucking. Probably a little bit of everything. I cannot believe how brazen I am around him. It's not my usual style, but something about Blue draws this sex kitten out of her box. I'm sure it's all thanks to the confidence I feel when I'm with him. I've worked hard on finding my own self-worth over the years. I'm not dependent on the judgment and acceptance of others like I was when I was in my twenties and early thirties. But it still feels good to receive all this positive attention from him. Verbal praise is for sure one of my love languages.

Standing back to get a better look at myself in the full-length mirror hanging on the door to the bath, I take stock of my forty-six-year-old self. If I blur my eyes a lot, I could pass for a twenty-one-year-old me.

Maybe.

Pilates has been a miracle worker for my muscle tone over the years. I am going to have to pick up a little gift for my favorite instructor, Tamara while I am on vacation, I think as my eyes get caught up on the little hickey resting in the hollow of my hip.

A memento from our first night together. I smile and start thinking up sexy ways to wake him. My eyes continue up my body and I notice two more little hickeys on the underside of my left breast. When did he give me those? I wonder, as I replay the night.

Oh!

And I feel the flush of blood rise to my chest, before I see the color flood my skin. Turning around, I check out my back to see if the scratch marks I'm remembering are still there too. Nope. I'm both glad they are not, and a little disappointed. They would be much harder to hide, I decide. So, I choose to be grateful.

I wish for my toiletries as I scan the counter for his toothpaste. Thankfully, I notice a mini bottle of mouthwash and take a swig. Much better. Morning breath is not sexy. Finger combing my hair, I toss half over my shoulder, and it honestly looks amazing falling in big loose curls over my breast. I turn off the light and quietly open the door to try to sneak back into bed.

Standing in the dark hall, I can hear the steady rhythm of his breathing, and know he is still asleep. I check the clock and see that it's 10:00 am already. I tend to be an early riser, so 10:00 am feels like half the day is already gone. But then again. I have nothing to do today.

Except Blue.

I crawl back under the covers and his skin is hot against mine. My fingertips are ice cubes in comparison to the molten lava of flesh along his ribs. He moans in his sleep and I can feel his morning wood grow against my stomach. I wonder how far we can go before he wakes up?

It becomes a game in my mind as I very gently, stoke one finger along his dick, watching it grow with every inch I touch. He moans again and his hips move against me, but he is still asleep. I roll my hips into him and his arm wraps behind my back pulling me tighter against him still. He gives a little snore, mumbling my name, sill in his dream world. Pressing my breast flat against his chest, his heat radiates through every cell in my body. A rainbow of fireworks explode in my mind and my soft touch turns slightly more possessive, as the lust between my thighs becomes a grabbing clawing need. I throw my leg over his hips, shifting him onto his back and positioning myself on top of him. I slowly lower myself onto his cock and his hands slide up my thighs, gripping my hips. His eyes still closed, he smiles and exhales my name.

I don't know if he is still dreaming or if he is awake.

The mystery is its own aphrodisiac as I slowly start to move against him.

I touch myself, imagining it's his hands roaming up my stomach and over my breast. Pinching my own nipple, a spike of amazing zips to my lady bits and I'm already close. Then I do feel his hands, as his thumb rubs little circles against my clit. I open my eyes to see if he is awake, and his blue eyes are dark indigo, as they stare at me playing with my breast. His nails dig into my ass as he pulls me closer. Thrusting deeper, my legs shake from the vibration of my orgasm as it ripples through my body.

I collapse on top of his chest, his dick still deep inside of me, panting.

"Good morning." he says. His voice was deep and gravely from sleep.

"Mmmmmm….Phhhffttt." is all I can get out.

"I've never been woken up like that before," he says.

"I've never woken anyone up that way either." I smile lazily at him. "When did you finally gain consciousness?" I ask, kissing a line up his neck to his ear lobe.

"Not long before I started touching you. I think I was fighting between the dream and consciousness for a while as I watched you pleasure yourself with me."

He thrust into me again slowly. Still hard, he had not cum yet. "I couldn't believe you were real and not just a dream." He thrust again, then flipped us so that my back was against the mattress. Grabbing my legs, he threw my knees over each of his shoulders. The angle allowed for me to watch as the head of his dick pushed deep inside of me. Each thrust is a little harder and faster. The pressure for release building back up, I climaxed again crying out his name while feeling him shake, as his own orgasm overcame him.

Releasing my legs, he fell against my side, pulling me by my waist to face him.

"That may be my new favorite position." I say kissing his chest. "I like being able to watch you fuck me."

"Ainsley..., the things that come out of your mouth." He hisses. "If it was physically possible to fuck you again right now, I would."

"It's a shame you can't have multiple orgasms. It really is a lovely way to start the day." I brag.

"Watching you have multiple orgasms is just as nice." he laughs, kissing my shoulder. "Do you know what time it is?"

"A little after 10:00 am." I yawn.

"Really?" he perks up "I never sleep in this late. I feel like half the day is already gone."

I smile at our shared thoughts. "Do you have any plans for today?"

"None. How about you?"

"Nope." I answer distractedly as his lips trail kisses over my breast.

"Oh, wait! Sarah and I have massages booked at noon." I was almost disappointed, but... Massage. So no, actually, I was very excited.

"That sounds nice. Anything else you want to do today? Anything with me?"

He makes me feel giddy. "Yes." I smile "Other than more of what we just did, I would love to spend the day with you. We could lounge by the pool and swim. Or play a round of putt putt golf, or gamble in the casino? I don't really care what activity it is."

His smile lit his entire face. "We can learn how to fold towels into little animals or go buy some art work in the gallery."

"We could take tango lessons."

"Or learn how to make ice sculptures."

"Or an air hockey tournament in the arcade."

"We should definitely do that." He smiled this big grin that reminded me of a playful little boy.

"Should we see if Sarah and Brent want to join us?" I ask, hoping he would say no.

"Maybe later. I think I want you all to myself right now, if that's okay?" His fingers stroked the side of my cheek. "Sarah is going to get you for an entire hour, I don't really want to share you before that."

"Ninety minutes."

"What?"

"Our massages are for ninety minutes. It will give you a chance to miss me. Besides, I'll come back to you all dewy and relaxed."

"Fine. I suppose I will make the sacrifice for the greater good." he smirked with half a grin.

I laugh out loud. "Very considerate of you, good sir."

"Until noon, may I have you?"

"Greedy." I tease some more.

"With you, yes. Five days is not a lot of time, and I want as much of you as you will let me share."

His words make me feel like a love sick puppy. "You make me want to say yes to booking the chapel, when you say things like that." I know I'm blushing. There is a fire in my chest and I feel absolutely nauseous over the fact that I just brought up the chapel. But it's a good nauseous. Besides, he was the one to bring up getting hitched first.

"I would." His voice is so low and deep I almost don't hear him. "I'm so insanely crazy for you Ainsley, that if you said yes, I would put pants on and go book the ceremony."

Taking his face in my hands I kiss him. "You're fucking crazy." I laugh.

"I would have married you in Vegas too!" he smiles.

"What? No, you would not have." I was still laughing. Thinking back, If I was drunk enough, I probably could have been talked into it. I was wild for him then too.

"You shouldn't have left so early." he says matter of fact. "I guess, you'll never know."

I love that he teases and plays like this. It gives me the tingles. He is right. Five days really isn't enough. I'm going to want more of him. Marrying him would be one way to make sure this little romance doesn't end. But then again, there is a lot more than just the two of us to consider.

"Alice would have my head if she was not present at my wedding. And Bodhi would be crushed if he couldn't walk me down the aisle."

"Does that mean your father has passed?" he asked quietly, completely changing the direction of the conversation from a funny, light hearted one to a sad one. Getting to know one another has lows sometimes too.

"Yes. Both of my parents are gone now. How about you?"

"My mom passed away a little over a decade ago. My Dad is still kick'n."

"Does he still work with you on the properties?"

"He likes to give orders when he can. It makes him feel important. He is a smart guy, and while most of his ideas are a bit outdated, you never outgrow common sense."

I like the way Blue speaks of his father. I can tell he loves and respects the man.

"Tell me about your son." I ask, wanting to learn more about him too.

"Austin is the funniest person I know." Blue lit up at the mention of his son. "He has always been two hundred percent. Bright colors, loud voice, class clown, and student body president. He loves drama and live theater. Vanessa instilled that in him. She took him to see the Lion King when he was three years old and he was hooked. He is working on his BA in Theater now."

Blue glowed with fatherly pride. Not everyone supports the arts so completely, it was wonderful that he did. "When Nessa died, Austin went through a really, dark time. He lost himself. Up until that point, he thought his mom was the only one who really knew him."

Blue held back...

He bit his lip...

The tension from his pause could be felt.

"Austin is gay. He didn't know that I knew." He let out a heavy breath. I released my breath too, smiling for him to continue. "I've known Austin was gay since he was a little boy. And he has always been perfect. But until I opened up to him about how I felt, Austin felt alone. We learned a lot from each other."

"Bodhi is gay too." Flies out of my mouth. For some reason, around Blue, I have no filter. "He dated girls before Brian died. He would bring boys home too, but Brian never knew. Once he was gone, the girls stopped showing up. Brian would not have loved him any less, but there was fear of disappointment there. Bodhi once told me that on their morning surfing trips, Brian would help him scope out the cute girls. He just didn't want to let him down. We both learned to speak our truths a little better after Brian was gone. Not that it was his fault, his death was simply the catalyst for that life lesson." I finished sharing.

"Is it just me, or do we seem to have a lot in common?"

"Twilight zone vibes over here."

He laughed. "Oh no! I just had a horrible thought. Quick, when is your birthday?"

"June 8th? Why?"

"Thank goodness. Mine is April 22nd. Just making sure we are not twins separated at birth."

"Thank heavens for that." I agree.

"What about your daughter? What is she like?"

"Alice is a go-getter. She is studying fashion design at FIDM. She designed the dress I'm going to wear to dinner tonight." I smile.

"Wow, I can't wait to see it."

"It is pretty spectacular. I may be slightly biased, but really, she is very good."

Then Blue's room phone rang, interrupting us. Reaching over me, he picked up. "This is Cody."

"Hey Sarah. Yeah, she's here. Okay, I'll tell her. (Laugh, laugh, laugh) You couldn't pay me enough (Ha, Ha) Sure. Bye."

"What was all of that about?" I ask intrigued.

"Sarah, wanted to remind you about your spa day. She said check in is at 11:45 am"

"What time is it now?"

"11:00 am"

"I've never been so disappointed to have to leave for a massage." I pout. He took my pouty lip into his mouth and my body instinctively rolled into his.

"Come back to me all pliable and … what did you call it? Dewy?"

"Yeah." I smile against his lips.

"I think dewy is my new favorite sexy word."

"I promise to come back as dew-able as possible. But now, I better go shower first."

"Want help?"

"There is no way two people can fit in one of those showers. Two people can't even fit in the bathroom at the same time." I laugh.

"We could try." He wiggles his eyebrows at me. But I just continue laughing and shake my head.

"Meet me after by the pool then? Brent and I will be waiting with whatever fancy drink you like."

"That sounds nice." I smile. "I'll take whatever the daily special is."

"You're adventurous." He grins.

"Gotta try everything to know what I like and don't like."

"That's a good philosophy. Is there anything you won't try?"

"Maybe heroin."

He chokes on his laughter. "That's a good standard."

"What's the craziest thing you have ever done?" I ask.

"Probably skydiving."

"Was it fun? Would you go again?" I question excitedly. I love his outdoorsy thrill-seeking nature. I miss having someone to go on weekend adventures with, finding that adrenaline rush of riding a roller coaster or the excitement of seeing something new for the first time. I can imagine the rush of jumping from a plane with him by my side and I pray that the image in my mind might come true one day.

"It was an amazing adrenaline rush. I only went once on a tandem jump with the instructor. I think I would tandem jump again. It was my fortieth birthday gift to myself. My own little midlife crisis.

This time I choke on my laughter. "I got really into Meditation and Yoga during mine." I grin.

"That sounds like a much healthier extreme."

"Life changing." I beam up at him.

"Oh yeah, how so?"

"Well, I started getting into breath work and discovered my higher self through deep meditation. I studied Anthropology in college. Not much you can do with that. But it was the spark that got me into reading about ancient philosophies and religions. I started piecing everything together in the quiet of my mind, finding truth in the commonalities. Then I stumbled upon metaphysics and it all fell into place for me. I guess I found my flow."

"The more I get to know about you, the more I like." He tells me, pulling me back under the covers and kissing me sweet and slow.

"So, what is the craziest thing you've ever done?" he asks, as his eyes study my features and his fingers play with my hair.

"There was this one time in Vegas that I judged a kissing contest."

His grin lights his face. "One of the best nights of my life. Although, the last forty-eight hours have been right up there too." I kiss him this time and we melt into the sweetest make out session for the next twenty minutes.

***

As the clock nears 11:30 am, I reluctantly slide out of the bed to get a fast rinse in, since I no longer have time for a real shower.

"May I borrow a towel to run next door? I don't want to get dressed again to walk five feet if I don't have to."

"That's like a whole new level to the 'walk of shame'" he jokes.

"I like to think of it as practical." I stick my tongue out at him before popping into the bathroom to steal a towel.

Coming back out, his presence next to me surprises me and I give a little jump. He stands there holding up my bra and panties.

"I really like these." he says, handing them over to me. I take them as his hand tactfully slides behind my neck. He pulls me in for a deep, sexy, goodbye kiss that has me considering skipping my shower totally. His body is hard and hot against mine and I claw at him, wanting more than just his tongue in my mouth.

"I love the way you kiss me." I say dreamily as he slowly steps back.

"I love you, …the way you kiss, too." He stumbles over his words and I can see his ears turn red for a change.

I love it.

"I'll see you up at the pool when we are done." I grin, kissing him again.

"Good." (Kiss, kiss, kiss) Enjoy." He says, not letting me go.

"Thank you." I finally turn to leave, picking my dress and shoes up as I exit.

Peeking outside to make sure the hallway is clear; I run next door and swipe my keycard, slipping inside without being seen. My heart races. Not from the five-foot sprint. But from the way Blue makes me feel.

This can't be love already.

Infatuation??? Perhaps.

Whatever it is, I love it. I love every moment with him. My heart is full.

# 17.

## Girl Talk

Ainsley:

I enter through double doors to the soft warm glow of candle light and the scent of lavender. Sarah is already waiting in the tiffany-colored relaxation room. She looks all snuggly in her white robe, sipping tea, when I arrive for our massage. Looking up she greets me with a smile and pats the chaise next to her, inviting me to sit. The cushion is squishy soft, and I snuggle in, getting cozy.

"You're glowing." she says as I take a sip of my own tea.

"You have a bit of a glow about you too." I reply "Tell me, did you and Brent have fun last night after we left." I wiggle my eyebrows at her.

"Oh my God, Ains, he is amazing!" she fawns "Last night. Wow! I don't think I knew what good sex was until last night." I giggle alongside Sarah, sharing in her joy.

"I think this singles cruise has worked out well for both of us."

"Totally. This trip was supposed to be about getting my rebounds out of the way, but I think this could be it."

"Seriously?"

"Absolutely. He is perfect. He is so adventurous and fun, he has been to all the places I want to go already. Brent lives the life I've always dreamt of. And he makes me laugh so hard. I've never been around such a happy person. Well, you're pretty happy Ains. But Brent...," she was practically swooning. "He is like the exact opposite of Wayne. He is so kind, and sexy, and he likes my ideas, and he thinks I'm amazing too." She rambles on dreamily.

"Well, Wayne is a narcissistic asshole, so he is a horrible standard to base anyone off of." I remind her.

"True, but Brent really is something special."

"I agree. The little bit of time I've spent with him has been great. He does seem truly wonderful. I have never heard you laugh so much in the seven years I've known you. I think an optimist in your life would be good for a change."

"You don't think I'm rushing into things, do you? I kinda jumped into the pond head first with Wayne and that didn't end well. What if I make the same mistake again?"

"You have to listen to your heart. Do what makes you smile, Sarah."

She nods and gives me a smile. "He makes me really happy, Ains. Freakishly happy. He has such a good heart. Did you know that he donates his time, building communities with Habitat for Humanity? He spent a month in Nigeria and three weeks in Chile helping others." Sarah's eyes glisten as she brags about her new crush.

"Definitely a total one-eighty compared to Ass face." I agree.

Ass face is my favorite nickname for Sarah's ex-husband. He was cruel and abusive and controlling. A complete nightmare for Sarah and all of us around her. But she is tough, and has emerged from his dark influence a glorious butterfly. Just like Blue said, like energy attracts like energy. Sarah is so pure and good, it's only right that she would attract someone just like her.

"I love the light dancing around in your eyes right now my friend. I say you keep him."

"My heart is seriously buzzing right now. Maybe it's just an orgasm hangover, because, Oh my God, Ains!" She leaned closer to me and I mimicked her move, leaning in a few inches, to hear the really good gossip. "He went down on me and broke my brain."

I burst into laughter. "Sweetie Pie, I fucking love you hopped up on broken brain."

"How about you and Mr. Blue eyes?"

"I'm just as head over heels as you are." I grin. "We just seem to vibrate at the same speed, you know?" I didn't know if she would get what I meant. But how else could I explain it. A twin flame? A matched soul?

"I get that. It's like you just melt into one person." Sarah says melting into the chaise a little more.

"Yeah, that's what it feels like. Like we are waves on the ocean, swirling together in a hurricane of incredible sex." I sink a little lower in my chair too, and take a little sip of tea.

"I have noticed the way you can't keep your hands off each other. Honestly, it's indecent Ains." That had me cracking up and nearly spitting my drink out all over my soft white robe.

"I don't think I can keep from drowning in him." I say as I dab my chin clean.

"We can both dive head first together. I'm pretty sure I'm going down with the ship too."

As we are laughing, two Masseuses in matching gray outfits, walk in giving us the side-eye over our apparent conversation of sinking ships.

Never a popular topic on a cruise.

"Sarah and Ainsley?" they ask hesitantly.

"That's us." We stand and follow the ladies out for our ninety minutes of pampering.

My sore muscles appreciated every moment as I relaxed and reminisced about all the fun wonderful ways Blue made me laugh. Or the way he surprised me with a clever thought or common interest. I thought about Sarah and Brent, hoping that their little romance flourished too. It would be so fun if my best friend was dating one of Blue's best friends also. Double dates were always hard when Sarah was with assface, back before Brian had died. Since her separation and now divorce, she and I have been having fun being single together. But it would be more fun, if we could just put yesterday on repeat indefinitely. Enjoying vacation life with two kind, funny, smart, and handsome men by our sides. I imagine the four of us hanging out enjoying a couple's game night, or going to a concert together. My imagination takes off as I picture one fun activity after another.

I'm a very good day dreamer.

# 18.

## Single No More

Ainsley:

Standing in front of the desk and mirror back in my room, I run the brush through my hair a final time before slipping on my sandals and grabbing my sarong to wrap around my bathing-suit-clad self. Today my suit is a black one piece. It's one of those specialty cut suits that is supposed to accentuate the good while tucking and hiding the not so good. It's simple but flattering.

I grab my floppy sun hat, sunglasses, and a beach bag full of books and head for the pool deck. Sarah is meeting us there too. I'm actually excited to spend time as a foursome. I want to see Sarah and Brent in action. We spent so much of our time together yesterday separated into pairs. And to be fair, I've been so lost in Blue's eyes, I haven't really been paying attention. It's wonderful seeing her so happy. She deserves a little beauty too.

I arrive on the pool deck and start scanning the crowd for Blue when I hear my name called. But it is not Blue's voice. I turn and see another man waving at me. It takes me a moment, before I recognize him as one of the guys I met at the speed dating event the first night. He stood out amongst the men, due to the fact that he is a professional axe thrower up in Washington state. A one-armed axe thrower! Born without it, he told me. But I overheard him tell Sarah that it was lost when he was training an underling. What was his name? Jimmy? Jack? Whatever his name, he had jogged over to me, grabbed my hand, and kissed my cheek before I could come up with it.

"I missed you at the last two events. Where have you been hiding?" he asks with a grin.

"I uhhh…," I stumble. "I'm not participating in the singles activities any more. I ran into an old flame and the spark is still there." I explain, as nicely as possible.

"Your blue wrist band is still on. Maybe you should give me a proper chance before you shut the door to our flame."

"Wow." I blush "I am so flattered. If things don't work out, I promise to come find you."

"He's a lucky guy." He kisses my hand in farewell.

"Thank you."

Slightly flustered, I turn around and head towards the center of the ship. I find my little group and quickly walk over to Blue. The pool deck is packed and Sarah and Brent are sharing a lounge chair. Blue kicks his legs to the side and makes room for me with a welcoming open arm. I sit down and snuggle into his side. Content.

"Who was that over there?"

"Oh, just your competition." I tease. "It's this blue wristband. It's like a homing beacon."

"I cut mine off this morning." Blue says nonchalantly.

"Really?"

"Yeah, well, I don't really feel single anymore."

There go the butterflies. "Maybe I should cut mine off too." The look Blue gives me blocks out the other five-hundred people on deck.

"Julio!" Blue yells, without breaking eye contact. A moment later a waiter stands over us smiling.

"Sr. Cody, ¿Un trago para usted, encantadora dama??" *Mr. Cody, a drink for your lovely lady?

"Julio, my man, this is Ainsley." He smiles at me with mischief and longing in his eyes. "Sí, por favor, ¿Podemos traernos una de las bebidas especiales de hoy y unas tijeras, por favor?" *Yes please. One of today's drink specials, and a pair of scissors please.

"Si, ahora mismo." *Yes, right away. And he dashes off.

OMG, Blue speaks perfect Spanish. Another piece of him for me to love and fawn over.

"So how was your massage? Are you all relaxed and dewy?" He asks, as his eyes devour my body.

"It was wonderful, and yes, I am. My skin feels so soft now."

Blues finger runs a line up from my ankle to my hip. Slipping under my cover up, like he has the right to. It turns me on so fast that I fear my blush will give me away to the rest of the ship. He makes me feel beautiful and desired unlike anyone else. Sure, it was flattering when the stranger on the deck approached me a moment ago. But, Blue... The way his eyes seem to consume every inch of my body. The way his gaze over my skin makes me hungry for him... Wow. Just wow!

"Very soft." He whispers, kissing my jaw, chin, then mouth. My nerves are on fire every place his lips touch me.

"You two are gross." Sarah jokes from the lounge chair next to us.

"He is just trying to show off to the competition over there." I say teasing.

"Am I that obvious?" Blue says as he continues kissing my neck. Brent throws a wadded-up napkin at Blue's head, followed by a wadded-up straw wrapper in jest.

Julio returns a few minutes later with my drink and a pair of scissors, interrupting their play fight.

"Thank you, Julio."

Blue holds my wrist gently, sliding the scissors between my skin and the band. He looks me in the eyes as he snips through the plastic. The action carries a weight of permanence to it. He leans over and kisses my wrist where the band had been.

Right against my pulse. I wonder if he can tell it is racing.

"So, are you two, like going steady now?" Brent asks in a fake valley girl accent.

"Yes." Blue replies with confidence. "Ainsley, will you be my girlfriend."

"That all depends on how many goats you're offering in your dowry." I joke.

"I will buy stock in Goats-R-Us for a yes."

"It's a yes, even without goats." I smile up at him.

"What do you say Sarah? Should we count our blessings and cut off our blue bands too?" Brent asks her.

"Yes." She claps, smiling up at him and bouncing in her seat. Blue passes over the scissors and Brent cuts off Sarah's band, and then his own.

"Now we are all properly spoken for." he says placing the scissors back on the table between us.

"Did you guys have a chance to check out the itinerary? Any soap on a rope demonstration we should check out?" I question.

"Brent and I each made dinner reservations for two at La Cave for 7:30 pm tonight. There is also an adult comedy show that is supposed to be pretty great." Blue responds.

"And tonight is the midnight buffet!" Brent pipes in excitedly.

"With so many activities, when will there be time for sex?" Sarah teases, and we all brake into laughter until Sarah and Brent get distracted making out.

Blue follows their lead as his hands start to slowly remove my cover up. His fingers sneak and tickle the fabric apart in an extremely sexy and intimate way.

"Yoga, gave you this body?" he asks as his eyes roam over me.

"Yoga, Pilates, and long nature hikes."

"You like hiking?" He perks up.

"I love it. I would much rather spend my time in nature than with people." Once again, the words fall from my mouth. "Not that, I'm anti-social." I try to back track, my self-conscious inner voice yelling at me, to 'please stop saying weird things around my fantasy man'.

"I like hiking too. It's one of the reasons I bought the camp ground. All the trails back to the national park, and there are a few fingers of the creek that run through the property. I walk the camp with my dog Fluffs, nearly every day. She likes to bark squirrels up the trees and chase rabbits and lizards. The canyon is filled with lots of cottonwood trees, oaks, and pines. Some days, I spend more time talking to them than I do other humans."

"You talk to trees?" I ask intrigued. "I talk to trees too, but people look at me funny when I say things like that."

He laughs "They make good therapists. But I find I learn more when I listen to them." He winks.

I can't breathe. This man is too perfect. How can anyone check so many of my quirky little boxes? "You scare me a little." I whisper with a smile.

"You scare me too." he whispers back, studying my eyes like he can read my soul. Then we kiss. Sweet and slow and perfect. His lips send fire racing through my spine. My fingers clutch at the waistband of his swim trunks, as I both pull him closer and hold him back. Both of us worked to restrain from dry humping him in public. We both slowly pull away before our minds lose control and our bodies take over.

Running a hand through his thick hair and letting out an exhale that says 'I wish I could have more' he asks "What's in your little bag?" nodding towards it at my feet.

"Just a few books. I wasn't sure if we would be relaxing or running amuck, so I prepared for both."

"Oh yeah, what has captured Ainsley the reader's attention this time?"

"I'm working on three at the moment. I have Mel Brooks' memoir. The Midnight Library. And Dirty, Sexy, Things."

"I've read that one." He points to the Mel Brooks book 'It's All About Me'. "Actually, I listened to it on Audiobooks. Mel reads it himself and it's hilarious. He cracks himself up half the time. Added a whole new element."

"Really? I don't usually listen to audio books, but that sounds like it would be even better that way."

"And what is this one? Dirty, Sexy, Things?" He picks up the little red paperback with nothing but suggestive shadows on the cover.

"That is where my filthy mouth comes from." I say grabbing it out of his hand.

"I love your filthy mouth. Read that one." He grins.

"Do you have anything good to read?" I ask him.

"Actually, I do have a good book. I'm reading 'The Secret Life of Plants.' But I think I want to read this one with you." he says pointing to my Dirty book. "Maybe I can pick up a few pointers."

"Like you need to. I don't think I have ever had more enjoyable sex than the past two days with you."

"I can feel my ego growing."

"Funny, I was noticing another part of you growing." I laugh nudging my thigh against his swelling cock.

"Ainsley, you make me feel young again, vibrant like I was back in my twenties. I can barely control myself around you." He says as he squeezes me tighter against his side. "But I never had sex like this, back then. And this morning. Fuck Ainsley, my wildest dreams don't compare to you."

"It's the Kegels."

He chokes on a laugh. "The what?"

"We do a lot of core workouts at Pilates. Lots of kegel strength." I grin up at him.

"I'm grateful for it." He smiles this wickedly sexy half smirk at me.

We four spend the last few hours of the afternoon relaxing, as well as swimming and having a race against some teenagers across the pool. After joining in on the conga line and voting for the hairy chest contest, the boys cleaned up on the sports round of the trivia game. Next, we all went inside to see who could best who, at air hockey. A little after 6:30 pm, Sarah put a halt to the party declaring that the two of us needed extra time to gossip while getting ready. The guys kissed us sweetly as we said goodbye and we headed back to our rooms while they headed for the tiki bar near the pool.

Stopping just outside of our doors, Sarah leaned over. "Ainsley, I'm really serious. I think I just might up my entire life for him. Have you ever been to Chicago? It doesn't really seem like my kind of place, but I would give it a try for Brent. No one has ever made me feel so wonderful." She says wistfully.

"Isn't he retired? Maybe he would move out to California."

"That's what I'm hoping for. But I'm afraid to ask if he would consider it. We have only been dating for thirty-six hours. I'm sure I'm jumping the gun, but I have never been so head-over-heels before." I'm struck by how similar Sarah's emotions and thoughts are to my own about Blue, and it makes me feel a little saner.

"From what Blue tells me, Brent is head-over-heels for you too. And honestly, what I have seen proves it. He is exactly the type of person I would like to see you end up with Doll. Someone who recognizes how amazing, and funny, and smart you are."

"Aw, Thanks Ains. I want the same things for you too my friend. So, what are you and Cody going to do?"

"I don't know? We haven't talked about it too much yet. Other than that, we both want to give it a try and see where it all goes. We have been too busy shagging to get into any details." I grin.

"So, you are going to try the long-distance thing?"

"Yeah, he wants to book a trip out to San Diego soon. Taos isn't as far as Chicago. I'm sure I could swing it as a midweek trip; but it's still not just a drive up the block. I'm not really sure what I expect our future to look like, just yet."

"Why can't the good guys be local?"

I shrug. "Maybe there is more for us elsewhere."

"I like that idea." she says as she opens the door to her room. "Bang on the wall when you're ready for hair."

"Thanks Sarah, I will." I say, opening my door to start getting all gussied up for tonight.

# 19.

## Clinking Wine Glasses

Cody:

Brent and I met at the pub a little after 7:15 pm as had become our standard. I don't feel the need for an extra shot tonight. My nerves are gone. Since waking up this morning, which was the best wake up of my life, my mind has been made up that this is the Divine at work. Gaining consciousness in the middle of that dream…, A real dream I have fantasized about in the past; not just this morning. The weeks following meeting Ainsley in Vegas, I imagined many fantastic naked moments with her. Then again, when I started my hunt for all of my missed opportunities.

But that one…,

I have pictured Ainsley riding on top of me, touching herself, hair tumbling over her shoulders…, just as it was in real life. I think that is what took me so long to focus on actual reality. It was exactly like my dream.

Exactly.

This feels like that old movie, The Secret. I set my intention. I imagined the feeling of gratitude and joy upon finding her again. And according to her, she prayed or manifested me too. This is how the universe works. Like energy draws like energy. This undeniable pull and magnetism between us, is the universal energy. It's the chi that flows through us all. I have full faith, and feel so sublimely at peace, that when Brent orders our standard double of whiskey, I almost decline.

But the look in his eyes tells me not to.

"I happened to be walking by the shops on my way to the pub and this caught my eye." He drops a little white box in front of me.

"For me? You shouldn't have." I joke, picking it up and opening the lid to look inside. There sat a solitaire diamond engagement ring, with a massively large rock glistening in the low light of the bar.

"Holy fuck man." I look at him in awe.

"I don't really know what came over me. I'm not even sure when or how I will ask her."

"But you know you want to ask her?"

"The only other thing I have ever felt so completely sure of was selling the business and retiring. And we both know how well that worked out for me." he grins.

"I don't mean to play devil's advocate here, but she just got out of a marriage. Are you sure she is ready for this?" I ask, thinking of the pull back I received from Ainsley when I mentioned eloping in the ships chapel.

"I told her last night I was going to marry her one day. She made me pinky swear." his grin reached all the way into his eyes.

"So should I start working on a speech for the wedding?"

"Obviously, you do get credit for hooking us up on our double date."

"Excellent. How about a toast to your upcoming engagement? May you and Sarah share all the joy and adventures of life and brighten each other's dark moments. Cheers Mate."

And we drank "Thanks Cody."

\*\*\*

Arriving before the girls, Brent and I check into the front desk of La Cave, the on-board fancy restaurant that is not included with the cruise. The place is low lit and quiet. Perfectly romantic. I put a fifty percent likelihood on Sarah walking out of this restaurant with that ring on her finger. It's that type of place. I'm almost jealous that I don't have a ring in my pocket too. But then again, that doesn't feel right for Ainsley and me. She already put a nix on the elopement thing due to the kids. Brent and Sarah don't have children and the mixing of families to consider with their whirlwind romance.

I imagine popping the question for real. I picture us out under a canopy of trees, alone. Something personal and private vs. a public display. Brent is the type that would propose over the loudspeaker at a ball game. And while I don't know Sarah that well, I'm pretty sure she would lavish that kind of attention.

From the little bit I've gleaned about her past marriage, Sarah had been held under the thumb of her ex-husband out of jealousy. He was always picking her apart and tearing her down. Afraid that she would realize that she was worthy of more, and run off with someone better. Ainsley called him mean. But it was more than the word itself that instantly made me hate Sarah's ex. It was the look in her eyes when she said it.

Pain.

Words hurt, and it is obvious that Sarah's ex-husband crossed the line into verbal abuse.

Brent is the exact opposite. He is optimistic and happy, and always has a good word for everyone. I imagine he would treat Sarah like a queen and spoil her at every opportunity. I'm sure she deserves to be spoiled.

My wandering mind comes to a halt as Ainsley and Sarah round the bend and into view. They are both stunning, but Ainsley is so lovely I forget to breathe. Her dress is a deep rich indigo that hugs every curve, then flairs soft and flowy at her hips. Short on the sides but long in the front and back. It is classic and edgy at the same time. Her hair looks like it has been professionally styled in a braidy-knotty thing that looks like it took hours to fashion. Yet, I know the girls only took one hour to look this amazing.

"You look ravishing." I say, pulling her into my arms for a kiss.

"Thank you. You're rather dashing yourself."

"You said, your daughter designed this dress?"

"Sewed it too."

"Wow. She is talented."

"I agree." She smiles warmly and full of love and pride. I like that look on her. A lot.

The hostess directs us to our table with a lovely view of the ocean.

"This is fancy." she says as the Sommelier introduces himself and offers suggestions to pair with the chef's menu for the night.

"I imagine you see many fancy meals in your line of work."

"Oh, I do. I often get to eat them too. Even the vendor meals at weddings are typically amazing. But the ambiance of this place and the energy is so classically elegant and romantic."

"I wouldn't be surprised to see a proposal here tonight." I say, half wondering how many of the men in here have rings hidden in their pockets too.

"I bet Sarah and Brent could be one of them. She is crazy about him."

"He bought a ring."

"What!" she whisper-yells. Her fingers covering her mouth at her outburst. I nod and lean in close so that I can speak low.

"He doesn't know when, or if it will be on the cruise, but he is crazy about her too."

"I feel good about them." she says sitting back, nodding her head with approval. "Really good. I normally wouldn't condone engagement on the second date, but those two have a shared energy. I think they would be happy for a very long time together."

"I don't think they are the only ones that have a shared energy."

She looks over at me. A small closed mouth smile on her face as places her hand in mine. "No, they are not the only ones." I can feel the electricity shoot up my finger-tips and down my spine, before settling in my chest.

"How does he plan to handle the long-distance thing?" she asks.

"I don't really know." I shrug my shoulders in response.

"Do you think he would move out to California? I know Sarah would be willing to relocate for him, but her business is here. The wedding industry is all about who you know and referral contacts. She might struggle to establish herself out there."

"I don't think he would expect her to work if she moved to Chi Town with him. Honestly, he would probably like her to retire, if she wanted to, even if he came out to California."

The questions about Brent and Sarah feel like they could be about us too. My answers would be the same either way.

"Brent is a really active guy." I continue, "I'm often jealous of how much he travels. He has been just about everywhere and knows all the best spots and fun activities. He is really good at enjoying every minute of life. I'm sure he would like for Sarah to join him as much as possible."

"I think Sarah would like that too. She binges on travel shows."

"Brent could host his own travel show. He has been my travel guru over the past year. Every time I need advice on where to go or what to do, I go to him. 'Cuz chances are, He has already been there and done it. He lives by the same philosophy as you. Try everything."

"Smart man."

"He is. He's a great guy. Easily one of my closest friends. And if Sarah is one of yours, then I have full faith they will be happy together for a long time."

"How often do you and Brent get to see each other living so far apart? I thought you two were just travel friends."

"We have become more. We call each other to check in every month or so. But usually, it's meeting up in Chi town to catch a Cubs game and eat amazing pizza. He came out to Taos last winter for the Wine and Food festival too."

"That sounds fun."

"I would like to take you to the festival next year. It's every January."

I watch the blush stain her cheeks, my favorite color as my suggestion for a date six months from now sinks into her brain.

"I would like that." She smiles.

"I was serious about coming out to visit you in San Diego. Maybe you could show me around your town too. My schedule is flexible. I'm happy to work around you."

"I'd like that." she smiles coyly. "I'm booked with weddings and playing a little catch up due to my time off on this trip, but I do slow down in August. San Diego is full of just about anything you could want. Or we could go check out the Temecula wine country where I usually work."

"I'm sure I would have fun anywhere, so long as I'm with you. Case and point, I'm in the middle of the Pacific Ocean, and I'm having the time of my life."

"I'm sure the cruise ship has a little to do with that. We don't even have to make our beds." She was cute in her excitement about not having to do chores.

"It's all you Ainsley. One hundred percent, because of you."

"I'm having the time of my life because of you too Cody."

"Cody? Not Blue?" I ask as her blush deepens.

"As I get to know the real you, I like you better than I ever imagined. Blue is only the daydream of you. Cody is the man sitting in front of me that contains so much more."

Now it was my turn to blush. "You have exceeded all of my expectations as well." I squeeze her hand trying to keep my pulse from exploding out of my veins.

***

Lobster, jumbo shrimp, scallops, and oysters arrive on the table a moment later interrupting my heart palpitations.

"Well, this doesn't look horrible." She licks her lips.

"Much better than the medium shrimp the peasants in the main dining room are stuck with." I joke, taking a bite of one of the shrimps.

It was divine.

"Good?" She asks in response to the look of sheer pleasure on my face.

"Mmmmm." I pick one up off the plate to feed to her.

"Are we the couple that feeds each other across the table?"

"Yes." I grin as she takes a bite and the same look overcomes her face.

A loud squeal interrupts us, and has the entire restaurant looking over at Brent on one knee, and Sarah crying "Yes" in delight.

"Oh my God. He did it."

Ainsley starts laughing with joy at Sarah's reaction. "And they lived happily ever after." she whispers in disbelief.

Sarah rushes over to our table dragging Brent behind by the hand. "Oh my God you guys, we are getting married!!!" She is vibrating ball of energy. Her aura glowing so brightly, I swear I can see it radiating from her. Ainsley stands to hug and congratulate the bouncing Sarah and I stand to give Brent a slap on the back, which quickly evolves into a bro hug.

"Oh my God, Oh my God. I can't believe this is happening. I can't believe how happy I am. I'm tingling all over."

"You're shaking." Ainsley holds Sarah's hands and laughs. Tears of joy falling down both of their cheeks. "You two are so amazing for one another. I know in my gut this is going to be the most wonderful union. I'm so happy for you both." She says looking over to Brent, including him in her congratulations.

"Brent wants to come out to California and we will keep his Chicago pad as a vacation home. How amazing does that sound? It's all so perfect it feels impossible."

"The only impossible thing, would be for me not to try move mountains to have you in my life." Brent says as he takes Sarah's hand pulling her back into his embrace and kissing her in a manner more suited for the privacy of the bedroom. But on a night like tonight, no one in the restaurant seems to mind. A few wine glasses clink in the background, and a few awe's sound through the crowd.

"We are probably going to cut the evening short after dinner." Brent tells us while keeping his eyes locked on Sarah. "Maybe we will see you two at the midnight buffet. I am planning to burn off all these calories from dinner and will probably need to refuel."

I laugh. "No worries if you don't make it out of your room tonight, Mate." I say slapping him on the back. "But we will keep an eye out for you just the same. Congratulations Brent and Sarah."

"Yes, congrats you two. I know this is the start of something amazing."

They walk back to their table receiving congratulations from strangers as they pass, and we sit back down laughing and smiling at the joy that still lingers in the air about us.

"I'm completely in shock and awe of what just happened. And maybe a little jealous that he proposed first, even though we have known each other so much longer." I joke as I dip a tender piece of lobster into the butter and continue to devour our meal.

"I feel an odd sort of wonder and envy too. But I had been placing the blame for my conundrum of feelings on my hunger pains." She smiles at me. Picking up an oyster, she shoots it back like a pro. Her shoulders give a little shake as the oyster slides down her throat.

I laugh "You look like you shoot oysters often."

"I took a trip to Boston a few years ago; had my first taste there. Then Sarah and I found an oyster bar in San Diego we sometimes hit when we go down there. But other than that, not really. Do you like them?"

"I've never tried them." I answer. Honestly, the idea grosses me out.

"These are very good. Now would be a good time to try one." She urges. "And you know what they say about oysters."

I know what they say. But I want to hear her say it, so I play dumb.

"No, what do they say about oysters?"

"They are an aphrodisiac."

"I don't need an aphrodisiac with you." Her cheeks stain pink in response. Every time I make her blush, I feel like I'm scoring points and winning a game. "But I'll try one anyway."

Scooping up an oyster shell, she stops me, and adds a squirt of lemon. "There, now try it." She encourages. "Just let it slide down your throat."

It is gross.

I make a face and she laughs. Not just a little laugh, but a big belly laugh that has me eating another one just to keep her infectious giggles going.

# 20.

## Manifestation Work

Cody:

After dinner, and a shared tiramisu for dessert, we walk the ship talking about her photography career and the team she has put together over the last fifteen years in the business. We stop to take pictures at the photography station, and sing along to Elton John and Ricky Martin at the dueling pianos lounge. In-between, we share funny parenting stories and our goals and ambitions for the future. The number of times one of us says, "Me too," becomes comical, and within an hour we are throwing up our hands at the way our lives and interest seem to run parallel.

Walking out to the deck, she leans over the railing and watches as the waves rush pass the ship. The wind sweeping her hair and dress to the side, she looks like a classic oil painting. A stunning work of art, just smiling and enjoying the moment. I am simply enamored with this woman. I stand behind her and wrap my arms around her waist, tasting the salt air on the back of her neck. Sighing, she leans back into me, exposing more of her beautiful skin for me to devour. My hand slides up her ribs and between her cleavage. I stroke her neck and jaw, pulling at the back of her hair just enough to angle her mouth towards mine. She responds by sliding her tongue into my mouth and I am now ready to call the night quits, just like Brent and Sarah had.

She gives a little shiver in my arms, so I pull her closer, spinning her around to face me. Her breast pressed against my chest and her hips pushed into my hard on. I am lost in the feel of her body against mine as we make out under the star filled sky, alone on that big open deck for what seems like a lifetime. She gives another little shiver and my hands rub up and down her arms to warm her. Her skin is freezing somehow, despite the heat radiating off her lips.

"Are you cold?"

"Yeah, a little. Can we stop by my room so that I can grab my pashmina?"

"Of course." Taking her hand in mine we walk back inside and down to her room.

***

Once inside, she tucks into the closet while I head out onto her balcony. It isn't as cold on this side of the ship. The privacy walls between the adjoining rooms' balconies providing some extra protection from the wind. She joins me a moment later, on the deck, with a beautiful blue and silver scarf wrapped around her shoulders.

"It's much nicer out here. I don't even need this now." she says, noticing the pleasant weather as well. She tosses the scarf on the chair and smiles up at me. "I think the love birds must be in Brent's room. I can't hear any sounds coming from next door."

"Then let's sleep in here tonight." I wink.

"Okay." She says moving closer to me, her fingers walking up my chest. A vixen's smile on her lips. That smile was all the motivation I needed. I was pulling her close and spinning her against the privacy partition. My hands up her dress and roaming along her thighs, I lift her, helping her wrap her legs around my waist. My hands found her panties and my fingers slid the little piece of fabric to the side as I pushed two fingers inside of her. She is so hot and silky soft that I feel dizzy as the blood quickly drains south from my brain.

"Cody, that feels so good." She moans in my ear.

I need to get my pants off, I need to feel her under the stars.

Sliding her down my body, feet back on the earth, I kiss her sweet lips as I pull down my pants, just enough. Lifting her back up, I give her my best wicked grin and slide slowly inside of her. She makes this sound that vibrates though my body and I see stars in my mind, not just overhead. Quickly we find our rhythm, despite the awkward angle. Her sounds of pleasure increased with each thrust. My fists hold tight to the fabric of her dress as I barrel towards sweet release.

"Fuck. Oh fuck. Fuck Cody. Fuck! Oh, holy mother fucking, Yes! I'm cumming. Fuck." She bites my shoulder.

Her potty mouth is fucking perfect.

As I feel her body clench and pulse around me, I find my release. Grabbing onto her, holding her close, growling incoherent words, I cum undone under the star filled sky.

"I love your potty mouth when I'm fucking you." I whisper into her hair as she readjusts her dress.

"Cussing is very healthy. It releases endorphins."

"Does it?"

"It does. Not that I needed to cuss to release any endorphins a moment ago. You took care of all those needs. But I'm guessing all the wonderful things you make me feel sets off that link in my brain, filling my mouth with naughty words."

"Well, fuck Ainsley, you make me feel all kinds of wonderful too." I grin and she laughs.

"I need to freshen up a little, then do you still want to go to the comedy show?"

"Yes, that sounds perfect."

"Okay, I'll be right back." She heads into the bathroom as I recline in the lounge chair zipping my pants back up. I stare out at the stars, picking out constellations. Orion's belt, the Big Dipper, the North Star..., which reminds me of wishing on stars. So, I decide to spend this moment working on manifesting my future with Ainsley.

I imagine standing under my favorite old oak tree near the creek back home. I picture us speaking our vows to each other. Promising to love and cherish till death and beyond. I envision our first kiss as husband and wife. The feel of her hand in mine, her ring cool against my palm. I feel the joy in the future moment right now, and I thank the universe for having brought Ainsley back into my life.

The door to the balcony reopens and she walks back out, sitting down in the lounge chair next to me. "You look peaceful. You're not too tired to go out again, are you?"

"Not at all. I was just daydreaming."

"About what?"

"You." I grin looking over at her.

"More filthy words?"

"Not this time."

"Well, are you going to tell me, or are you going to make me guess?"

I laugh. "I like that idea, let me hear your guesses."

"Were you planning our day for Ensenada tomorrow?"

"No, but we should talk about that later."

"Sexy naked time?"

"While that consumes ninety percent of my daydreams about you, No."

"Maybe a future trip together?" she says in a slow quiet voice. I think I can hear a little hope behind her words and it makes my heart warm.

"That's not it either. But we should also talk about that later too." I looked over at her imagining that she was already my wife.

"I was doing a little manifestation work." I told her. "While Brent may be the impulsive one to buy a ring and pop the question, he isn't the only one thinking about forever." She turns a new shade of red I have not yet seen. I can't keep the smile from reaching my ears as she bites her lip and smiles up at me from under her lashes.

"I've been meditating on our forever too." she says. And I leave my lounge chair and kneel next to her, my knees to the ground. Our eyes lined up just right, I held her face in the palms of my hand and I kissed her just like I imagined in my day dream. All of the wonderful emotions of joy and gratitude filling my being.

"Wow." She whispers as I pull away. "Your kisses always give me the tingles."

"You give me the tingles too." My heart is still buzzing with them. "Ready?" I ask holding out my hand to help her up.

"Ready."

Leaving our love nest for the comedy lounge, my spirits could not be any higher.

## 21.

## A Few Laughs

Cody:

Our old friend Sven is the MC for the night. He starts his intro with a few jokes about the singles group and all the romance that can be found on board the ship. He pulls the audience in with a little game of 'Who's been married the longest' and 'Who are the newest of newlyweds. Scanning the crowd, his eyes land on us, a smile of recognition overcomes his features.

"Speaking of love on board," he continued. "Just two nights ago, I had a couple fall so madly in love they left in the middle of our speed dating event!" Sven announces to the crowd, receiving a loud response of laughs and a few whistles.

Ainsley beams up at me. "Gee, do you think he's talking about us?"

"We have become cruise ship legends." I wink.

"Maybe they will write a love song about us and duel it out at the piano bar." She continues with the jest.

"I bet they will rename the bar after us." I say, making her laugh. I love making her laugh. The way her eyes laugh in equal measure with her lips is contagious.

The headliner takes the stage and our laughs continue for the next forty-five minutes. After the show, as we make our way out of the theater, Sven comes up to speak with us.

"I see you two really did hit it off. Your blue wrist bands are gone." he says, smiling at us. I wrap my arms around her waist and kiss the top of her head in confirmation of his impression. "This makes me so happy." His blond hair flops against his forehead as he nods his pleasure at our relationship. "Maybe we will see you at the couple's event tomorrow night instead of the singles events from now on, Ja?"

"What event is that?" Ainsley asks politely.

"We are playing the honeymooner's game. It's always a hoot."

"I'm down for a hoot." she says, looking back up at me.

"We will try to make it. Thanks for letting us know."

"You kids have fun tonight." He says as he walks off towards some other crew members, smiling then pointing back at us.

"He's fun." she says.

"Yeah, but I don't really want to play the honeymooners game tomorrow night. I think I would rather spend every possible second of our last night together as just us."

She leans into my chest and sighs long and slow. "Me too." Looking up at me, her fingers move up to glide along my jaw. "Madly in love he called us." she whispers.

"I don't think he's wrong."

"No, I have a feeling he knows what love looks like."

My heart buzzes. We both keep dancing around that four-letter word. She makes it so hard to do things slow. But I try. Despite the people moving around us, I take the moment just for ourselves and my fingers trace along her jaw. I kiss her with all the love I am feeling, pouring out from me into her. Saying, I love you, without words.

# 22.

## Stock in Oysters

Cody:

We make our way to the midnight buffet, keeping an eye out for Brent and Sarah. Ainsley fills up on fresh fruit and a chocolate mousse, and I grab two plates containing one of everything.

"Hungry?" She questions looking at my plates.

"A boys gotta eat to keep up with pleasing you." I smirk.

"You have been pretty stellar." she winks. "Here." She adds a few pieces of pineapple to one of the plates.

"What's that for?"

"If we are going to start talking about forever, I'm going to need you to eat some fruit and stick around past sixty."

"Oh, I thought the pineapple was for…, taste."

She laughs. "Such a man. Head always in the gutter. But well, yes, I did give you the pineapple over the watermelon for that reason." She smiles a sexy little pirate's smile at me and wiggles her butt in her seat. Then her smile turns to one of greeting.

"It's Sarah and Brent. They made it out of their sex cave." She gestures behind me, waving to them.

They join our table with hugs in greeting, then go to load their own plates full of food.

"Did you two have a good night out enjoying the ship?" Brent asks, once they are back and situated.

"The comedy show was great, and we did a little sing-along at the piano bar." Ainsley tells them.

"That sounds nice. But I bet Sarah and I had more fun staying in." He gives Sarah a heated look, which she turns bright pink in response to.

"So, what's the plan for tomorrow, kids? Anyone know what's good in Ensenada? Other than the tequila that is." Brent asks.

"Have either of you guys ever been to Ensenada before?" Sarah questions. Neither of us have.

"I think we should take a tour then. The ship's excursions are all booked up, but I can google reputable tour companies. Maybe we can find a local group once we disembark.

"I like that idea." Ainsley agrees and Brent nods.

"Sounds good to me. We can meet at 8:30 am for breakfast then leave the ship a little after 9:00 am?" I suggest.

"Great" everyone agrees.

We all walk back down to our rooms together saying goodnight. A buffer of empty walls between us.

"Do you want to get anything from your room?" Ainsley asks as she opens her door.

"Good idea, I'll grab my tooth brush and something suitable to wear for my morning walk of shame." I grin, before briefly slipping into my room.

After grabbing my things, I gently knock on her door. "Who is it?" She answers from behind the door in a silly voice.

"Housekeeping." I joke back in a high-pitched, even sillier, voice. I wonder if she will get my obscure Tommy Boy movie reference.

"We don't need any towels." she replies keeping up with the game. My heart leaps when she opens the door, laughter on her face. There are no words to describe how happy this little discovery about her makes me. So, I kiss her sweet mouth.

Pulling me in the room we kiss against the door until our lips are swollen.

"This dress is so beautiful on you. I almost don't want to take it off."

"It wouldn't be very comfortable to sleep in. Besides, I am wearing pretty underthings for you."

"Mmmmm" I groan. "I love your pretty underthings."

My hand slides the zipper down her back and she gracefully steps out of the dress. I kneel down to pick it up and hang it on the hook at the back of the door. This dress is too special to be left in a crumpled mess.

As I stand my eyes become glued to the lacy indigo bra and panties set that match her dress perfectly. Little vines of silver decorating the edge. I practically rip the buttons from my pants, stripping down to my boxer briefs, so that we can be equally nude.

"You are stunning." I say practically drooling.

"I think the same when I look at you." She smiles up into my eyes.

Holding her hand, we walk over to the bed. Pulling her under the covers we kiss and fondle with our underwear still on, just like we had all those years ago in Vegas. No matter how amazing she looks, I am still a forty-six-year-old man. The fact that I've had sex five times in seventy-two hours is amazing. Six is definitely pushing it. But I can still bring her pleasure. Sliding the straps of her bra down her arms, I gently unhooked and removed the pretty, little, lacy thing and replaced the soft fabric with my lips over her nipple. My hands massaging her as my tongue flicks and plays.

Moving down her stomach, I slide her panties down her legs, then crawl between her thighs.

She is beautiful.

My hands slide over her, spreading her lips, and my tongue sucks and plays. I drew little circles over her little pleasure spot with my tongue, and my fingers slid inside her warm universe. Her hips raise against my mouth and her fingers pull and push against my hair as the happiness cuss function in her brain goes into overdrive. Her pleasure drives me wild. And as her thighs tighten around my head, and her legs begin to shake from her release, I am so hard and ready that I am already cumming as I push into her on the heels of her orgasm. I feel her body spasming as I release with a groan of amazing inside of her.

Holy Fuck.

Maybe I should put a little more stock in oysters.

# 23.

## Cerveza Por Favor

Ainsley:

I am beginning to grow accustomed to waking up spooned in Cody's embrace. He is big and warm and firm against my back. I snuggle in deeper before peeking at the clock. Thankful that it is only 7:00 am, I close my eyes and fall back to sleep feeling happy and perfectly safe and at home in his arms.

8:00 am and a voice comes over the loudspeaker, waking me as it announces that we have landed and guests may begin to disembark for Mexico. Stretching and preparing to take first dibs on the bathroom, Cody's hands stretch along with my body. One moving up to cup my breast, the other moving south, cupping the heat between my legs.

"We are going to be late if you keep touching me like that." I moan indecently.

"Remind me again what day it is?"

"Ensenada day."

"Are we going to do body shots at Senor Frogs?" he asks.

"I might after a few margaritas." I grin playfully. "But we have to get dressed and meet Sarah and Brent for breakfast at 8:30 am first."

"Who was the bloody idiot who chose that time? So early." He shakes his head in disgust.

"That bloody idiot would be you." I smile, kissing him before popping into the bathroom.

We arrive at breakfast five minutes late, but still before Sarah and Brent. Halfway through the meal, a sex glazed Sarah plops down in the chair next to me.

"Good night?" I ask.

"Oh Ains, I'm so smitten. I think my heart is going to explode!" I smile knowing the feeling. Brent sits down a moment later with two plates. Passing one to Sarah, they dig in like they haven't eaten in days.

Sex is great cardio.

"So, I did a little digging and found a few fun tour excursions." Sarah mumbles between a mouth full of eggs. "It seems our choices are:

"One. We can watch the cliff divers." Sarah holds up a finger.

"Two," a second finger joins the first, "La Bufadora, also known as the Blow Hole. It's a really big water spout against a different cliff.

"Three," the fingers continue, "the flea market.

"Four. Guadalupe Valley for a wine tasting tour."

"Or five, drinking along the downtown strip and shopping at the tourist traps. What sounds good to everyone?"

"Everything sounds fun. How much can we do?"

"Well, if we do the trip out to Guadalupe Valley, it takes most of the day. So that might make it hard to view the cliff divers or La Bufadora. We can find time to go downtown for an hour or two, whichever activity we plan."

"Since you boys haven't been here before, how about you choose."

"Sarah and I talked about wine tasting when we get back home. So, since we will be doing that soon, maybe the other La Buffy and cliff diving things. I also enjoy drinking cerveza in bars along the main drag."

"Sounds good to me too." Cody agrees and I nod.

"What are your plans once the ship docks in Cali? You're not going back to Chicago?" I ask Brent

"No, I canceled my flight. I have no need to rush back. Sarah is taking me home with her." he winks. "We are going to practice being newlyweds and she is going to show me around San Diego and the Temecula wine country."

"That sounds like a lot of fun." Cody smiles. "I'm planning a visit soon too. Think you'll still be around? Maybe we can all go out together again."

"I'm not going back to Chicago until Sarah is free to come with me." He oozed sappy love from every pore.

"I'm booked with weddings the next few weekends, so Brent is staying through the middle of August." She smiles.

"That is over three weeks away. Ainsley and I were planning for me to come out in early August."

"Oh fun!" Sarah Exclaims. "We will set up a tour of all our favorite haunts for you guys when you visit, won't we Ains?"

"We do have some great craft breweries we can go tasting at." I suggest knowing the guy's preference for beer.

"I like the sound of that." Brent agrees.

I was feeling jealous that Brent and Sarah would not be saying goodbye tomorrow like Cody and I would be. It will make this time together more special; I try to convince myself over the jealousy. The idea of simply merging my life with Cody's from the moment we step off the ship sounds fantastic. But I am pretty sure I have dirty laundry on the floor in my bathroom, and the fridge is nearly empty. I would feel anxious and overwhelmed with a spur of the moment house guest. Having time to prepare keeps me calm. Plus, what would Bodhi say if I brought a strange man home? I chuckle to myself as I imagine him standing mouth agape.

"What are you giggling about?" Cody whispers in my ear.

"I was just imagining the expression on Bodhi's face if I was to bring you home with me."

"Is he protective of you? Should I be worried?"

"He is, but no. He is going to love you. Alice is the one you need to worry about." I grin teasingly.

"Maybe we can pay Bodhi to be our DD when we all go out on the town." Sarah interrupts.

"I don't know that I'm ready to subject him to our PDA yet." I quickly decline to Sarah's frown.

"I can ask Jordan if her wine trolley has any availability and book us a tour with her." I suggest instead.

"Good idea. Jordan loves you."

"Who is Jordan?" Cody asks.

"Jordan is a friend of ours. She co-owns a wine tour trolley that does comedy tasting tours. She is super funny, and her tours are always like a comedy show on wheels, with wine. Lots of wine."

"That sounds like a fantastic day." We all agree as we finish our meals and head to the lower level of the ship to disembark.

***

A sunny seventy-two-degree day greets us as we walk through customs. We hop on the $4 bus that drops us off on the main drag of Ensenada. At the corner, are a slew of different tour guides and taxi services asking for business.

"Hey guys, this is one of the tour groups recommended on yelp. They will take us wherever we want to go. Like a private hire, but the driver is also your tour guide." Sarah tells us.

"I like it." Brent agrees, grabbing his wallet and walking up to the driver. "?Quanto es coche dia, por favor?" *How much is a car day, please? Brent tries to speak to the driver in broken Spanish. Which has Sarah gushing all over him. It is nice that he is trying to speak the language, and a bonus that his new fiancé finds it charming. They are cute together. Brent is like a ray of sunshine, and I see my friend glowing brighter by his side. He is the exact opposite of Sarah's ex who was dark and gloomy, and angered over the smallest things. Sarah deserves lots of sunshine in her life now that hurricane Wayne is long gone. I sigh, a smile settling across my face, as I watch them from across the square. Feeling content and happy for my friend.

After a quick exchange, Brent books the mini tour van for just our little group of four. Our tour guide, Enrique, was born and raised in Ensenada and he knows everyone and where all the best deals are. If we want Mexican leather, he will take us to his cousin's shop for the family discount. If we want silver, he will take us to his uncle's shop for the family discount. If we want the best fish tacos in all of Ensenada, he will take us to his wife. He pats his big, round, happy belly. Enrique suggests we go to see the cliff divers first, as the best divers like to jump early in the morning. We all agree and hold on for dear life, as the crazy traffic has us all a little white knuckled until we get out of the heart of the city.

Up at the lookout, we hang over the railing watching these amazingly brave men cliff dive into the crashing surf below.

"Would you jump?" Cody asks me.

"Maybe off a smaller cliff into calmer, warmer, water. These guys are professionals. Baby steps up to greatness."

"I hear Hawaii has some good places for novice cliff jumpers. Shall I call my travel agent and book us a trip?"

"That sounds lovely. Is it really that easy?"

"It can be."

"Then let's plan it when you come to visit. So long as my cooking doesn't scare you off."

"I have lived off top ramen and mac-n-cheese for the past five years." he responds laughing.

"Those are delicacies in my home as well." I replied. "I do have a few dishes I make pretty well. Chili and Potato leek soup. And my mac-n-cheese is actually kinda amazing. I bake it, then add those little fried onions to the top." I told him.

"That sounds spectacular. Good comfort food."

"And cinnamon roll apple pie." I'm just bragging now.

"That also sounds amazing."

"Pick one and I promise to be domestic and make it for you."

"Can I pick two?"

"Greedy." I grin. "Yes, what would you like?"

"May I place my order for some of that mac-n-cheese and cinnamon roll apple pie, please?"

"Gladly. Maybe we will make that a movie night and make out to our favorite films on the sofa."

"You're perfect." he smiles at me, kissing me on the tip of my nose.

"I think you're pretty perfect too." I kiss his lips, full and warm and as greedy as his appetite.

"Hey you two!" Brent calls out to us. "There are children present."

Cody sticks his tongue out at him in defiance and Brent shoots him the finger. Sarah and I share a laugh at our immature men, behaving like boys.

"So, since we need to keep things PG, what's your favorite movie?" Cody asks me while tidying a stray strand of hair the wind had blown in my face.

"I'm not telling. You will have to wait and see."

"Then you will have to wait to know my favorite movie as well." he grins back at me.

"Fun, but if it's not streaming, you'll have to bring it with you."

"I'll bring it just in case."

Our future date's taking shape nicely.

Next, Enrique takes us down a scenic drive, stopping along a beautiful beach where we all run and play in the surf. I get out my camera and take a few shots of the coast, along with a bunch of candid pics. Ricky, as our tour guide asked us to please call him, offered to take a few group shots of us all, our feet in the water.

Peeking over my shoulder, Cody watches as I run though the photos we had taken.

"These are really beautiful. You have a great eye."

"Thank you." I say smiling. Compliments about my art work or my kids are the best.

"May I?" he asks motioning for the camera. I hand it over to him to let him scroll through the pics to his heart's content.

"Wow, Ainsley. You're really good. These pictures are even prettier than the place is in real life."

"Ains is totally wasting her talent in the wedding industry." Sarah pipes in. But I won't let her leave me, so it's a moot point." I laugh, climbing in the back seat of the van. Sarah has always been one of my biggest supporters, despite her jest of holding me hostage in the wedding industry.

"Everybody ready?" Ricky asks from the driver's seat.

"Punch it, Chewie." Cody jokes and my heart stops.

I know he likes Sci-Fi. What red-blooded American boy didn't grow up watching Star Wars. But for him to choose that quote. My quote. It is too much. A chill overcomes me and goose bumps raise the hairs on my arms as I shiver.

"Are you cold?" Cody asks, surprised.

"No. It's you. I always say 'Punch it, Chewie'. You stole my line." I look up at him feeling like a deer in headlights. My heart is pounding over this simple coincidence. One of so many, yet a very important, quirky coincidence, that has my head spinning.

"No shit?" He laughs. I was shaking my head, No as his hand moved warm behind my neck and his tongue slid between my lips in a kiss that turned my chills to hot flashes.

"Fweet, fweet" Brent whistles, teasingly. Cody gives him an evil grin, then kisses me again even harder.

# 24.

## Caught A Sparkly

Ainsley:

After a stop at La Bufadora, we head on to the best jewelry shop around. Owned for over thirty-five years by Ricky's Uncle Enrique; whom he was named after. While Brent is picking out pretty things to spoil Sarah with, Cody and I walk around quietly, admiring all the large silver art pieces decorating the gallery. Some of the sculptures and vases probably weigh over five hundred pounds! Gorgeous platters, and candelabras are showcased amongst beautiful turquoise necklaces and bracelets. Moving to a long display case, my eyes catch a shiny. Two stunning chips of blue, so perfect a match to Cody's eyes, that it catches my breath and I look at him to confirm the similarity.

"See something you like?" he asks me.

"Those earrings are the same color as your eyes." I show him.

"What kind of stone is that?" he asks. He also seems enamored by the color of the little solitaire's brilliant blue crystals.

"I don't know." I shrug.

Like magic, sensing our interest in a sparkly, Uncle Enrique greets us with a glass of champagne for me, and a bottle of Corona for Cody.

"Gracias." We both thank him.

"Do you two see something you like?" he asks us.

"What kind of stone is this blue one, right here?" Cody questions.

"That is a blue diamond, Señor. You have very good taste. These diamond stud earrings are a total weight of one point two carats. Set in white gold. Would you like to know the price?"

"No thank you," I interrupt. "I was just wondering the type of stone because it matches his eyes so nicely." I smile. I do not want Cody to feel any kind of pressure to spend money in the shop on me. Jewelry feels so intimate and personal a gift. And those are not going to be fifty-dollar crystals. Those are one point two carats of fancy exotic blue diamonds. I don't want to touch that awkward scenario with a twenty-foot pole.

"Yes, it is a striking resemblance." Enrique agrees as he tells us a little bit about the mine where the blue diamonds come from. It is actually very interesting information and we spend the next five minutes engrossed learning about the boron levels of the crystals. After wandering around looking at all the lovelies in the store, I settled on a bracelet for Alice and a small silver and turquoise vase for my bookkeeper.

After we all check out, Sarah and Brent picking out matching pinky rings, Ricky takes us to his nephew's margarita stand. His nephew, Julio does not speak English very well, so Ricky makes it his duty to brag about him on his behalf.

"Julio, has been making bootleg tequila from the agave plants growing in his backyard since he was twelve years old. Said he YouTubed it! Can you believe that?" Ricky slapped his knee to exaggerate his point. "Now, he is a pro. Julio makes a few specialty flavors, if you would like to see the list." Julio passed out the list with a shy smile. "You won't even need to chase it with salt and lime. It is so smooth it will make your knees weak." Ricky bragged, working the sale.

I was excited for a little tequila tasting. This sounded amazing. So long as we don't all go blind. But the little roadside stand looks totally legit with stray dogs and cats lounging across the patio tables, enjoying the sun shine. A mismatch of different brightly colored umbrellas dotted the terrace with a lovely view of the ocean. Animals wouldn't hang out around poison or bad energy, so I take it all as a good sign.

"Four shots of your best Tequila, Por Favor!" Brent request.

"Señor, the best tequila is thirty dollars a shot. Are you sure?"

"What do you say, gang? You only live once? My treat."

I look to Cody to gauge his reaction. "Don't worry about Brent, he's loaded." Cody teases.

"You are?" Sarah looks back at Brent in shock.

"That's an opinion question." Brent shoots Cody a look. "I don't hurt for money." He tells Sarah and I. "I sold my business and made a nice profit. Enough to treat my friends and fiancé to some fancy ass tequila."

"Cheers to that! Thanks Mate. Sorry for putting you on the spot."

"No worries pal, I'll pants you at the pool later to pay you back." Brent threatens and we all laugh.

A moment later, our laughter is interrupted by a shy Julio. He produced a silver tray with a beautiful blue bottle and four shot glasses. He served us ladies first, but we all waited to cheer and drink together.

"Salud!" We all cheer, before throwing back the smooth warm liquid.

It is fucking amazing.

I slide down in my chair as the buzz tingles up into my brain. The smooth heat warmed my throat.

"Wow. We all four say in unison."

"I'm buying a bottle of this and we will all drink it at our wedding." Brent announces.

"That sounds like a perfect use for a thousand-dollar bottle of tequila." Cody jabs while Sarah bounces up and down in the seat next to Brent.

"It's so sexy when you talk about our wedding. It reminds me this isn't all a dream."

"So, when is the big day?" Cody questions.

"Oh, I have to check with all my favorite vendors and the venue too. I have my perfect wedding all planned out after being a part of so many."

"Are you going to have Ainsley do the photos?" Brent asks.

"No silly, she is a guest. But one of her henchmen can shoot it. I know she will be behind the camera at any opportunity anyway."

I smile. Sarah knows me well.

"Do you have your dream wedding all planned out too?" Cody asks me quietly as Sarah starts discussing the wedding menu with Brent.

"Not like Sarah does. I imagine something small and intimate. Outdoors. Somewhere beautiful, surrounded by nature."

"I like that image with you and I in it." he says, and I get the feels. I imagine us sharing our first kiss as husband and wife under twinkling lights that hang like fire flies from the branches above us. I can picture it so clearly. I can practically feel his kiss on my lips.

This I want.

I am going to have to meditate on this future, because this image makes my heart beat stronger.

"Where would my favorite passengers like to go next?" Ricky asks, pulling out a chair and sitting in it backwards.

"What do you suggest?" Brent questions.

"Flea market?"

"Yes!" Sarah pipes up.

"Okay, you just let me know when you all are ready. No rush."

***

After another twenty-five minutes enjoying the view and the best spicy margarita with tajin along the rim, we all loaded back in the van for a little shopping. We arrive at the market to find aisle upon aisle of vendors selling every trinket imaginable. We spent a little over an hour picking out a few souvenirs to take back home. Then on to our final stop along the main drive downtown. Ricky points the way and tells us that it is an easy walk back to the dock with shops and restaurants along most of it. We thank him for an awesome day with a nice big tip before starting our bar crawl.

Halfway down the street, we found a great little place with a patio bar. Dollar bills with signatures and dates from past guest's wall-paper every empty surface of the walls and ceilings. We order a gigantic plate of nachos to share and devour them in under ten minutes. Followed by a round of tacos.

"Shall we add our dollars to the wall?" Cody asks, grabbing his wallet to pull out a couple of ones."

"Of course, we should." Brent replies, taking the extra dollar offered in Cody's outstretched hand.

There is a black marker sitting on the stand near the entrance and Cody leans over and politely asks the server, in perfect Spanish, if we can borrow it. I love that he's bilingual. So cool. There are so many little things I love about him already and so much more for me to learn.

Cody covers the bill as he writes like it is a secret, then passes the marker to Brent.

"Now where should we hang these?" he asks while scoping out the wall for a free spot.

"Are you going to let us read them before they are up on the wall?" Sarah questions.

"Nope. You will have to wait like Ainsley." Brent replies. The boys teamed up against us.

"Well Ainsley and I have secrets too." she adds jokingly. "Come on, Ains, ladies' room."

"Be right back." I say as I follow Sarah inside.

After five minutes gossiping about how giddy in love we both feel, we come back out to the patio to find the waiter helping the guys tape the bills onto the lighting fixture above our table. I look up and can read Sarah and Brent's bill first. It has their names and today's date. Along with a little heart and quote. "You call it madness; we call it Love." Sweet, funny, and slightly true.

Cody finishes hanging our bill and I look over to read what he wrote:

## Blue + Ainsley the Reader = Love

At the bottom are two dates. Today, and New Year's Eve twenty-five years ago. It is perfect in its simplicity with our inside joke.

"Perfect." I say smiling.

We walk back to the ship hand in hand, Sarah swinging her shopping bags while Brent carries his bottle of tequila like a baby. After a long day we are all in need of a good shower before dinner. And with dis-embarkment starting at 8:00 am tomorrow, we still need to pack up too. We walk to the rooms together, then each of us, for the first time, go into our own separate rooms. Alone.

# 25.

## Remember This

Ainsley:

After brushing my teeth, I hop in the shower and let the sun and salt wash off my body. I was tired and if it wasn't for this being our last night, I would have wanted to crawl into bed right out of the shower. But I don't want to miss a minute of my time left with Cody. Even this time alone in the shower feels like a waste.

God, I have it bad. I think to myself as I shut off the water and start to towel dry.

Walking out to the main cabin, the small 200- square foot room feels so cold and empty without Cody in it. I've become accustomed to him, and his energy, and expect to see him legs stretched long on the bed with a book in hand. But the only thing on the bed is a towel folded into the shape of an elephant and a chocolate mint on the pillow. I pop the chocolate in my mouth and start getting dressed, packing my things as I go.

Thirty minutes later, a small knock raps against my door and my pet butterflies wake up. I rush to the door and Cody is standing there in a black suit, looking sexy as hell, leaning against the door frame. Clean shaven and hair in place, he reminds me a little of a sexy spy. 007. His arms wrap around my back as he pulls me in for an amazing kiss, ruining the lipstick I just applied.

"You look beautiful." he smiles, twirling me in a circle.

"You clean up pretty well yourself." I smile, kissing him again. "I'm not ready yet. Almost." I say moving back to the mirror.

"I'm early anyway. But I have a little something I wanted to give you for tonight. I turn to look at him holding a black box in his hand.

"Oh my God Cody." My fingers cover my mouth in shock. There, in the little box, are the blue diamond earrings from the jewelry shop this afternoon.

"I liked the way they immediately reminded you of the color of my eyes. I hope you think about me every time you put them on."

"Every time I look in the mirror, I'm going to think you're standing here next to me."

"That was my goal." He kisses my cheek.

"These must have been a fortune. You really shouldn't have."

"I got the family discount." he winks. "Besides, I like seeing you wear them."

"I love them. Thank you."

I can actually feel the tears in the corner of my eyes. The way he looks at me has me so flustered that I can hardly put the blue diamond studs in my ears with my shaking hands.

"When did you have time to buy these?"

"When you were distracted checking out yourself. I slipped Enrique my card and he threw the box in with Brents purchase."

I look at my reflection in the mirror. They are so pretty. My dress tonight is just a classic black cocktail. Nothing special, but with these glittering in my ears I feel amazing. Cody's head pops up in the reflection over my shoulder and the color match of the earrings to his eyes is uncanny.

"You look stunning." He kisses my neck just below my ear. Spinning in his embrace to face him, I hook my arms over his neck, pulling him close.

"Thank you. I love them so much."  But as I said it, in my mind, 'Them' was really 'You'.

"I'm jealous of Brent getting to go home with Sarah," he admits. "I don't want you forgetting about me next week. So that means you can't take these off."

I laugh. "There is no way I could forget about you."

"Good."

"I suppose I should find something to give you to remember me by." I say scanning my luggage.

"You don't need to give me anything. Everything I need is right in here." he says, patting his chest.

Be still my heart.

I think the butterflies living in my stomach have been replaced by full sized birds. He makes me nauseous in all the right ways.

I finish getting ready while Cody looks under the bed and out on the balcony for me, to make sure I didn't forget anything. He comes back in with my bag of books.

"Oh, thank you! I would have been really sad to leave those."

"Were you reading the dirty one to get new ideas on how to wake me up tomorrow?"

I laugh out loud. "Maybe."

"Perhaps I'll read a few chapters while you finish up, and I can wake you up tomorrow."

"Assuming you wake up before I do."

"A challenge." he grins "Where should I start? What chapter is good?" he asks, leaning back against the headboard with my naughty little romance in his hands.

"Hmmmm. I'm pretty sure they are fucking by the second chapter. And just about every other one after that. Take your pick."

"Any request?"

"I'll let you surprise me. Assuming you're the first one awake."

"Yes, assuming I win the race to wake."

I grin then reapply my lip stick and put on my shoes.

"Ready." I say a few minutes later. He holds up one finger requesting a pause. His attempt at short hand sign language.

"I just need to find out where he puts his throbbing member."

I laugh and hit his shoulder. "It doesn't really say throbbing member, does it?

"No, I'm just teasing. I think that was a joke in a movie I saw once. The basis of my preconceived notions about books like this one. This is awfully spicy. I think I like it."

"Want to zoom in on our book club meeting on it at the end of the month?" I ask in a tease.

"You discuss this kind of stuff in your book club?" He acts scandalized.

"Sure do. It was Brandine's turn to pick a book. She is feisty like Blanch from the Golden Girls. We all drink sangria and talk about what gave us the feels. These books make for some of our best meetings."

"Maybe, I will zoom in." he winks.

"You look really pretty tonight."

"You already said that."

"Well, I thought about it again." he half grins at me, standing up from the bed in one smooth fluid motion.

I smile as my heartbeat quickens. "I guess I should be telling you how handsome you are every five minutes then too."

"Oh yeah? You think I'm handsome, do you?" He squeezes my waist and gives me a cocky grin that plays all the way up into his eyes.

"I'm pretty sure you know you're good looking."

"I think you got more sun today than you realize."

"And he's modest too." I grin. "Shall we go?" I nod my head towards the door.

"And she is punctual." I laugh as Cody opens the door and leads the way to Sarah's room, then knocks.

"Hey lovebirds. Are you two ready to refuel?"

Brent peeks his head out while stuffing the shirt tails back in his pants. "Just need two more minutes." he grins.

"Want us to go get a spot in line to check in?"

"Sure, we will be there in a moment."

Cody takes my hand as we walk towards the elevators. "I figured they would be more than two minutes." He squeezes my hand. "And I didn't want you to be late." I elbow him playfully and he laughs. "I'm going to miss you." he says, as he kisses the top of my head while we wait for the lift.

"I'm not looking forward to good bye either." I frown. "When does your flight leave tomorrow?"

"3:00 pm."

"Do you need a ride to the airport?"

"Yeah? You would drive me to the airport? I warn you; I flew into LAX."

"I'll take whatever extra time I can have."

The elevator came and went, but we were too busy kissing to notice. A moment later, I feel a tap, tap, tap, on my shoulder. Pulling away from Cody's lips, I see Sarah grinning down at me.

"You two could have done that back in your room."

"It was more fun out here." Cody grins.

"While you two are working on dessert, I need some real food in my belly. Let's go!" Sarah says in her no-nonsense coordinator voice.

# 26.

## Evil Clocks

Ainsley:

The elevator pings open and we all step in and ride down to the dining room. Dinner is excellent as usual, and after we decide to attend the deck party, complete with fireworks. At around 11:00 pm the yawns start going around our group. I was already so tired; my eyes were blinking a little too long when Cody nudged me. "You sleep'n?"

"Just thinking about sleeping." I say, still not opening my eyes. We all decided to end the night. Well, end the part of the night where clothing is necessary at least. I was praying for a second wind. This is not how I want to go out on our last night together. Well, our last night until Cody flies out to visit in about a week and a half from now.

Cody pops into his room to grab his packed suitcase and moves it into my room. There is already a little info sheet about disembarkation procedures and times under my door. I am set for 9:45 am tomorrow morning. That works well for me.

"What time is your disembarkation?" I ask.

"I can leave any time after 8:00 am because of my flight." He tells me.

"We will have a few hours to play around the area tomorrow before we need to get you to LAX. Is there any place you would like to go?"

"Nothing I can think of at the moment. That's a question for future Cody and Ainsley to worry about tomorrow. Now we need to get those sleepy eyes of yours into bed." He holds out his arms and I walk into his hugging embrace.

"That sounds good, but I don't want to go to sleep yet." I yawn.

He laughs his reply. "Oh yes you do. It's been a long day, I'm tired too."

"If I fall asleep then tomorrow will be here sooner and I'm not ready for tomorrow yet."

"Tomorrow will be here in about forty-five minutes no matter what."

"Boooo." I moan into his chest.

"I believe you said that absence makes the heart grow fonder."

"I'm full of shit sometimes. Besides, I don't think my heart is capable of feeling more than it already is. I'm going to miss you. I don't want to say goodbye, even if it is for only for a short time."

"Neither do I." He kissed the crown of my head. "Come on, let's go to bed. We can talk until we drift away." I look up into his smiling eyes.

'I love you.' I think, and I feel.

Every cell of my being exudes this undeniable love for the man standing in front of me. But I can't say something like that so soon after meeting him. I feel frivolous, and infatuated, and silly. I hold back the words and instead tell him with a kiss. My lips tell his lips that they are the only ones I want to kiss for the rest of my life, letting him decipher my actions, any way he pleases.

We help each other out of our clothes and crawl into bed. This isn't like our previous nights together. This is slow and sweet. The potential of hot sex is still here, but this is more comfortable, and lazy. Soft caresses instead of greedy hands. Whispers instead of cuss words.

***

I'm not sure if I made it to midnight before I fall asleep. Nor am I sure how long I've been out. Could be five minutes or five hours. What I am sure of, are the hands caressing my back and shoulders. I'm fully aware of the fingers that massage me gently into consciousness.

"Hmmmm...." I sigh, as his fingers weave magic along my skin. His hands move up to my neck and shoulders as the massage starts to get really good. I roll onto my stomach to give him better access.

"You win the wake-up battle. This feels so nice." I say against my pillow.

He laughs. "You are a light sleeper. I'm nowhere near finished waking you up yet. Although I'll take the early win." I can hear the smile in his words as his fingers dig into the muscles along my traps.

"Ohhh, right there." He rubs, and I purr my gratitude.

"Did you just purr like a cat?"

"Mmmmm Hmmmm. Consider it a compliment..., Oh God Cody, harder, right there." I sigh. He digs in with his elbow and I moan a little louder.

"I think I like the sounds you make while I give you a back rub as much as I do when we are making love." His lips replace his elbow in a gentle kiss, followed by the feathers touch of his fingertips relaxing the muscle he just worked. Then he repeats the deep tissue massage on the other shoulder.

I'm in heaven.

"Now that I know you give good massages, I'm going to have to keep you."

"If I had known that was all it took, I would have given you a massage back in Vegas." He laughs as his thumbs rub little circles down the sides of my spine. I rolled around to face him.

"I was already crazy for you back then also. If a back rub back then didn't remind me to leave you my number, then it would have at least gone into the stack of bonus points you had been racking up." I smile up at him.

"Can I still use my bonus points? And if so, what can I turn in my points for?" He wiggles his eyebrows at me.

"Lots of naked things."

"Oh, I like naked things." He growled in his sexy 'I want to devour you' way.

"Ainsley." He says my name slow and deep, his fingers tracing the shape of my face. "I want you to keep me."

His comment is my end. Our lips lock and our bodies merge into one. His hands continue roaming and massaging my body, as we start to make love. His fingers, lips, and eyes all make love to me as if I am a Goddess to be worshiped. The pressure of his large hands pull me closer as our rhythm becomes more incessant. The pleasure blinding, my nails dig into the muscles along his back and I bite his shoulder as the pressure and need for release build inside of me. My thighs clench tight around his hips. Only my head touches the bed as I practically levitate into him in orgasmic bliss. A rainbow of colors exploding through my mind as wave after wave of rapture washes through my body.

I'm brought back to consciousness to the fantastic sound of Cody cursing my name. I feel the vibration of his orgasm inside of me, and see flashes of light brighten to neon behind my eyelids. My orgasm renews and intensifies brighter, and stronger, and longer, than I have ever experienced in my life. We fall to the bed, his hands still holding me tight against him. I'm so spent I can barely breathe.

"My God, Cody. The things you do to me."

He chuckles and kisses my neck. "Ainsley, I think I may be addicted to you."

"That's a good thing, right?" I kiss his chest over his beating heart, which I can hear strong and fast.

"The best thing." He pulls me up to his lips and kisses me like I have never been kissed before. He tells me he loves me without words.

At least that's how I read it.

**27.**

**Debarkation**

Ainsley:

We spend the next hour lazy in bed. Kissing, touching, and talking about our plans for L.A. today. We decided to go to LACMA (L.A. County Museum of Art) before his flight home. Packing up our final items, we head up to the pool deck's breakfast buffet and find Sarah and Brent finishing up their meal and enjoying coffees.

"Hey Mate." Brent calls as we take our seats with them. They are still all cuddles and giggles, a glow of romantic bliss.

"What are your plans today, kids?" I ask while sipping my coffee.

"Just a home day. I'm absolutely giddy about doing nothing but Brent and sleeping in my own bed." Sarah bounces.

"I'm envious." Cody replies with a smirk.

"What time do you need to be at the airport?" Brent questions, sympathy in his voice.

"Flight leaves at 3:00 pm, so 1:00 pm. We don't have long. Ainsley and I are going to hit a museum in our free time."

"Oh, that's fun. Which one? I hear MOCA has an amazing interactive exhibition right now." Sarah responds.

"What's MOCA?" Cody asks.

"Museum of Contemporary Art. It's right next door to LACMA. It's smaller, maybe a better fit for our time frame. Are you up for a little bend-your-mind contemporary art?" I ask with a hopeful grin.

"Totally into it. What's the interactive part?" he looks to Sarah.

"I think there is bouncing and bright colors." A friend went and posted pics, but I haven't been myself.

"Want me to look it up?"

"No, let's be surprised." He smiles and kisses my cheek and my heart gives a flutter. I love his sense of fun. This really is love. All of these feelings he invokes in me come from the real him. This isn't just vacation Cody, this is who he is, adventurous and spontaneous. The way he speaks about his family and the people in his life is sentimental in a way that can't be faked. That's real Cody too. And he makes me laugh. You can't fake being funny. It all feels too good to be true.

The 9:45 am call for departure is made over the loud speaker and we all move to join the line off the ship. At the parking garage we say our goodbyes and wish each other well. Brent hopping into Sarah's little, black, sporty car and Cody jumping into my Jeep.

"I have a Jeep Wrangler too." he grins at another one of our many similarities. "But it's an old beater we use around the camp, more than an everyday vehicle."

"Who is, We?" I ask.

"Mostly my caretaker Charlie and I. But the agents and my dad will sometimes use it too."

"How many agents do you have in your team?"

"There are six of us in total. We are like a little family. Bill has been my partner and right-hand man for many years. He is also a broker. He handles most of the sales. Charlie looks after the grounds, and we have two agents that handle the rentals. Dad bosses everyone around and I socialize mostly." he tells me.

"Is that how you have so much time to travel?"

"It is. Who is going to feed and water the pup is typically my biggest hurdle to overcome. Austin is watching her now."

"That's a good son." I smile.

"I would like to get to that point with my team too. I know I can do it. After Brian died, I took a little break from weddings. It was too hard emotionally to be there." I said, staring out into traffic along the freeway. It's easy opening up to him while hypnotized by the white dotted lines. "I worked

~ 172 ~

behind the scenes for a few years. Did a lot of school photo shoots and Bar Mitzvahs instead. It's really just a scheduling balance."

"So, what you're telling me is that we can ditch all of our adult responsibilities by pawning them off on someone else, and go run away together?"

"I'm sure it could be done." I grin.

"Will you be my travel buddy, Ainsley?" he pleads, with big puppy dog eyes.

I laugh. "Won't Brent be hurt to be replaced so fast?"

"He ditched me for Sarah the moment he set eyes on her."

"It's true. Brent was drooling for Sarah from the moment they met." I giggle.

"Just as I was for you. Hell, I still am."

# 28.

## Stinky Socks

Ainsley:

We arrive at the museum and buy our tickets to go inside. The interactive portion requires socks, which conveniently can be purchased in the gift shop. Cody and I are both in flip flops; sans socks. So, I pick up some Klimt socks featuring 'The Kiss for me', and a pair of 'Dogs Playing Poker' for Cody and go to check out.

"I got you a little gift. When you put them on, I hope they remind you of me. I would say don't take them off until you visit me next week, but that's gross." I say presenting Cody with the little gift bag.

"Socks! With dogs' playing poker. You shouldn't have."

"I wish I could tell you that I got the family discount, but alas, it's a tourist trap." I say, shrugging my shoulders.

"I'll cherish them. Thank you." He holds the socks to his chest, hugging them like a teddy bear. And that is it. He wins the joke and I break into laughter, disturbing the quiet of the museum gift shop.

Sneaking out, we both giggle like school kids up to something naughty as we make our way to the exhibits.

The interactive display is a massive gallery room that feels like you have walked onto the set of Willy Wonka. A rainbow of bright colors surrounds us on a bouncy floor with marshmallow pillows and gumdrop beach balls for tossing at the other patrons. The room is filled with people ages five through eighty, bouncing around, all acting like little children on a sugar high.

Cody and I climb the foam chocolate mountain to the candy cane castle at the top, then slide down the licorice slide. Then we do it again, sliding down head first. After thirty minutes of play, we move on to the other exhibits for a bit before grabbing some lunch and heading to the airport.

I park in short term and we both walk in together holding hands. At 1:00 pm in the afternoon, LAX is surprisingly slow. There is still a small line at check-in and I wait with Cody. But it goes much faster than I would have liked.

Where is overcrowded, noisy LAX when you need it?

Security is as far as I can go. And as the time ticks away, the anxiety in the pit of my stomach grows.

This is it.

We stand before the line entrance, just staring, neither of us speaking. Afraid to break this little pause in time and move forward to the next moment.

"Nine days," he says. "I'll see you in nine days." It was practically a whisper and it made my bones chill, as I suppressed the shiver threatening to race through my chest.

"That feels like a lifetime at the moment." I fake a smile, into those blue eyes. "Blue, I'm going to miss you."

His grin lights his face. "Ainsley the reader, I'm going to miss you too."

We kiss all our goodbyes, missing, and anxieties, out of our bodies there in front of TSA and the drug sniffing dogs. I want to say I love you, but I don't. I feel it, but I'm also afraid that this is too good to be real; too good to last. I don't want to speak a partial truth no matter how much I believe it with all my heart. Love at first sight has never been a terribly believable story line for me. But after the past five days with Cody; and after watching Sarah and Brent. I'm considering the possibility more and more. However, I keep the words to myself, biting my lip and holding back, as I try to convey my feeling though just the look in my eyes.

"Oh Ainsley." he whispers as his thumb gently pulls my lip free, and his mouth kisses me soft and sweet. His hands softly pull my hair as they slide down my back. "I feel it too." He kisses me soft and gentle, once more on the lips and shivers light my heart with sparks of light.

"I'll call you tomorrow." he says, as I nod up at him. I'm out of words. I'm still too afraid to speak. The pressure in my heart building to a painful level. As if he knows just what is going on inside of me, he places the palm of his hand over my heart and my pulse jumps. I place my hand over his heart too, and we say our goodbyes in one final perfect kiss.

"I'll see you soon."

"See you soon."

He walks into the cue and waves, blowing me a kiss. I pretend to catch it and pull it into my heart. Then I sent him a kiss through the air too. He smiles, catching it and placing the floating kiss in his pocket for safe keeping. I stood there for a moment just watching him shuffle through security, my feet glued to the floor. But once he has passed through, there is nothing left but for me to walk back out to the parking garage and drive home.

The hope to beat traffic is my new focus as I finally get moving.

# Part 3

**Soul** Searching

# 29.

## Wake and Bake

Cody:

It's already sunset when I walk through my front door. Fluffs wags her tail, and half her lower body along with it, over her excitement to see me. Fluffs is the best dog. Nessa and I bought her as a Christmas gift for Austin, when he was twelve years old, a tiny little fluffy golden retriever with a red ribbon tied in a bow around her neck. We woke up at sunrise to sneak her into his room so that her puppy kisses could wake him up on Christmas morning. He was so happy he cried for twenty minutes. The memory almost brings tears to my eyes now. We named her Goldie, but the nickname Fluffs soon took over and by the time she was two, we officially changed her name tag to Fluffs. She wouldn't know who Goldie was if we called her that anyway.

I rub Fluff's ears and chest and speak in my dog voice that I reserve just for her. "I missed you. Did you miss me? What a good girl you are. You didn't peepee in my closet, did you? No? Such a good girl. Where is Austin? Did he remember to feed and water you?" She wiggles and tries to kiss my nose.

Standing up, I yell to the house "I'm home!" I hear some shuffling and the chorus to Popular from Wicked in the background as Austin's bedroom door opens and he comes out in his pajamas.

"Hey dad, welcome home." he says, stretching with a yawn.

"Hey buddy, are you waking up or getting ready for bed?"

"Closer to option number one. I've had a lazy day just playing video games. Didn't feel the need to create more laundry by getting dressed." His comment reminds me of Ainsley stealing my towel to cross the hall back to her room. Practical she described it. She's going to like Austin, I smile.

"That's very practical of you."

"Gee, you must have had a great vacation, I would have expected you to tell my lazy ass to get dressed."

"I did have an amazing vacation." I grin.

"Oh yeah, did you meet my new Mommy like I told you to?"

"I hope so. Her name is Ainsley."

"No shit! Does that mean you got some?"

"Austin!" I glare at him. "Inappropriate." This boy has no filter. But the grin staring back at me makes it pretty obvious that he can read the blush that now flares on my skin as a rush of memories of Ainsley fills my mind.

"I'm going to fly out to San Diego to visit her in about a week." I answer instead.

"Spill, I want all the juicy gossip."

Moving to the kitchen I make us both grilled cheese sandwiches as I give him the PG version of our story, starting with Vegas twenty-five years ago.

"What is she like? Is she the same now as back then?" he asks, elbows on the counter and head held between the palms of his hands dreamily.

"Better than I remembered. Better than I imagined." I say back just as dreamily. "She is smart. She knows all these little fun facts. And she is creative. She's an amazing photographer, and has an artist's eye. And she has a great laugh." I smile and close my eyes remembering the tingle it gives me to make her laugh. "She's funny in an undercover kind of way, like the joke is just meant for you." I add, eyes still closed.

"Shit dad." Austin says in a wispy, dreamy, dramatic way which is totally Austin.

We talked until midnight. I don't think Austin and I have ever had a conversation that lasted over an hour let alone four hours. It wasn't all about Ainsley and I. Austin opened up about his on-again off-again boyfriend Phillip, who he was pretty sure had been cheating on him even when they were on again.

"A second chance is important. People usually will learn from their mistakes and grow. But some people ignore life's lessons. They get stuck in a loop and the behavior becomes a pattern. Those are much harder to evolve out of. If they are not growing along with you, they will hold you back too. It's up to you to decide if you want to keep with his influence and energy in your life, or if you want to find someone better suited to you." I try to give my best advice without sounding too preachy. No one likes being told what to do. I just want to open his eyes to more possibilities.

Austin is quiet, a rarity for the boy. "Thanks Dad. I think I'm going to go crash now. I'll see you in the morning."

"K, good night. Love you."

"Love you too."

As he left for his room, a wave of tiredness swept over me also. It had been a long day. I take a fast shower then crash into bed, asleep before my head hits the pillow.

***

I can't sleep. I've been trying since 4:00 am. It's nearly dawn now anyway, so I make some coffee, grab my jacket, and head for the front porch to watch the sunrise over the mountains that shelter the village of Taos. Passing by Austin's forgotten smoke box, I steal a joint and the lighter. It has been years since I had a proper 'Wake and Bake' and a little weed seems like just the thing to help me sort through my jumbled mind. I light up. The end of the joint glow's orange just like the sun as it peeks over the crest of the mountains. I exhale slowly letting all the magic cannabis plant knowledge and energy glide into my cells.

I was mad about Ainsley, crazy madly in love. But how could I be so insanely infatuated with someone I have only known for a total of five days? Five and a half including our night in Vegas. I probably spent more time daydreaming about her during our twenty-five-year hiatus than I've actually spent with her.

Is that it? I think. Am I in love with the idea of her? I don't like that thought at all, so I start a list of things that I know about her.

Let's just get the physical out of the way and lump that into its own category.

1. She's fucking Hot!

My mind starts to get lost in the memory of her nipples rubbing back and forth against my chest. The feel of her body. The feel of her skin under my hands as I try to consume every inch of her. Magic cannabis plant, you make these memories feel sooo much better. I can practically feel myself inside her and I shudder, then I inhale again.

Getting back to my list...

2. She is smart.

She studies metaphysics and ancient philosophies for fun and reads many of the same things I like. More even. If she learned all that dirty talk from those romance novels she also likes, I may need to expand my library. I can learn a lot from her. I smile at the memory of her voice filling the dark cabin. "Let me be your sex toy tonight."

Fuck. She makes me dizzy. I take another drag from the joint. Dirty-talk is definitely on the list.

3. Dirty talk.

But I don't let myself get distracted by the memory of her smell. Or the way she bites my shoulder right before she cums.

Fuck.

I shake my head and think;

4. She is creative and has an amazing talent for seeing beautiful things in the ordinary.

I remember her crouched down low, taking pictures of the waves bubbling against the sand. Who looks at that stuff? She does. And the image she created… Wow. The potential she saw in that tiny snippet of the universe was breathtaking. I can feel my heart smile.

5. She is active and does fun things.

I like to do fun things. I love all of the fun things we did in Catalina and Ensenada. I loved watching her swing through the trees ziplining and the way her arms flexed as she paddled the kayak; beads of water magnifying the color of her sun-kissed skin. I like drinking in bars and seeing new things. But I loved watching her take shots of coffee tequila and the surprise on her face over how smoothly it slid down her throat. I liked the cruise, but I loved all the fun things we did on the ship, and in bed. Mmmmm in bed. Fuck, there is my heart again and my penis is awake again too. I take another hit.

6. She loves to travel.

I love traveling with her so far.

7. She enjoys nature and hiking.

Hiking is my number one hobby. I love that she is healthy, and active. It means she can keep up with me. I want to go and see and experience the world. She wants to do the same. She said it herself; she is a free spirit that wants to see and experience all that life has to offer. But she is still practical. Not a heroine user.

8. Not a heroine user.

I want to go, and see, and experience everything except hard drugs with her. I want it bad.

What if she wants more than what I have to offer her? Anxiety spikes through my veins. What if she is too free a spirit to want to turn this into more than just vacation hook ups? Travel buddies with benefits. I stop that train of thought before I derail into depression or lusty daydreams, neither of which will help me with my list, that I keep derailing from.

Let's see…

9. She likes the same music I do.

That is important. Back in college, my first year in the dorms, the campus advisors chose roommates for the year based solely on every one's music preference. My old roommate Nate is still one of my best friends. I can't wait to take her to a concert. I wonder what kind of movies she likes, or if she binges any TV shows. My mind starts to wander as I take another hit. This weed is smooth, I think, twirling the joint through my fingers. My kid has good taste; this has got to be top shelf, my thoughts derailing once again.

I wonder if Ainsley gets high on occasion? I bet she would be a riot. What bad habits could she have? I wonder. Will she judge my bad habits? We haven't exposed the skeletons in our closets to each other yet. This is still the honeymoon phase. That also explains why I'm so thrown by her.

I wonder how she unwinds at the end of a hard day, when the dishes are piled up in the sink, the kids are bitching and the bills are late because no one remembers to pick up the mail. What does she look like when she isn't relaxed and on vacation? What is she like when she is sad or angry? I know she drinks alcohol, but she was controlled on the ship and never over did it like we did back in our twenties in Vegas. Just a glass of wine with her meal, or a single fancy drink by the pool. She doesn't strike me as someone who has dealt with substance abuse. I've spent three years learning those lessons after Vanessa's death. Honestly, I'm still learning. It's all about a healthy balance and staying within my limits now. I wonder if she has such control now because she had to learn that same lesson.

We do have our histories in common, sad as they are. Both of us losing our spouses suddenly five years ago. Both of us raising teen-age children on our own while trying to glue the holes in our lives together. I'm not the same person I was before living through that grief. I evolved. The way she explained the life lessons she has taken with her from those struggles proves to me that she is focused on her growth as a human too. Like I told Austin last night, it's important to surround yourself with like-minded energies. I feel like Ainsley matches my energy perfectly. We have so much in common, even our sons, sharing in their emotional highs and lows. Watching them discover who they are and navigate a turbulent social and romantic environment is both painful and exhilarating. She gets that. Both of her children sound wonderful and successful in life. I realize I'm excited to meet them. I'm excited for Ainsley to meet Austin, and all of my people too.

I turn my head right towards the still dark sky in the west. I imagine her snug and warm under a pile of blankets still sleeping, and wish that I was spooning her. I have plenty of reasons to already love her, I decide, grabbing my device and pulling up my Expedia browser. And I can't think of any dark secrets or bad habits that would make me want to cut and run. I type in flights to San Diego, CA.

# 30.

## Playing Catch Up

Ainsley:

I wake to the sounds of birds chirping through the open window in my bedroom. The early morning sunlight, my alarm. I missed my bed while on the ship. But now that I'm home, I miss Cody's warm body spooning next to me. At least I do have two warm balls of fluff at my feet, and I sit up and stroke both of the cats. Mouse and Zoomie, their little motors purring loudly. Mouse giving me her squeaky little meow that she is named after in greeting. Seems the kitties missed me while I was away.

Today is my first day back to normal life. Really, it is a massive catch-up day and I feel the anxiety of overwhelm, already building within me. I take a deep breath and get out of bed to freshen up. While brushing my teeth, my usual routine is to run my calendar through my mind to get organized. But I keep getting distracted by memories of Cody from the first time I noticed him on the pool deck before sailing, to our amazing goodbye at the airport.

My focus is zilch.

There is a Zen proverb that says:

*-You should sit in meditation for twenty minutes every day, unless you are too busy. Then you should sit for an hour.*

Today should be an hour day, I think to myself. I compromise at thirty minutes and head out into my garden to Zen-out.

Once in my favorite spot, under an old oak tree, I find my peace and take and extra fifteen to meditate both on my schedule, as well as on Cody. He calls it manifestation work. I call it focused meditation. Some people call it Prayer. But it's the same thing. Focus energy on the outcome you desire. I desire him.

The last few days could have been a story in a romance novel, except for the lack of a plot twist. Maybe the twenty-five year separation counts for all the suspense that a good story usually has. Perhaps it's all happily ever after from here on out. I let my fantasy mind take over enjoying the whirlwind romance in my imagination.

But I am a realistic romantic too. I know that "Vacation" Ainsley is a little different than everyday Ainsley. All people have different sides of themselves depending on their environment. I'm sure Cody is the same way. The honeymoon phase always fades. The new face becomes familiar. The sex is no longer new and exciting. The chores and to-do list start to take precedence over one another, because you expect the other to always be there.

I remember years of neglect in my relationship with my husband Brian. Both my neglect of him, and he of me. When the kids were tiny, I was so tired all the time, I pushed him away. Then he stopped trying. The romance died long before he did. Brian's death taught me not to take anyone's presence for granted. I know some dimming of this honeymoon phase is bound to happen, but I promise myself, that I won't let the mundane task of life take precedence over him the way I had Brian. I won't repeat the same mistake.

I go inside to finish getting ready for my day and pass by a pile of dirty laundry, I stop to pick it up. Most of my day will be in the studio going over photo edits from the previous week, as well as preparing for my upcoming wedding tomorrow. I need to get chores done in whatever empty space I can find. It looks like 7:30 am on a Saturday is going to be laundry time.

Tossing the load in the wash, I change into a pair of shorts and choose a teal blouse in honor of Cody. Then I put in my new blue diamond earrings. I still can't believe he bought these for me. Receiving gifts usually makes me feel awkward. But remembering the look in his eyes when he held them out to me, makes me feel nothing but warm gooey love. I throw my hair up into a fancy messy bun like Sarah taught me, to show off the earrings. I add a little mascara and lip gloss, and I'm done.

Grabbing a Monster Mean Bean coffee from the fridge (One of my guilty pleasures) I pick up the bag of gifts I bought for my team and my purse, then head out the door. I blow a kiss towards Bodhi, still probably fast asleep in the studio above the garage and I head towards the 15 freeway.

Tonight, Alice is driving down from Long Beach for dinner with Bodhi and me. I'm excited and nervous to tell them all about Cody. They were both all for me going on this singles cruise with Sarah, and I know they will be happy, if I'm happy. But I'm still nervous as a few worst-case scenarios pop into my brain. I flush them out with an image of what I want to have happen instead of the one I don't.

Then I start to think about the kids and their love lives. Bodhi had a first date last night, and I'm excited to hear about it. Hopefully his romantic life is picking up like mine is. Alice has had a steady boyfriend for the past six months. Eric. I have only met him once, but he makes Ali happy, so I'm happy. I should invite Eric over for dinner again soon, I think. Then I add picking up take-out to my mental to do list for the day, knowing I'm not going to want to cook tonight.

***

Saturdays in July are always busy in the wedding industry. Careful scheduling is the only reason I have today off. It's not even 9:00 am and already the office is full of life. Photo shoots can start as early as 6:00 am for the bridal party and a few of my staff have already left for shoots. As different photographers grab their gear or work on last night's photos, I walk in feeling like Santa passing out little shot glasses, or bracelets, or abalone shell trinkets to all my employees. They are my work babies. Seven of us in all, and I love them like family. Walking to the editing studio I pass by Malinda's office. She is my bookkeeper and I would be 100% lost without her. I do not have a mind for numbers. Without her, I would be bankrupt.

"Hey Lindi, I got you a little something pretty." I pass her a bag with the little silver and turquoise vase that I picked up at Enrique's silver shop in Ensenada.

"Oh, Ains, it's stunning. Thank you." She stands up and gives me a gigantic, tight hug. Lindi gives amazing hugs for such a tiny person. Her silver hair, styled long and wavy, picks up the gleam in the vase.

"I'll bring you a flower from my garden when you're back in the office on Tuesday." I smile. "Are you free for a fast lunch around 1:00 pm today? I can't wait to tell you all about my cruise."

"Of course, but does it have to be a fast lunch? I've missed you."

"I've missed you too. We shall see how much I get done before then." I smile. "I'll be in the editing dungeon if you need me." I wave as I walk out the door.

Setting up my computer, I start with my missed calls and messages. Opening my phone I see at text from Cody.

> Cody: "Morning, Beautiful. I missed waking up to you warm in my arms."

The sweet text makes me feel giddy.

> Ainsley: "I missed waking up next to you too."

I respond, then sit staring at my phone waiting for those little reply bubbles to turn into words.

> Cody: "I found a flight arriving at 2:00 pm next Monday. Should I book it?"

> Ainsley: "Hell YES!!! . 😚"

The happy face emoji was nowhere equivalent to my joy, but I sent it anyway.

> Cody: "Consider it done. Do you have a busy day?"

> Ainsley: "I do. Playing catch up at work and meeting my progeny for dinner tonight."

Cody: "I told Austin all about you last night."

Ainsley: "And.....????"

Cody: "He is very excited to meet you."

Ainsley: "I'm both excited and nervous to tell Alice and Bodhi about you tonight."

Cody: "You'll do great. So, what are you wearing???" 😜

I take a selfie of the side of my face, my earrings, jaw, lips, and neck the only visible part showing. It is artsy, and after a quick lighting edit, I send it along. I look at the clock on my phone. 9:30 am already, and I haven't even opened a single file yet. I roll my eyes at myself. It is too easy to get distracted with him.

Ainsley: "Your turn to send me a selfie, then I need to get to work."

He sends me a picture of a dog, head resting in his lap. I can see the bend of Cody's knees and his hand against the dog's neck, like he has been stroking her. The look of love in those chocolate brown eyes is melt-my-heart adorable. A Golden Retriever, just like our dog (Bodhi's dog) Pippy.

Ainsley: "Is that Fluffs?"

I was proud of myself for remembering the dog's name from his stories of home. I'm horrible with names.

Cody: "The one and only."

I shuffle through my phone for a picture of Pippy. I find one of her playing tug-of-war with Bodhi and Alice. Both fighting against her, two to one. Pips is winning.

Ainsley: "Our Golden Pippy. One more thing we have in common. Our dogs."

I find another picture of Pips cuddled up with Mouse and Zoomie from last Christmas in front of the fire place and send that one too.

Cody: "Is that from a photo shoot?"

Ainsley: "No, but it's one of my favorites. Pippy, Mouse and Zoomie. My fur babies. I hope you like cats, they come with the package."

Cody: "Cats, dogs, goats... I'll take it all."

He has me laughing out loud. He is so funny. Goats! I shake my head in laughter.

Ainsley: "Maybe we can get the pups together for a playdate too."

Cody: "Really? Can Fluffs come out to California also?

Cody: "Please feel free to say no if another dog would be a stress for you or your pets."

He is so thoughtful. Fact is, I think Pippy would love another puppy friend. And the cats are chill. We tease that Bodhi is a dog whisperer. He would be in Seventh Heaven if Fluffs was to visit. Cody would instantly score points with my son. The thought makes me smile.

Ainsley: "Yes. I think that's a fun idea. I have a fenced yard where the dogs can play and they have free roaming privileges in the house and in Bodhi's studio above the garage. I'm sure you would score a few points with Bods if you were to bring Fluffs with you. He loves dogs, plans to become a veterinarian."

Cody: "Thank you. I will buy Fluffs a ticket too. I can't wait to see you."

Ainsley: "I can't wait to see you either."

Cody: "Now, stop procrastinating with cute pet pics and get to work."

Ainsley: "Uploading work files now.

Cody: "I hope you have a productive day."

Ainsley: "Thank you. I hope your day is wonderful too."

Setting my phone down I dig into my email messages. But a moment later my phone buzzes again.

Cody: "Will you call me tonight after your dinner with your offspring?"

Ainsley: "Yes. I'll tell you how it went. Please do your manifestation thing for a smooth night for me."

Cody: "Of course. *♥*"

My heart did a little emoji too. I heart emoji'd him back. Then I got to work.

# 31.

## Take Out and Small Talk

Ainsley:

The day had been long, but I got a ton of work done. My lunch with Lindi was full of all the dirty little tidbits that she lives for. She was swooning and fanning herself through half our meal as we laughed and giggled like teenagers over sandwiches from the local deli.

Now at a quarter past 7:00 pm, I'm finishing up paying for our take out as I get a text from Ali.

Alice: "Bodhi and I are home. Where you at?"

Ainsley: "Just finished picking up Dinner. Home in 10."

As I pull into the garage, Bodhi comes out, followed by Pippy, our (his) dog, to help me bring in my bags. Bod's is wearing one of his muscle shirts and his tan buff arms make easy work of all the bags. Despite being shy, the kid still likes to show off.

"Smells great. Trupiano's?"

"Yup, all our favorites." I smile, kissing his cheek in thanks for the help.

"How was your vacation?"

"Amazing." I beam "I'll tell you and Ali all about it over dinner. I'm starving." I say patting my stomach and ushering him inside.

"Hey Mom!" Ali waves from the kitchen sink as we come in through the side door.

"Hey Baby, you look lovely." She gives me a little twirl of her sun dress. It is ombre orange and magenta. She looks like a sunset. Her long wavy brown hair swirling around her face in time with the dress. "Very pretty. A new creation."

"Yup." she smiles. "Oh Mom, I love your earrings. Did you get those in Mexico?"

"Thank you. I did."

"Can I have them when you die?"

I laugh out loud. "Sure baby."

"It's such a nice evening, shall we dine on the patio?" I ask.

"Sounds good. What are we having?"

"You are having the chicken alfredo. Bodhi has a personal pepperoni pizza. And I have eggplant parmesan, along with a side of cheesy bread and a Caesar salad to share."

"Yum. Thanks Mom."

"I'm just so happy to have both my babies' home and to have someone else cook the meal. I think I got a little spoiled on the ship."

After we made ourselves comfortable, and fed the pets, so that they wouldn't be at our heels the entire meal, conversation turned to my trip.

"How was the singles cruise? Meet anyone interesting?" Ali asks, mouth full of pasta.

"It was amazing. And yes, I did meet someone. Sarah did too. In fact…," I figure I should start with the biggest news first. It might make my story easier to tell. I lower my voice, leaning into the table like I have a big secret to share. "…Sarah is now engaged."

"What?"

"No way!"

I nod my head.

"Tell all!" Ali says, eyes big as saucers.

"Well, I guess I should start at night one and the speed dating event." I smile remembering the moment he said, 'Hi', and those blue eyes staring back at me. I feel the blush starting to stain my cheeks and take a drink of water.

I have to drink a lot of water as I intertwine bits of my blossoming relationship with Cody in between the love story of Brent and Sarah. I tell them how we recognized each other from our chance meeting in Vegas so many years ago. Although, I do not go into detail about Vegas. But I do tell them about how much fun I had with him, and how he made me laugh, and about all the things we have in common. I tell them about Brent and how perfect he is for Sarah. How he popped the question after only 48-hours and canceled his flight.

"He is at Sarah's house as we speak."

"What about your guy?" Bodhi asks "You're going to see him again, right?"

Here goes nothing. "He is coming out a week from Monday for a visit."

"He is staying here?" Ali asks in an accusatory tone that spikes panic inside of my gut.

"He is."

"You're letting a complete stranger stay in our house?"

"Alice, he is far from a stranger. I've known him for over twenty-five years." I visibly cringe as I hope my joke will lighten the mood. "It's not like I got engaged like Sarah." I send Sarah a silent apology into the air, for throwing her under the bus.

"I know you miss Dad and all, but isn't this a little fast?"

"He's not moving in honey." Yet. I think.

I skip ahead hoping to move this awkward conversation into safer territory. "We have plans to go out wine tasting with Sarah and Brent while Cody is in town. And he would love to meet both of you if you would like to meet him. One night I'm going to make mac-n-cheese and a cinnamon roll apple pie. I would love for you both to join us. Ali, you could bring Eric too."

"Sure, I want to meet this guy." Bodhi chimes in, before shoving another slice of pizza in his mouth. "So long as it's not Friday, I've got another hot date." Bodhi says, mouth full. "This time with Alex."

"Oh, how do you know Alex?"

"We met at a party."

"Good. I'll make sure it's not Friday. How about you Alice?"

"Gee, this isn't too fast at all, Mom." Ali shakes her head and rolls her eyes. "Yeah, I can come down that Wednesday. I'll see if Eric is free too."

I ignore her eye roll. "Thanks kids. I'm really excited for you to meet him." It is a small victory. Their opinions mean so much to me, and giving him a chance is a step in the right direction.

"Gosh, the new guy is already meeting the family." Bodhi shakes his head with a small half smile. I send him a pleading look asking him to cool it with the drama. Then I follow that with puppy eyes that beg him to be open to this new person in my life. Hopefully in all of our lives.

I understand why Alice is nervous. This could mean a profound change for them too, assuming things progress with Cody as I hope they will. I realize I need to be as gentle with Ali and Bodhi's feelings, as I am hoping they will be gentle with mine.

"How long is he going to be here?" Ali asks.

"I'm not sure yet. Cody said he was planning to book his ticket today. But I've been so busy playing catch up at work, that we haven't spoken more than a few texts."

"Oh, my goodness." Alice giggles. "Bodhi and Cody rhyme. How cute is that."

"Ewwww. Maybe I'll have to go back to calling him by his nickname." I joke.

"What's that?"

"Blue, for the color of his eyes. When I met him in Vegas, I didn't know his name. So, I nicknamed him Blue. For the first two days of the cruise, I found it hard to think of him as Cody, he was still Blue to me. But as I got to know the man he is now vs. who he was back then, he transformed from Blue into Cody." I tell them, a wistful smile in my eyes.

"Mom, I can tell you really like this guy. It's almost a little scary. Like, I'm super happy for you and all. I just want you to be careful with your heart." I grin at Ali's 'Love Advice' to me. It is good advice. But I am afraid it may already be too late.

"Thank you, sweet heart, I will do my very best. Now, enough about me. How was your date last night Bodhi?"

"Blaaa. There won't be a second." He said taking another slice of pizza and biting it nearly in half.

"Oh well. Better to know on the first date than the tenth."

"I guess."

"How about you and Eric?" I look at Alice.

"Great. He wants to take me up to meet his parents for their 30th wedding anniversary in a few weeks."

"Wow, that's like a whole new level. So, you're meeting the family too." Bods nudges her.

"Yeah."

"You feel good about that?" I ask.

"I do. I'm just nervous about making a good impression on his closest fifty relatives."

"You're amazing, who wouldn't love you?"

"Mommmmm," she moans "You're biased. Your opinion doesn't count."

"I beg to differ. I know your soul better than anyone. I see amazing."

"Ugh, please don't get sappy."

"Okay, okay. Where do his parents live?"

"Ventura county."

"That's a pretty drive once you get past L.A. I'm sure you're going to have a great time."

"Thanks." she mumbles into her food.

After dinner, Alice took off and Bodhi and I turned on some reruns of Friends.

"So, just how serious is this guy? Are we talking wedding?"

"It may have come up a few times."

"Seriously? You're already talking about it?"

"The proposals were all in jest."

"Proposal(s)? as in plural?"

"Well, weddings were a popular topic with Brent and Sarah with us." I was feeling nervous to tell him just how serious our talks had been. Not as nervous as if Ali had still been around, as Bodhi is a bit more 'chill' than Alice is. But I still feel like he needs to meet him first, before I go into how completely head-over-heels, I am for this man. I want the kids to see for themselves. Maybe I want to see it again too and make sure it's not all just a vacation fling. But I don't think that's what this was or will be. Cody said it himself. "There is some kind of wonderful cosmic connection between us." I feel it even now just thinking about him.

"So, is he like Dad?"

I think for a moment. "In some ways, yes. He is very active like your father was. Although, not a surfer. Not much surf in New Mexico. We went ziplining and kayaking, and he's been skydiving. He loves adventure and that adrenaline rush, same as your dad and I. He's funny like your father, but a different kind of funny." I smile as memories of laughter fill my brain.

"Mom?"

"Hmmm?"

"Didn't you hear my question?"

"No. I guess I was distracted."

"It's nice to see you distracted in this way." he smiles, "I asked if I could steal a beer from the fridge?"

"Oh, sure honey."

"Want another glass of wine?"

"Just half. Thanks, Sweets." He takes my empty wine glass and heads for the fridge.

While he is in the kitchen, I check my phone and am happy to see a missed text from Cody

Cody: "How was dinner?"

Ainsley: "Great, Bodhi and I are just watching a little Friends. I'll call in an hour if that's not too late."

Cody: "Counting the minutes"

I smile and put my phone down just as Bodhi peeks his head into the den.

"You're glowing. Was that him?" he asks, nodding to my phone as he hands me my full glass of wine.

"It was. He was just asking about dinner." I smile.

We stay up watching one last episode, then Bodhi goes back to his studio, Pippy in tow.

# 32.

## Phone Sex

Ainsley:

After getting ready for the night, I snuggle into bed and call Cody. He picks up on the first ring.

"Hi." He answers. His voice is so deep and sexy, it does things to my insides with just his 'Hi'. I didn't realize how much I had missed the sound of him until right now, and a sigh of relief sounds loud across the line.

"Oh Ainsley, I've missed that sound." he groans into the phone.

"How was your day?" I finally manage to ask.

"Productive in that I was able to confirm that no one at work truly needs me. The place runs like a well-oiled machine. Also, I booked my flight out with Fluffs. Monday arriving at 2:00 pm, return flight Friday at 3:00 pm."

"I can't wait to meet your dog."

"What about me?" he fake-whines, pouting his lower lip out at me.

"I suppose Fluffs handler is pretty cute too." I joke, "So tell me, how was your chat with Austin?"

"That boy is ready to call you Mama. He says he takes full credit and will accept our gratitude by way of large fancy Christmas gifts or Bitcoin."

I laughed hard at that.

"Ainsley?"

"Yeah?"

"I really missed hearing your laugh today. I missed your voice, your energy…, I missed being able to touch you."

I sigh in response. He makes me feel all kinds of wonderful. "My drive home from work was spent remembering sexy naked time."

"Mmmmm. I've missed that too. Tell me about your dinner with Alice and Bodhi."

"They were both happy that I had a great time and met someone. Alice is a little nervous with how fast we are moving. So, I didn't go into too much detail. I think once they meet you, they will get it."

"But they both want to meet me?"

"Yup. They are both free Wednesday night and want to join us for dinner. Really, they probably just want pie."

"Pie is a good bribe. Have you talked to Sarah?"

"No. Have you spoken with Brent?"

"Not yet. I'll drop him a line tomorrow."

"Me too, with Sarah. I also forgot to call Jordan today, I was so busy at work. But I'll give her a ring tomorrow after I check to see which day works for BrentRah. Hopefully, we can steal Jordan and her trolley on Tuesday or Thursday."

"BrentRah?"

"Yeah, Brent plus Sarah. You know, Like BradJolina, and BenNifer...?"

His laugh made me tingle. "I like BrentRah. So does that make us CodSley?"

"CodSley is actually kinda cute." I smile.

"Yeah, I think we won the obnoxious couple's name game."

"Won't BrentRah be jealous." I jest. "So, what else would you like to do and see while you're visiting?"

"I want to do what you like. A week in the life of Ainsley. I want to go to your favorite restaurants and watch the movies you want to go see. Show me your favorite places. Think of it as time with me, not for me."

"Does that mean I will get a glimpse into your life when I come out to visit you in Taos?"

"Oh yes. I will share all my favorite haunts with you."

We chatted about nothing and everything for over two hours before the yawns started.

"Do you have a busy day tomorrow?" he inquires.

"I have a wedding shoot starting at noon. I probably won't get home until 11:00 pm."

"Wow, are wedding shoots always that long?"

"I try to divide long days up between the staff. Usually, one photographer does pre-wedding and then a second will join in for the ceremony and main events. Photographer one takes off after dinner and the second finishes up the night. But I will often do a shoot from start to finish. It's almost always a fun and very happy day, even if it is long."

"It's important to enjoy what you do for a living."

"Yes, it is. Do you enjoy your job?" I ask him.

"Sometimes. When I first got into real estate the adrenaline rush of a sale had me loving it. But it can be very stressful too. There was a point when I despised it. Getting into rentals stabilized me for a while. But being the middleman for complaints started to wear on my nerves. I had been contemplating a shift when Nessa died. Then the shift happened out of necessity.

'Life often waits for some crisis to occur before revealing itself at its most brilliant.'" –

He quoted and my skin prickled with goose bumps at the familiar phrase. Oh my God, did he just quote Paulo Coelho and my favorite book, 'The Alchemist'? He just keeps getting better and better. Cody seems so self-aware, so sure of himself. I hope he is sure of me too.

"I'm happy now." Cody continued. "I can get most of my work done from my device anywhere that has service. I go into the office fairly often, but that's more for moral support and comradery. Most of my time is spent around the campground, out in nature."

"So, you are like the broker who oversees everyone else?"

"I share that job with my partner, Bill. They call me Pops at work, even though Bill is older than me."

"It sounds like they like you."

"They better, I'm an awesome boss." I hear him yawn his reply.

"I think it's bed time for us both. It must be really late where you're at."

"1:00 am."

"Oh no, I'm sorry to keep you up so late. I wasn't thinking about the time difference."

"I would stay up all night to hear your voice."

"Awe, you make me feel all warm and gushy inside." I smile into the phone.

"I know you didn't mean it like this, but now I'm thinking about your warm insides and I'm wide awake."

I laugh hard enough to wake Zoomie, who was asleep at the foot of my bed. She gives me an evil lip, then goes back to sleep. "What kinds of naughty things are you thinking about?"

He groans into the phone. "Ainsley, do you have any idea how amazing it feels to be inside of you."

I shudder. "Only as much as my fingers can feel."

"Now, I'm imagining you touching yourself."

"I am."

"Fuck Ainsley," he growls "Please tell me how you touch yourself."

"Are you asking me for a naughty bedtime story?"

"God yes."

"Okay," I pause composing myself. I have never done this before and feel a little nervous and flustered, unsure of just what to say. "I'm in my room with the lights low," I start. "I can already feel how wet I am for you through my panties." I add quietly into the receiver as I touch myself. Imagining that he is here with me, pretending that my fingers are his fingers sliding under the edge of my undies. "I'm sliding my middle finger between my legs and it is so silky, wet, and hot. It must be over one hundred degrees." I hear him groan into the phone and tingles shiver down my spine at the sound. "I'm sliding my finger up to my clit, spreading the moist heat over myself and rubbing little circles with my thumb, pretending it's your tongue."

"Holy fuck Ainsley. I'm going to change my flight to this Monday instead of the next. I'm so hard for you it hurts."

"Then tell me how you pleasure yourself." I say in my sexy voice.

"Right now, I'm remembering how you woke me up on day number three of the cruise. That was so amazing it seems unreal even now. But if I focus hard enough, I can almost feel you hot and tight around me. I can feel your body quiver from your orgasm." He shudders an exhale. "I tighten my grip on my dick as I imagine your body clenching around me. I've never felt in sync with anyone the way I do with you." he breathed heavily against the phone.

My chest tingles with a rush of heat from just his words. Already, He has me on the brink of release. "Don't stop." I say in a rush as my imagination kicks into overdrive and my body responds.

"I imagine my hands around your hips, the feel of your soft flesh as I thrust deeper inside of you. I can practically feel your nipples tighten from my imagined kiss."

"I'm playing with my breast imaging that too. I'm picturing riding you, grinding against you. God, I feel flush all over. My breasts tingle, and I'm… so…dizzy."

"Are you close?" He whispers deep and slow.

"Yes." I pant in a rush.

"Let me hear you cum."

"God Cody, it's so tight, so intense, I'm....oh... fuck!" and I let myself scream my release next to the phone.

I lay back against the pillow panting, listening to the sound of him cum across the line with a shiver.

"Ainsley?"

"MmmmHmmm?"

"That was fucking amazing."

I sigh. "I'm dragging my wet fingers over my nipples and up to my mouth to taste myself."

"Fuck, Woman. Please, tell me what you taste like after you cum." he begs.

"Like a sweet warm buttery biscuit."

He hisses in a long breath at my description. "Ainsley, the only way I'm going to make it until next week is if you promise we can have phone sex every night."

"I'm going to have to read a lot more filthy novels for that." I laugh back.

"Please read them all. But first, get some rest. You have a busy day tomorrow."

"After that, I'm going to sleep like a rock."

He laughs. "Me too. Sweet dreams, Ainsley."

"Good night, Cody."

Disconnecting, I slide under the covers and let my fingers continue to trace my body, imagining the postcoital caresses that Cody always delivers. This after sex loving may be my favorite part with him. It's so unlike the 'Wam bam thank you ma'am that I had grown accustomed to in marriage. Wednesday night sex night, assuming there wasn't a game on or we were not too tired. Then it was back to packing lunches or doing the dishes. But Cody isn't like that. He loves me after the act as much as before. The orgasm itself being the pinnacle in the middle.

# 33.

## California

Ainsley:

The rest of my week flew by. As Monday approached my excitement grew to the giddy levels of a child the night before Christmas. Cody feels like my gift from the Universe. I have our week all planned out. We will start with an evening in Old Town San Diego, including a dog friendly walking Ghost tour, while we wait for traffic to dissipate.

I wake with the sun and start my day with my usual routine of meditation in the garden. Then I do a quick tidy up around the house. I hit Pilates at 9:00 am with Sarah. We gossip about her steamy days and nights with her new fiancé, and she helps me decide what to wear when I pick up Cody this afternoon. Then I run to Trader Joes and stock up on food and drinks for the week. I take a fast shower, then drive down to San Diego to pick up Cody.

Thanks to Fluffs, Cody is one of the first passengers to leave the plane. To be honest, my attention is torn between the man that I admittedly love, and the golden retriever wiggling excitedly next to him. He spots me a moment after I noticed him and his smile absolutely gives him the win. We both double-time our pace, as we hurry into each other's arms. Cody dropped his carry on so that he could hold me properly. His lips touch mine with an electric fire that zings all the way down to my toes.

Not wanting to be left out, Fluffs stands on her hind legs wrapping her paws around us both, licking our arms and elbows. My left arm transfers from Cody's shoulder to the mop of golden fur atop of Fluff's head. I pet and scratch behind Fluff's ears in greeting, as Cody's tongue continues to reacquaint itself with my mouth.

"I've missed you." he says, leaving baby kisses over my lips, cheeks, nose, and forehead.

"I'm so happy you're here, I'm practically shaking." I move the hand that had been petting Fluffs to his heart and kiss him again. His heart beat is just as fast as mine. It even feels to be in alignment with the pounding of my own in my head.

After a quick stop at the pet relief area, we hop in my jeep and head for Old Town. We have lunch on the patio at a cute little Mexican restaurant off the main square, then walk up and down the main street appreciating the old Spanish architecture.

The ghost tour is a fun little glimpse into the history of the area. But other than Fluff's random barking at shadows, which we assume is the Ghost Cat of San Diego, the tour is Spector free. But the good-humored nature of the group has us laughing and all telling our own ghost stories even after the tour ends and we walk back to the car park.

"So do you believe in ghosts?" Cody asks, nudging my shoulder.

"I have never had an experience where I can say that I saw a ghost. But I do believe there are other dimensions existing around us that we cannot sense. And since energy never dies, maybe one of those other dimensions houses the spirits we refer to as ghosts. Maybe sometimes the veil between our perceptions and reality shifts or becomes thin. That's why some people who are in tune with those other worldly frequencies can see and communicate with those spirits." I pause trying to gather my words. "Human life is impossible by all scientific standards. So, if the impossible is possible, then everything we imagine has potential. So, yeah, just the fact that they are impossible probably means they are real." I smile feeling a little dorky. "You?" I ask, implying the same question he had asked me.

He grins a cute little boy smile that makes my knees weak and makes me feel a little less dorky and more confident. "Ditto. I like the way you explain it. Having faith in the impossible is a beautifully optimistic way to view the world."

\*\*\*

We pull up to my little California style bungalow in Fallbrook a little after 8:00 pm. The sun has already set, but a rainbow of light is still arching across the western sky, making the evening feel magical. The lamp is on in Bodhi's studio, so I send him a quick text inviting him and Pippy down to greet Cody and Fluffs. Pippy, sensing a new friend, comes running down the stairs from Bodhi's studio, the dog door flapping loudly, before I finish my text and can hit send. The dogs do their butt-sniffing greeting then start jumping and nuzzling and playing with each other. Running around in circles. They are so excited and cute that Cody and I can't contain our laughter at their shared joy.

"Who is this amazing creature?" Bodhi asks as he comes down the stairs to join us in the garden. Our cheeks pink from our laughter.

"Amazing! Wow, I'm flattered! My name is Cody." He teases.

I laugh even harder, doubling over on myself as my stomach starts to spasm from laughing so hard. Bodhi just stares at us, stoic in his expression as I grip my side trying to catch my breath. Then his grin brakes too as Pippy runs up to him and nudges his hand. As if to drag her human down to the garden to meet her new friend.

"That is Fluffs." Cody finally answers the real question between laughs, waving a hand towards his dog. Bodhi, bends down to let Fluffs smell his hand, then gives her a good ear scratch. She rolls over for an additional tummy rub and Bodhi's smile reaches his eyes.

After a proper hello to the dog, Bodhi finally walks over to Cody, hand outstretched in a friendly greeting. Cody grabs his hand and pulls him in for a hug. I am so grateful for Cody's welcoming energy. Bodhi tends to give back what is received, and this is a great start as Bod's returns the hug.

"Your mom has told me so much about you, I feel like we are friends already. It's so nice to finally meet you." he declares in a warm voice.

"Yeah, you too." Bodhi opened up to Cody's welcoming, happy energy and the true smile that had been reserved for the dogs, returned almost at full volume.

But that's a big win in my book. To be fair, we humans really can't be expected to compete with dogs.

We all move into the kitchen via the French doors that open to the back patio. Everyone settling around the bar area while I get refreshments.

"Did you two have fun in San Diego today?" Bodhi asks.

"We had a great time. I have never been outside of the downtown area before." Cody says. "Old Town is like a little piece of the city that time has forgotten."

We talk about the day and our plans for the week, reminding him about dinner Wednesday night with Alice.

"Got any tips for me, when I meet your sister?" Cody asks Bodhi.

"Don't let her sense your fear." Cody chuckles as Bodhi's phone starts going off from his upcoming date for Friday.

After Bod's finishes his drink, he politely excuses himself for the evening and retreats to his studio. Fluffs and Pippy both following behind.

"I feel a little jealous that Fluffs just ditched me without a second glance for Pippy and Bodhi." he says in mock heartache.

"Bodhi is a dog whisperer. Canines will just follow him home. Fluffs didn't stand a chance."

"So long as he doesn't mind the extra company."

"He is probably wishing you had two dogs. The more the merrier." I smile.

"I do wish you had two dogs!" Bodhi yells from the bottom of the stairs as he waves a final goodbye.

We wave goodnight from the deck and finish our drinks under the twinkling night sky. Then Cody takes my hand and we walked back inside.

"It's been a long day. Especially for you. Are you tired?" I ask.

"It has been a long day; and yes, I am tired. But I'm not ready to go to sleep." His fingers trace the shape of my jaw as he says it. My pet butterflies, the ones that live in my stomach, wake up at the thought of what we could be doing instead of sleeping. "I wouldn't mind a shower followed by a tour of the bedroom." He says softly against my ear.

Grabbing his bag, I lead him back to the master suite. He drops his duffle bag on my side chair and I start helping him undress for his shower.

"Join me?" he asks as he starts unbuttoning my shorts.

I answer him by sticking my hand down his pants and my tongue in his mouth.

He growled, deep and primal.

God, I have missed that sound. We stumble around each other, as piece by piece clothing falls to the floor. Leaving a trail like Hansel and Gretel on our way to the bathroom.

Turning on the water, we make out against the bathroom wall until the steam of the shower fills the room. Stepping into the water, Cody pulls me in front of him so that both of us are facing the shower head. He pours some shampoo in his hands and rubs them together to create a foamy lather. Then he starts washing my hair. His fingertips massaging my scalp feels amazing and I close my eyes, letting the bubbly lather slide down my body. His hands follow the bubbles down my shoulders and over my breast. The slick feel of his fingers has my nipples hard immediately. He slowly lathers my stomach and hips. Between my thighs he takes his time, his fingers slowly teasing me. Finishing my front half, he spins me around so that my soapy self is pressed hard against his chest. I'm surprised to find his cock is fully grown already and I haven't even started to lather him up yet. I feel like I need to catch up. Grabbing the soap, he fills his hands with more.

"Me too? For you?" I ask. Cody smiles and squeezes some in the palm of my hand too. I go to work, starting with his abs and moving up to his chest, over his shoulders and down his arms. Memorizing the defining lines of his muscles as I go. He is in great shape, hard in all the right spots.

"Sit" I command, nodding to the little ledge that I believe was built specifically for shower sex. Standing between his legs, I wash his hair too. He pulls me closer as my fingers scratch and massage his scalp; my breast directly in front of his face.

"You are even more beautiful than I remember." His hands gently cup my breast, his fingers tracing the shape of me, removing the soapy suds from my nipples before replacing them with his mouth. His lips, tongue, teeth...he knows just the right pressure to make me see stars. I close my eyes leaning into him. Lost in the feel of him. Forgetting for a brief second all about the soap running down into his eyes.

"Up" I direct him in a panted whisper. Obedient as ever, he stands and I switch places with him in front of the shower head. He's too tall, so he has to rinse his own hair, but my fingers find something else to do, as they follow the soapy bubbles washing down his pecs, abs and groin. I slide my hand over his dick and I can feel him grow even bigger in my palm. The vibration of his groan against the shower walls reverberates in my bones and I'm ready to climb on top of him.

I start to make a move but he stops me. (The nerve.)

"The shower is for a fast fuck. I want you in OUR bed. I am going to take my time making love to you all night."

He kissed me and my brain shut off. I know there was lots of kissing and groping as we finished rinsing off. I vaguely remember us toweling dry before stumbling into bed where we indeed took our time making love. All night we spent studying each other's bodies. Coming together, then apart to simply kiss and snuggle or cat nap for thirty minutes before coming together again. Cody would whisper something sweet into my ear. I would whisper something naughty. Then he would make one of his sounds I like so much that turns my blood to fire. Then we would be going at it again.

Now as I lay here half awake, dawn coming in through the window, I can't help but wiggle my butt against his groin. I snuggle myself into his chest as the sultry memories of our night together bombard my mind. He must be dreaming of me too, because I can feel his cock pressed long and hard against the crack of my bum. Stirring at my movement, his hand, which rested against my stomach, slid up to cup my breast. His lips greet my neck in a good morning kiss. Cody's hand slides from my nipple down my stomach and between my legs. I moan as his fingers press inside me.

"Fuck, you're already so wet." His voice is gravely and needy and oh so very sexy. Moving his hand to my thigh, he gently adjusts my leg and I feel him come inside me from behind.

Oh my God.

The angle goes straight to my G spot and he knows it. The palm of his hand moves over my abdomen and he presses firmly and groans into my ear.

"Fuck, I can feel myself moving inside of you." And he takes my hand and places it flat on my tummy under his, pressing my palm against my own soft flesh. My God, I can feel his cock sliding inside of me through my muscles. Every thrust pops against my palm. The sensation breaks my brain as his lips fall to my neck and his teeth bite into my shoulder. I cum with a ferocity that makes me extremely grateful for an empty house.

# 34.

## Ainsley Day

Ainsley:

The amazing vibration and sound of his orgasm brings me back to earth, as he holds me tight in his arms. Gentle kisses now in place of the biting teeth of a moment ago.

"Good morning." he says, kissing my cheek.

"Mmmmmphhh." I blubber into the pillow, unable to form a single word. I grin and snuggle into him some more. He laughs pulling me closer.

"So, are you ready to start your 'Day in the life of Ainsley?'" I yawn dreamily.

"I think I just did." He nuzzles my neck pulling me tighter against him still.

I giggle at his play on my meaning.

"Let me hold you a little longer before we get up, then I will be at your command."

"Deal." I agree. But Zoomie and Mouse were not in on this deal and five minutes later came in meowing and pawing at our noses to feed them. Mouse takes to Cody right away, which I take as a very good sign. Zoomie showered Cody with affection by racing through his legs as he walked down the hall. Nearly killing him.

True love.

"So, tell me what does my Ainsley day consist of?" he asks over a cup of coffee as we head out to the garden for meditation time.

"I thought after Zen-time and breakfast we could go for a little hike, then to the studio. Malinda will kill me if I don't bring you by. Then dinner at my favorite Pad Thai restaurant."

"Sounds like a great day to me."

We round the side of the house and sit under a one hundred and fifty year old California oak. We sit together in meditation listening to the sounds of nature. The dappled sun warms our skin against the chill morning air. The gentle sound of the wind rustling the leaves of the tree. I expected it to be more difficult to "Zen-out" having the distraction of Cody by my side. But it is not. I fall into my rhythm easily and a vibrant joy fills my soul to have him next to me.

***

Cody:

Sitting, eyes closed, under this magnificent old tree that has watched Ainsley raise her family over the years, I feel an overwhelming sense of wellbeing and peace. Like I'm right where I'm meant to be. I felt this when I found the campground too. But this feeling has more to do with Ainsley than it does this beautiful oak or even being in California itself. Love radiates from my heart. I feel my aura grow with it, an amazing tingle in every cell that feels bigger than my body. I imagine sending my energy over to Ainsley sitting only inches to my left. I want to envelop her in this feeling. I want to scream my love for her at the top of my lungs. But right now, this energetic transfer is all I can manage. The words themselves don't feel powerful enough. Those three little words just can't contain this emotion.

As my mind spins, I feel her fingers take hold of my hand. I peek one eye open at her and I swear she is glowing. Her eyes shut and a slight smile on her closed lips, she holds my hand linking our bodies in meditation. Just as I had linked my energy to her. I give her hand a small squeeze and close my eyes again, doing my best to send the words 'I love you' through the ether and into her heart and mind.

The slapping of the doggy door and the rushing of eight paws down the stairs breaks our concentration as Pippy and Fluffs come up to both of us, licking our faces in greeting.

"Good morning, ladies." Ainsley laughs as Fluffs wiggles between us knocking Ainsley onto her back assaulting her with kisses. Pippy joined in the attack and I laughed even harder as I tried to rescue her from all the puppy love.

"Are you girls ready for a nice hike this morning?" she asks the dogs, rubbing their bellies. Pippy barks a 'Yes' as if she understands. We stand and head back into the house to feed, water and leash the pups for our adventure.

It is a quick drive to the Santa Margarita Nature Preserve and a beautiful day for a hike along the river. The trails are fairly empty of people, so we let the dogs run for a little bit off leash to chase lizards and smell all of the wonderful smells. As we walk amongst the trees enjoying the glory of nature, Ainsley is constantly stopping to pull out her phone and take pictures of mossy logs or bees on daisies along the way. She marvels at the dew on a leaf or the way the sunlight filters through the trees. She sees magic and beauty in the mundane and through her eyes, the world becomes an even more beautiful place to me too. Skipping ahead of me, I stand there on the path lost in the wonder that is her.

"You coming?" she spins around, a brilliant smile shining in her eyes.

I swallow the marriage proposal that is sitting on my tongue and nod, forcing my legs to move from the spot they had rooted.

After a four-mile loop, we jump back in her Jeep and head to her studio in Temecula. The little photo studio is in an old Victorian house off of one of the side streets in Old Town Temecula. A cute little part of town filled with tourist shops, trendy restaurants, and tasting rooms. People walk and mingle along the busy streets. Music and laughter spilling from the windows. Pips and Fluffs noses sniff high into the air as the smells of food waft about us.

"This place is cute." I say as we walk up the ramp and through the front doors of her studio.

"Thank you." She smiles at me before greeting the receptionist with a friendly hello.

"Marta, this is Cody and Fluffs."

"Oh, it's so nice to meet you!" She greets us in a lovely Spanish accent, standing and walking over to us from behind the desk. Her short brown hair bounced in time to her step. I reach out my hand to shake a greeting, but she wraps her arms around my waist in a hug instead. Tiny little Marta squeezes me with the strength of a sumo wrestler. Which is surprising, since I don't think she is taller than 5'1" and 100 pounds. soaking wet.

"It's nice to meet you too." I say hugging her back. Marta releases me to give her love and attention to Fluffs and Pippy. Pulling two dog treats from her pocket.

"Can Fluffs have a treat too?" she asks.

"Of course." I smile at her thoughtful question. "I assume you bring Pippy by often, or does your receptionist keep treats in her pocket for all your K9 clients?"

"Pips is a regular. Jason, my web-designer and editor, brings his poodle Prince Pumpernickel in every day too. I'll take you back to meet them shortly."

"Enjoy the tour." Marta waves as the phone starts to ring. She excuses herself and gets back to work, brown hair bouncing.

I follow Ainsley down the hall, dogs at our heels, as she gently knocks on a frosted glass door.

"Lindi, I have a few guests who would like to say hi." She lets the two pups into the room first. Pippy bounces over to Lindi's smiling face which is surrounded by a desk of paperwork and framed family photos. A lovely woman with a crown of silver hair and creases around her eyes and mouth that speak of years of laughter, greets the golden ball of fluff trying to climb into her lap with a laugh.

"Hello Pippy my love. Who is your friend?"

"That is Fluffs, and this is Cody." Ainsley says, directing her attention to me as I emerge from the doorway. "Cody, this is Melinda. Lindi, for short."

"Now this is who I really want to meet." Lindi says as I walk over to her desk to say hello. "Ain's told me you were handsome, but Wow! Talk about a tall drink of water."

"Why thank you." I smile feeling the heat rise to my cheeks. "Ainsley tells me you are her math savior and one of her closest friends. I'm so happy to meet you in person."

"Awe, did she say a bunch of nice things about me?"

"All nice things."

"Well, you should assume they are all true." she grins. "She said some pretty nice things about you too. But I probably shouldn't repeat those things in public." She winks at me. I feel my ears turn red as Ainsley giggles behind me. I immediately liked Lindi. Her energy is all encompassing and full of good humor.

"Lindi, is my gossip buddy. She knows it all." Ain's gives me a little shrug.

"So, Cody…, do you have a single older brother or father to hook me up with? If they are half as handsome as you, I would be a happy lady."

"Actually, my father is a handsome bachelor too." I grin at her. I bet my dad would love this little firecracker of a woman.

We sit and got to know each other for a good twenty minutes before moving back down the hall and onto the 'editing dungeon' as Ainsley lovingly refers to it. We let the dogs slip out to the back yard to play and relieve themselves, before quietly entering the studio. The room is large and dark with TV screens and monitors over most of the walls in the room. The glow of a single computer off to the right is the only light.

"Hey Jason." Ain's calls out as we enter the room. A head of dark brown hair and a pair of glasses peek up over the screen.

"Yo."

"What ya work'n on?" she asks as we walk over to him, peeking at his screen.

"Bec and Mia's pics from the Schouner/Blanchet wedding Friday. They got some really great shots of the ceremony. Look at this."

She bends low and a smile graces her eyes. "Wow, I love this one." She points.

"I know, right? I don't need to touch up a thing. It's perfect raw."

"Is this from Bec?"

"Yeah, she's really good."

"Yes, she is." Ainsley looks up at me and waves me over. "Jason, this is Cody." Jason looks up, noticing me for the first time.

"Oh, hey man. Nice to meet you." He waves, unable to get up due to the little ball of white fur sleeping on his lap.

"Is this Prince Pumpernickel?" I inquire, gesturing to the dog.

"His Royal Highness is pleased to make your acquaintance too." he says as the dog snores once loudly.

Ainsley pulls her lap top out of her bag and sets it up at a desk near the window. "I'll only be about twenty minutes. You are welcome to look around or you can hang in the garden with the pups."

I move a chair and sit down next to her. "I'm happy here with you. I wouldn't mind seeing some of your photos."

She gives me half a smile and a tentative 'Okay' before turning on the large screen hanging on the wall above us. A series of thumbnail photos cover the screen for a brief second before she hits play and the first image of a waterfall fills the screen. I am transported into the image for three seconds before it starts fading into the next photo of a sunset. I sit there mesmerized as image after image crosses the screen. The majority of pictures are landscapes, not weddings. There are grand vistas as well as close ups of flowers and the veining of leaves.

"These are beautiful. Are they all yours?"

"They are. Mostly from my hikes each morning. Just a second." She pauses as she uploads a new file to the screen and opens it. A dozen photos from our hike this morning pop up on the screen, and the three second slide show starts rounding through the new pics.

"Wow, these are all from today?"

"They are."

"You're an artist. These are amazing."

"Thank you" she blushes.

I can't keep myself from kissing her at that moment, despite Jason only being only ten feet away. The beauty that she sees in the world, she captures in her photos. Maybe part of me expects to capture a part of it too with the kiss. I'm not sure where my mind is. I just know I need to touch her. Embrace her. Soak her up and make her mine.

"Maybe I can hire you to take some photos of the camp ground when you come out to visit me."

"I'm very expensive." She teases. "But perhaps we can work out a trade for back rubs."

"Deal." I grin.

After another thirty minutes, we finished at her shop and said our goodbyes. Walking the dogs along the main street, we stop in at a little Greek restaurant for a late lunch. Sitting on the bougainvillea-covered terrace we watched humanity walk by.

Two young men pass by wearing top hats talking and laughing loudly drawing our attention away from our appetizer of spanakopita.

"What do you think their back story is?" she asks in a low voice.

"Hmmmm." I think, "They are hipsters trying to find an antique store where they can buy a typewriter."

Ainsley laughs out loud. "They are time travelers and got mixed up on their way back to 1810." She contributes.

"Maybe they are ghosts." I add in a spooky whisper. Her boisterous laugh has me laughing too.

"You're good at this game. Making up histories for people is one of my favorite solitary games to play, I have to say, it's more fun with you to bounce ideas off of." She smiles at me.

"Me too." I say as the warmth of crippling love fills my chest. "How about those ladies over there?" I ask, pointing across the street to a group of three middle aged women all dressed in designer shoes and handbags.

"They are probably all named Heather, and are out for coffee before their Botox appointments this afternoon."

I choke on my water; I laugh so hard. "I can't compete with that. I think you nailed it." We play a few more rounds as we eat our meal then walk back to the car and drive home with enough leftovers for dinner, mutually agreeing to push off Pad Thai for another night.

Arriving back at Ainsley's house, bellies still full from our late lunch, we crash onto the sofa feeling the weight of the food coma settling into our bones.

"Did you remember to bring your favorite movie?" She looks up at me.

"I did. Should I go get it?"

"Yeah, I'm feeling to full and lazy for anything other than a book, nap, or movie. I figure, since Ali and Bod's will be joining us tomorrow night, we should do a movie and snuggle tonight."

"I like that idea. What's your movie?" I ask, ready to give her the third degree. But she's ready to let her secret out as she grabs the remote control sitting on the ottoman and pulls up her Netflix account. 'The Princess Bride' is the first movie in the queue. The same movie sitting at the bottom of my duffle bag. I am on her before I know what I'm doing. My tongue in her mouth trying my best to devour her. The palms of my hands holding tight to her as if I could absorb her into myself if I just pull her close enough. Her skin flushes my favorite color and I lick a line of kisses down the soft skin of her neck.

"Have a thing for Cary Elwes, do you?" She teases as she simultaneously angles her neck giving me more access to her flesh.

"I'll give you three guesses as to what movie is sitting in my duffle bag. But I bet you will only need one." She turns her head to look at me. Her eyes are as big as saucers. Her pupils dilated so large; I could tumble right into her soul.

"Really?" she whispers in a hushed tone of amazement.

"It's the perfect movie. A little bit of something for everyone. Sword fights, giants, love... actually, the movie is what turned me onto books as a kid. And there are so many great lines from the film that can be used in everyday conversation. It's inconceivable!" I say with a big excited grin.

"I don't think that word means what you think it means." she quotes in a perfect accent just like Mandy Patinkin did in the movie.

'I love you' I think. I want to say it for real, but it feels too soon somehow. Almost as if BrentRa stole the idea of a fast falling and now Ainsley and I are left with the responsible slow falling into love. Resigned to be the responsible pair. But just because I'm choosing not to speak it out loud doesn't mean I can't still tell her in other ways. I cup her face in the palms of my hands and do my best to tell her with my eyes and with my lips. We melt into each other with the opening scene of The Princess Bride playing in the background. We make slow intentional love there on the sofa. Every kiss holds the space of eternity. Because that is how long I plan to spend with her. My entire life, lived in this moment with her.

Afterwards, we snuggled and spoke our favorite lines along with the movie there on the sofa. We then followed up the Princess Bride with another 80's classic, The Goonies. Refueling with leftovers, we binged watched a few episodes of the Simpsons then went to bed kissing and whispering sweet nothings until we fell asleep in one another's arms.

# 35.

## Glued back together

Cody:

I wake to the sound of breaking glass and an empty pillow beside me. Sitting up, I rub my eyes against the sunlight pouring in through the windows. I stretch, then go in search of Ainsley.

Rounding the corner into the kitchen, I spot her leaning over the sink. She turns to look at me, giving me a fake smile. I have never seen this look on her before, and warning bells go off in my mind as the memory of breaking glass returns. I rush to her side and find her standing there with water pouring over her bleeding palm. The sink stained red from her blood.

"Oh no. What happened? Are you okay?" My concern for her is like that of a parent.

"Clumsy me. I wasn't paying attention and broke a glass."

"That cut looks deep. Do you think we should get you stitches?"

"No, no, no. It's not that bad. I have some super glue in the second drawer over there." She nods to a row of cabinets along the far wall.

"You plan to glue yourself back together?" I ask half amused.

"That's what super glue was made for. It was used by medics in the battlefield during World War two for fast wound care."

"Really? Wow, I learn something new every day. Where did you learn that little fact?"

"Books! Of course."

"How about a first aid kit or some bandages?" I ask, after I fetch the glue.

"Medicine cabinet, hall bath." she tells me over her shoulder. "Thank you."

I slip into the bathroom and grab the little first aid kit, then hurry back to the kitchen to glue Ainsley back together. The cut is about three inches long right across the palm of her right hand.

Very inconvenient.

She is brave and only cringes a little as I put the Bactine over the cut and dry it off. It isn't as deep as I originally thought, and a little glue seems to do the trick. I wrap a bandage around her hand and gently kiss the top when finished.

Looking into her eyes, a single tear trails down the side of her cheek.

"Did I hurt you?" I ask, worried. But she just shakes her head no, as another tear falls.

"I'm just so grateful you're here." she says, her fingers stroking my jaw with her uninjured hand. "Thank you for taking care of me."

I wipe the tears from her cheek and replace them with a kiss. "I will always take care of you Ainsley."

She shudders and the tears start falling in earnest. "Hey, what's wrong?" I ask, pulling her into my arms. Her tears wet against my chest.

She lets out a deep heavy breath and a sobbing laugh. "I don't know what's wrong with me. It's been so long since I've been taken care of. I'm the 'Mom'. I am used to being the caregiver. I guess I didn't realize how much I needed a little 'caring for' until now. It makes me feel a little weak and vulnerable."

"I have not witnessed a weak bone in your body." I smile down at her. "And there is nothing weak about needing to be loved and taken care of." She pushes up on her tippy toes and kisses me.

"Somehow, I love you even more today than I did yesterday. And yesterday I was on cloud nine." she tells me. "Thank you for gluing me back together."

She said she loved me!

It just slipped by, like she didn't even catch it, but I sure as shit did. My mind is all jittery as I try to figure out how to navigate an unintentional 'I love you'.

I go for humor.

"Starting your morning gratitude meditation with me, are you?" I ask.

She smiles. A real smile this time. "Every moment of every day since I've met you, I am grateful for you."

"Good. I have brainwashed you well." I joke, and am rewarded with a good healthy chortle in place of her tears. "How about, you go make yourself comfy and I'll make us some coffee."

"Okay." She kisses my cheek then heads outside. I was expecting her to go to the sofa, but outside in nature seems better.

A few moments later I go out to the patio, but don't find her relaxing on the deck. I round the corner of the house and find her meditating under her oak tree instead. I have a favorite oak tree I like to day dream and manifest under back home too. It feels like we live such parallel lives in so many ways. I imagine two parallel lines joining and running as one long, solid, thick line into eternity.

Quietly, I sit next to her, placing her coffee down in front of her and close my eyes, too. I like this habit of hers to meditate every morning. Perhaps I'll make it a habit of mine also. I send a little healing energy towards her hand and thank the universe for every day I have had and every day I have left to spend with Ainsley. Then I get to thinking of romantic ways to tell her how much I love her too. I'm no longer scared it's too soon. But I want it to be perfect, I want to be able to tell her everything I'm feeling. And I don't know how to do that yet. It's like trying to speak coherently while using only two letters from the alphabet.

***

After our meditation, I help her in the garden and then we take the dogs to the dog park. We spend the day reading on the deck, and I help her make dinner and dessert as the evening nears. At 5:00 pm a little black sports car pulls into the driveway. A beautiful young woman steps out of the driver's side, followed by a tall young man out the passenger's door.

"Hey Ains, I think Alice is here. And she has a friend." Ainsley peeks through the window and smiles.

"Oh goodie, she brought Eric with her. You'll get to meet everyone!" She claps her hands, then winces at her forgotten cut, before leading me outside and onto the deck to meet Alice and Eric.

I am terrified.

The appetite that had been building while playing cooks with Ainsley, quickly turns into a ball of nausea in the pit of my stomach. I had not been worried about meeting Bodhi, but Alice scares Ainsley, and her nerves have become mine.

Half way out, the dogs hearing the commotion come bursting through the doggy door of Bodhi's studio apartment and race down the steps to be included with the hellos. As expected, they steal the attention and lighten the mood. Giving everyone something else to place their attention on. Much better than the awkward greetings of,

'Hi, I'm the guy fucking your mother'.

Or in Eric's case,

'The guy who is screwing your daughter.' Thank you Pippy and Fluffs!

As Bodhi comes down the stairs, we all move into the house and proper introductions go round as I help get drinks for everyone. The evening is beautiful, so we decide to dine on the patio enjoying a bottle of Mourvèdre that Alice and Eric brought with them to share.

Eric and I bond right away, outsiders that we are. But we don't feel like outsiders for more than two seconds once the dogs start playing tug of war and all attention and laughter moves to them. It seems a few good belly laughs and half a glass of wine was all I needed to release the anxieties of meeting the most important people in Ainsley's life. The wine seems to relax Alice too, as her walls slowly dissolved around me and the conversation evolves from work, to play, then family.

After dinner, I gather the dishes to rinse inside and give Ainsley a little one-on-one time with her kids. Eric joins me a moment later with some empty glasses to refill. Both of us stand there quiet for a moment, staring out though the window watching Ainsley, Alice, and Bodhi laughing and enjoying one another's company.

"I think Ali likes you." Eric says handing me a plate to wash.

"Yeah, what makes you say that?"

"I haven't heard one snarky comment from her all night. That might be a record."

"So long as her love language isn't sarcasm, I'm gold then."

Eric chuckled. "Gee, I didn't think of it that way. She may actually hate you then."

That had me whooping out a loud laugh too. "Overall, I think the night's gone well. Yeah?"

"For sure. But I'll give you a heads up if she starts plotting your murder."

I laugh again. "Thanks."

This family is good, I think. I could be a part of this family. Austin would have fun here too. And just like that, a wave of love for my kid back home floods into my heart and I miss him, and wish desperately that he was here too. I love being in Ainsley's world, but I want her in my world also. I want our worlds to mesh into one.

Eric refills the wine glasses, then we head back out onto the deck to the sound of laughing.

"The dishes are done and the casserole dish is soaking." I tell Ainsley kissing her cheek as I sit down next to her.

"Really? You did the dishes for me?" She beams, her hands held over her heart.

"Okay. That clinches it. You can keep him." Ali says, looking at me with half a grin.

"Wow, did I just gain approval by doing chores?"

"Doing the dishes for Mom, you bet. She hates doing the dishes. You just scored major bonus points."

My mind zooms to the bonus points I cashed in during the cruise and I send Ainsley a heated look. From the flush that overcomes her skin, I'm guessing her mind is reliving those sexy naked moments as well.

"Gross you two. I don't know what that look is about, but save it for after we leave." Ali smirks and fake gags.

"Okay kids. Time to go home, then." Ains counters back.

"Not until after the pie you promised." Bodhi objects loudly.

"I have been told stories of the magic cinnamon-roll apple pie, and I'm excited to try it, too." Eric chimes in too

"Okay then, who wants ice cream with it?" Ainsley asks, as she stands up to get the pie. Everyone's hands go up.

I follow Ainsley into the kitchen and she takes the pie out of the warming drawer while I grab the vanilla ice cream from the freezer, meeting her at the counter.

"Bowls or plates" I ask, as she goes to grab a knife.

"Let's do bowls and spoons." She smiles up at me. The easy flow of working together in the kitchen just makes me love her more. She adjusts the knife in her injured hand twice before switching over to her left hand.

"Let me do that. How about you grab the spoons and napkins while I cut and scoop?" She hands over the knife and kisses my cheek. These little things shouldn't mean much. This isn't what novels are written about. But it's all these little moments of comfort and companionship that make me feel so happy and content in our flow.

After the most delicious dessert, we say good night and head into the house so that I can cash in on my points.

"Tonight was fun. I really like your kids."

"Thank you. I'm fond of them too." she grins. "Alice really likes you. I was a little nervous about her. She is kinda all or nothing."

"Yeah, I can see that about her. I'm glad I got her all vs. her nothing."

"Me too." she exhales.

"I wish Austin could have been here tonight. He would have enjoyed the evening as well."

"Maybe he can come out too, next time."

"He would love to come out to California. I may struggle to get him to leave."

"Well, maybe you'll both choose to stay."

"Maybe we will." I smile and my lips fall upon hers as I imagine staying put in California.

# 36.

## The Test

Cody:

Two days later and I was leaving California. My expectations of the visit superseded tenfold. Our day out with BrentRa seemed to solidify everything that has occurred over the past few weeks even more, confirming that this isn't all a dream. Sarah and Brent have already chosen a date and venue. July 22nd. One year and a day from when they met. They asked us to be their best man and maid of honor.

"We were the catalyst for their romance after all," Sarah said.

"Thank goodness Ainsley left without leaving her number that night in Vegas or Sarah and I never would have met." Brent had joked.

But that joke stuck with me. It was a good perspective. That something new and beautiful could come out of that missed opportunity. Obviously, we had our children too. I wouldn't trade Austin for anything, and he wouldn't be Austin if I hadn't married Vanessa. I'm sure Ainsley feels the same way about Alice and Bodhi. Perhaps the friendships between our children can be another bonus. I'm sure the kids will be fast friends. Just imagine if we can hook up Lindi with my dad too. So many potential blessings now have the opportunity to exist because we missed our chance way back when.

Before I left, we booked Ainsley's flight out to New Mexico for the Tuesday after next. Only a three day visit, but I will take everything I can get. I'm both excited and anxious about her stay and can now appreciate how nervous she must have felt the nine days prepping before my trip out. I want everything to be perfect for her. I want to make her feel as comfortable and welcome in my home as she had me feeling in hers. This entire experience feels like a part of a test.

Part one. Do we fit together?  √

Part two. Do I fit in her world?  √

Part three. Does she fit in my world? I'm betting 100% Yes.

I guess the final will be figuring out how to make it all fit together. How to blend our worlds which exist over nine hundred miles apart. We could do something like BrentRah. Share our time between the two places like snow birds. Perhaps we could spend the busy wedding season in California and the rest of the time here in Taos. Maybe she will consider going part time or retiring. She wouldn't have to work if she didn't want to. I've done well enough with my real estate investments not to have to worry about money. But I think she loves her job and I don't want her to feel obligated to leave behind something that she has built. I could leave real estate, but this camp ground and the land has a piece of my heart too. I want her to love it here as much as I do.

# 37.

## New Mexico

Cody:

I wait with flowers at the departure gate. Every minute feels like an hour. Then I see her. Soft honey skin, dark bouncing wavy hair, and a smile that melts my heart and gives me a hard on at the same time. Eleven days apart has felt like an eternity. I missed her constantly. We talked every day, but it's not the same as seeing her in person. Feeling her energy encompass mine. Tasting her lips... warm and soft and inviting.

I gun it home and make the hour and a half long drive from the airport in just under an hour fifteen. Absence has made more than just my heart grow fonder. My body has missed her too. She is so pretty sitting next to me in jean shorts and a floral blouse. It's been hard to keep my eyes on the road and off of her legs. Every time I look at her, I think of the taste of her, and my foot hits the pedal a little harder. But the adrenaline of speeding eighty-nine miles per hour down the highway is a drop in the bucket compared to the flash that ignites as I park and we climb the steps of my front patio.

Without warning, I sweep her up into my arms, before kicking the heavy wooden door open and carry her inside. I don't let her down, but take her directly to my room. Our room, for the next three days.

"I've missed you too." she says with a giggle as I release her onto the bed. But I'm not giggling. I'm a man on a mission, and my mission is currently encased in denim and some kind of Poly Cotton blend. This coming back together is what Ainsley had meant as the good part, where absence makes the heart grow fonder. Even if that absence is only a couple of days.

Our clothes come off fast but we make love slowly. Not emerging until nearly sunset when our stomachs finally start to protest for more fuel to sustain all the sex.

***

I gave Ainsley a tour of my home. I love this house. I helped build this house. It's a classic adobe with log accents. A large center courtyard and stained glass. The indoors and outdoors blend from one room to the next with floor to ceiling windows which show off a view of the campground and canyon below. I take her to my sunset deck off the back of the house. I love this spot. Now I get to share it with her.

I'm nearly giddy as she sits down with a plate of appetizers and a glass of wine, waiting for her reaction to the view. The sky is fuchsia and tangerine orange. A streak of purple along the belly of a rain cloud sitting lonely in the sky. She is silent as she places her things on the side table staring out towards the west. Then she slowly stands up again moving to the edge of the deck with her phone in hand.

She's taking pictures.

I think from her, that is the highest compliment. She turns to look at me and she is as radiant as the sunset.

"This place doesn't suck." she gleams, hands on her hips she walks back over to the sitting area and plops down next to me again. "I think I could spend every evening out here." she sighs, resting her head against my side and looking out towards the horizon.

"I usually do. The front patio is for the sunrise." I tell her as I wrap my arm around her shoulders and appreciate the passing of the day.

"Your home is really lovely. I see why you like it here so much." I want her to call this our home one day. My heart buzzes with it.

"I can't wait to show you the rest tomorrow." I told her. "I want you to love it as much as I do."

"I don't think that's going to be a difficult task." She looks out onto the vast horizon with wonder behind her eyes, and my heart does a little happy dance.

"One more surprise. I look down at her with puppy dog eyes. "Tomorrow my dad and Austin are going to join us for dinner. Don't worry," I wave my arms "I'm not cooking. We are going out to Doc Martins in town." She is speechless, so I continue. "And Charlie and Bill both want to meet you too, so I've promised a brunch date with them Thursday. But other than showing off the camp ground with a little hike tomorrow morning, I don't have any other plans for us outside of the bedroom."

"What you have so far sounds perfect. But I'm honestly terrified all of a sudden about meeting your family and partners. Did you feel like this about meeting all of my people?" She holds her hand to the pit of her stomach. The memory of fear and nausea at meeting Ali flashes through my mind and I laugh softly at her expression. I pat her on the hand in sympathy over the shared emotion.

"I did when Ali drove up. But the dogs helped lighten the mood when they started playing. I was lucky to have a distraction." She still looked a little green. "Don't worry, they are going to love you as much as I do."

My heart tightens over my inadvertent saying of the L word. We both let it slide, but I can see her slight flush. Can she see the way I am blushing too? Can she read in my eyes that I mean it? I want to say it so badly. But not like that. I've been finding the words, but this isn't the right moment for them.

I'm at least going to wait until she no longer wants to throw up.

We pass from dusk into true night, sitting arm-in-arm out on the deck, nibbling our plates of food. Ainsley drinking her wine while I enjoy a beer. Our conversation is light and funny and I feel so comfortable with her here that when we finally get up to go back inside, I forget that she doesn't know where she is going and she gets lost on her way to the kitchen. She fits in here so well, that I guess I just assumed she would know where everything was.

I find her in the game room looking through the trinkets, photos, and books lining the shelves of a floor to ceiling bookcase. I like her in my space. She fills every room with her aura. She lights it up like the sunshine on a warm spring day. The house has felt gray since Austin moved out. But now, there is this soft warm glow everywhere. The house feels alive again. As if, it had been hibernating in winter, starving for the warm light of Ainsley to wake it up.  And now here she is, standing in my home glowing warm and radiant, ready to be drunk up in abundance. I mentally add stopping by the jewelers to look at rings to my wish list of activities for this week. I know it's coming.

I imagine her leaving here with a ring on her hand.

That night, I fall asleep, manifesting our forever and thinking up ways to tell her how I feel.

## 38.

## Thunderstorm

Cody:

I wake up to a thunderstorm around 7:30 am. Looks like our morning hike is going to have to be postponed. Oh well, I can think of other fun things to do instead. I grin to myself as I grab the remote for the bedroom fireplace, turning it on. The ambiance of the crackling fire, along with the rain on the tile, roof and thunder in the distance is perfect. And as far as I'm concerned, the war for the best wake up sex is still on.

I slowly wrap my arm around her waist and snuggle against her. She smells like sex and strawberries. Her scent, mixes with the electric smell of lightning in the air, giving me goose bumps. The crack of thunder mimics the clap of my heart, as the familiar euphoric need for her pulses through every cell of my being.

I place my hand just above her arm and can feel the static electricity in the air raise her fine, baby arm hairs up to tickle my palm. The sensation is wild, so I test it out over her stomach, up her ribs, and over her breast. In her sleep, she sighs and shifts towards the energy of my hand. Inadvertently ending my game of 'not touching her' as her breast thrust into my palm. My thumb finds and gently toys with her nipple, and I feel a jolt of pleasure shoot through my own chest as if we are connected.

String theory or entanglement or something... She has me thinking in terms of quantum physics these days, because that's what this is; quantum in its bliss.

My lips gently hover over her neck as I get as close as possible without touching her. The electricity buzzes between our skin and she sighs.

"Hmmmm...Cody...muffle, blubber, nonsense..." She exhales a round of sleepy talk that ends my game of not touching her, as her flesh melts against my lips . I let my kisses sink in and I give my fingers free reign to softly roam her body. This experiment has been fun, but it would be more fun with her awake.

Thunder shakes the house as the storm nears and the sound pulls her fully into consciousness. Her hands begin to grab and grope with her own needs, as her lips find my collarbone and she kisses and nips at my skin. The room lights up for a flash, followed two seconds later by an enormous boom.

"Dear Lord." she exhales.

I don't know if it's in response to me or the thunder, but it's the 'Me' that lives for all the naughty, breathless, sounds she makes that responds. I crawl between her legs and take her breast into my mouth. I'm not slow or very gentle as I pull her hips against my erection. My penis brain has fully taken over and I am...

Needy.

I am desperately waiting for the next lighting strike and boom of thunder, as my hands glide up her rib cage and over her breast. I feel the energy in the air ramping up the fire between us with each second that ticks by. I glide the head of my cock back and forth, up and down, her soft, wet pussy. My heart beat races as I wait for the flash, wait for the boom.

*Flash!*

There it is. The room is temporarily lit, illuminating her rose gold flesh, and I watch as the head of my dick disappears inside of her, just past the rim.

*Boom!*

I sink fast and deep inside her sweet, warm, well of all that is good and holy. Her cuss of pleasure is both and inhale and exhale at the same time. Yet the moment stands breathless as the electricity in the air seems to vaporize it. Energizing our particles and amplifying every feeling in every nerve. Then another flash lights the room, and the flash is like a sneak peek at heaven. The image of her body stays burned into my retinas long after the lightning has faded. Her writhing hips, her hard pink nipples, the angle of her back... God, the way her fingers curl around the blanket in a fist.

We are rowdy and intense as she digs her nails into my ass pulling me deeper. Her teeth are sharp on my shoulder as she mumbles something that sounds like 'Fuck me harder' through her bite, and I go white with need. My hands grab her hips and the sound we make is *Fucking Amazing,* as skin slaps against skin. The wet slide of my cock pulling out and pushing back in again, has become its own raging storm.

"Oh my God, Cody..." she gasps. "Holy Fuck.... Oh God Cody, it feels so good."

**"You** feel so good."

I love this. Her voice sends shivers through my soul.

"Fuck! Now, now.... I'm ......cumming..." She cries.

And this is it.

The moment.

When her head falls back and her eyes close in bliss. When time stops and nothing but that ripple of magnificent energy engulfs her body, mind, and soul. I love seeing her like this. I love being the one to bring her here. I feel her body start to shake and spasm around mine. I try to hold on, but the feel of her coming undone has brought me to my own undoing. Cussing her name in time with the thunder, I crumble on top of her, spent and panting.

"Wow" she sighs, as I lay still sprawled across her chest. Too depleted to move or speak. "You are the most amazing lover." she whispers against my shoulder.

The best compliment ever.

"Loving takes two." I growl, before kissing her sweet plump bare lips. Sleepy and without make up, she is the most beautiful thing I've ever seen. Morning breath and all.

# 39.

## An Appetizer of Antacids

Cody:

Thankfully, the storm lets up at noon, so the day isn't totally ruined. We just have to re-arrange a few activities. Tonight, we are meeting my family for dinner. So, I decide to take her into town a few hours early so we can pop into some of the galleries and I can point out some of my favorite haunts. Maybe I'll coax her into a jewelry store as well. She still wears the blue earrings I bought her in Mexico. It makes me smile to know she likes them so much. Or maybe she has worn them all this time because she likes me so much. That is even better.

But as the afternoon turns to evening, I can sense her nerves rising. Now does not seem like the time to look at engagement rings when she is silently worrying about meeting my kid and dad. Honestly, it feels like that needs to be checked off the list first, before I go popping the question anyhow. I hold her hand and call out to the brave Ainsley I know is hiding under a bed somewhere in her mind.

I suggest getting to the restaurant early and we head to the bar to get us both a drink of liquid courage. After all, two shots of Whiskey have always been my go-to calm-down remedy. She gratefully accepts and orders a Long Island Iced Tea. My girl knows how to drink. Despite the hard liquor, I can tell Ainsley is still nervous, So I try to distract her.

"Didn't Alice meet Eric's family last weekend? How did that go?" I ask. She exhales a large breath with a smile. Grateful, I think, to have someone else to think about.

"She had a lot of fun. She and Eric's sisters really hit it off and she said she felt welcome by everyone. Eric's great-grandma kept commenting on her birthing hips and ample bosom for nursing babies. I guess she really wants to be a great-great-grandma before she kicks the bucket." she laughed at her own joke. I laugh too, as the doors swing open and my father and son walk in together, chatting secrets in each other's ears.

Here we go.

***

Ainsley:

I can tell they are behind me by the way Cody's expression shifts on his face. I feel nauseous again. I want this to go well so badly that I am afraid I'm going to puke all over them. Cody stands and comes over to my chair wrapping his arm protectively around my waist. "They are here." He whispers in my ear and gives me a little squeeze. He can tell I'm nervous. He can read me like a book. "You'll be great." he whispers encouragingly before reaching out for hugs, first with his son, then with his father.

Seeing the three men standing in a row is kind of amazing. First there is Austin. He reminds me of the statue of David. His golden-brown locks tumbling in a halo of angelic curls against his forehead. He has apple cheeks and dimples that would make any girls panties drop. Or boys. He has his father's bright blue eyes, straight nose, and hard jaw line. But he is still pretty in his flamingo pink shirt and designer jeans and shoes.

Cody's father is more rugged and gruff. A thick white and gray beard, along with a full head of hair, has him looking a little like Bad Ass Santa Claus. He looks healthy and strong for a man in his 70's. John strikes me as the type of man who has worked from dawn until dusk his entire life. Not because he had to, but because he wanted to. He probably still chops his own wood for fun.

Then there is Cody, a perfect blend in the middle. I feel privileged to be with these three as they hug and greet each other with love. My nausea settles and my heart feels warm and safe as Cody smiles at me, then lovingly introduces me to the two most important people in his life.

"Somebody better call God, because he's missing an Angel." Austin teases, pulling me into a warm hug. "Father, the photos you showed me do not do her justice." He snickers towards Cody. "Ainsley darling, whatever potion or spell you have slipped my father, please continue to weave your magic. The man has never been happier."

I liked Austin already. He's fabulous! "Your Dad makes me pretty happy too." I smile back.

"Oh good! Can I call you Mother then?"

"Austin!" Cody yells as John and I choke back a laugh. "You're supposed to be making a good impression not scaring her off."

"Oh please, we could see you two love birds through the window outside. You two radiate ooey gooey romance. And if she loves you, she's gonna love me even more." Austin smirks. "Mom, have I scared you off?" Austin looked at me pointedly. I tried my best to hold in my grin. Cody was so red in the face it was comical. I could tell Austin was pushing his buttons for the fun of it.

"No, I'm not scared off. Instead, I think you just shut down all my anxiety about meeting everyone, you sweet boy." I pat his hand. "Thank you, Austin." Cody harrumphs a sigh of defeat then his frown brakes into a laugh as Austin kisses my cheek for the win.

Cody's father John is a bit more controlled with his excitement to meet me and pleasantly shakes my hand in both of his, offering me his welcome.

"It's a pleasure to meet you, Ainsley. The kid wasn't exaggerating on how lovely you are. Nor was he lying when he said that Cody hasn't been this happy in years."

"It's true. I am like a butterfly on a spring day." Cody jokes, fluttering his lashes at me. These men have me feeling so much love that the anxieties that had been controlling my emotions have nowhere to go but away. Thanks to all their sweet words and attention, I feel like a Maharishi with a harem of men reciting her attributes.

"You are all going to give me a big head with all these compliments." I laugh.

"What's good for Cody is good for all of us." John beams.

I like what John says. What is good for one should be good for all. That's how families work. Everyone helping each other out on their life's journeys. I can tell this family is close and care deeply for each other's happiness. This is a good family. I bet Ali and Bodhi would feel just as comfortable and at home with them as I already do. And they are going to LOVE Austin. He has just the type of charisma to pull Bodhi out of his shell. And John seems so gentle under his burly mountain man exterior. A big teddy Bear. All three of them are like gentle giants and I feel warm and happy surrounded by their presence.

# 40.

## The Big L

Cody:

"Are you ready for my version of morning meditation?" I ask as she grabs her shoes.

"Totally." Her smile is everything and she bounces excitedly to go. Fluffs, seeing outdoor shoes being put on, bounces to her feet too, wiggling her butt with her gigantic tail wag.

"I'm not sure who is more excited for our walk. You or Fluffs."

"Fluffs has the butt wiggle of excitement down better than I do." she jokes.

"I beg to differ." I grin, remembering her fabulous ass wiggling in those little Cheeky's back on the cruise.

"My partner Charlie lives at the other end of the campground and has invited us and Bill, over for brunch. I thought we would walk over to his place this morning. Hikes are always the best the day after a rain, and Charlie and Bill are very excited to meet you."

"I'm excited too." She says, wiggling her butt at me playfully. No sign of nerves this time.

We head out through the back gate and onto a path that leads down to the campground. Cliffs of red rock, pine, and chaparral on our right. Cottonwoods and birch mixed with a few old oak trees on our left. I have become like a mini-Walt Whitman since living out here and working the grounds. My love for nature has grown exponentially. I spend most of my days outdoors and I know every rock and fallen log.

Ainsley has her pixie-like way of skipping and twirling and bouncing from one pretty sight to another. She takes pictures of all the beauty she sees. Her constant state of awe makes me feel like I'm experiencing my camp for the first time too. As if I had just gotten a new eye prescription and can now see all the colors brighter, or see the definition of the leaves on the trees which were just pretty blobs of green before her.

We talk about the Earth and God. Our spirituality and philosophies. Our politics and hopes and dreams for the world. It's wonderful to feel so open and free with such deep taboo topics. Our theories and perspectives are so in sync. She describes things in her own Ainsley way and I see old ideas in a new light. I hope I do that for her too. If I can read her smile, I think I do. I feel suspended in time with her, like the forest has come to life and everything glistens with magic.

I love her so much.

I love things about her I didn't even know I was looking to love.

As we near the creek, I usher her down a small path and through the low limbs of my favorite old oak tree. The creek comes right up to the roots after a snow melt, but now at the start of fall, there is just a small creek at its edge. This is my favorite place in the entire camp. I come here to collect my thoughts. I don't share this space with many people. Bringing her here, holds a weight to it. I want her to find the same peace and serenity here that I do. I want her to love it.

"Hello beautiful!" She spoke directly to the tree as we entered its shaded arms. A warm buzz fills my mind as she walks up to the trunk and strokes it lovingly. Then she climbs right up into the oak and makes herself comfortable in the joint of a large branch. The way the dappled sunlight glints off the crown of her head and shoulders makes her look like a forest spirit. A nymph or something magical.

She doesn't know this is my spot yet. She is not putting on a show for me. This is her real reaction. This is her spirit crawling into the arms and heart of my favorite space while proclaiming its beauty.

This is the ultimate moment for me. Right here.

This is when my heart and mind have both agreed that I am undeniably in love and am going to marry Ainsley. Sure, it has always been part of the plan, and I have been dropping hints about marrying her since our first night together on the cruise.

But this is different.

This is solid like stone, not wistful and dreamy like air.

It feels right. Everything about this moment feels perfect. Leaning her head back against the tree limb, she closes her eyes and takes in a big breath, then releases it slowly. "Can we pause here for a moment? This space feels good." she asks, eyes still closed.

"This was my destination. This is my favorite place in the entire campground."

Turning her head towards mine, she opens her eyes to look at me. Her eyes shine like diamonds and her sweet smile makes my knees weak. She holds out her hand towards me, and I walk over to her and wrap my arms around her; tree and all. We stay like that. Arms entwined and hearts pressed together. Embracing each other as we breathe in and out, meditating as one.

'I love you.' The words pound inside my brain louder and louder, the longer I stay here with her. My skin itches with the need to say it. In this space, the moment finally feels right.

"Ainsley, I am so awestruck in love with you."

The words fall out of my mouth and my heartbeat quickens. I nod my head as I look up into her eyes. "I do. I love you. I love everything about you, my sweet Ainsley. The way you light up a room with your positive energy. Your spirit, your mind, humor, compassion, and over all gratitude for life. I love how you see the beauty in everything. My world is so much more beautiful with you in it." I caress the side of her cheek, brushing the pad of my thumb over her full lower lip. I whisper it again. "I love you." I don't let her respond, I kiss her instead, I'm not done telling her yet. There are some things you just can't say with words.

She didn't need to say it back out loud anyway. She told me in other ways that this feeling's mutual. Her fingers told me when they linked between mine. Her lips told me as she kissed me back with as much admiration and love as I feel coursing through my soul.

We have shared some pretty intense and amazing kisses, but this one, it's full of every color in the universe.

"Cody." She whispers my name, her fingers soft in my hair.

"I love you too. So very much." Her eyes speak the words as loud as her lips, and the love in my heart intensifies beyond description. "I think I've loved you from the first time I saw you. Somehow my soul knew." she whispers.

"I feel like the universe is on our side." I nod in agreement.

"Yes. These feelings are so much bigger than just you and me. Bigger than just right now."

"I think you and I have tapped in on something really special and I can't imagine any part of my future without you in it. I've missed the last twenty-five years with you, I don't want to miss another day. Marry me. For real this time. I want you by my side for the rest of my life. I want to share all of the good moments, and work through all of the shitty ones, with you next to me."

"Yes. I want that too. It's what I've been dreaming about since first meeting you." she whispers, her smile growing to her eyes. My heart is on cloud nine and it only seems right that my feet need to be off the ground too. Because my heart is floating. I clumsily crawl up into the tree next to her and kiss her. Slow, passionate kisses that speak of all the years we have left.

***

We sit there in my tree, swinging our dangling feet. Hand in hand, we simply stare at one another. Memorizing every particle of this moment for at least half an hour. Studying each other's features and expressions. Sharing soft kisses and light caresses as we simply snuggle and hold each other in this perfect moment.

"How are we going to make this work?" She questions in a soft whisper. "Where are we going to live?"

I think for a moment, my thumb drawing little circles inside the palm of her hand. "You wouldn't have to work if you didn't want to." I quietly put out there. She looks at me, a soft light in her eyes, that I read as guarded interest. So, I go on. "I'm not loaded like Brent, but I've done well over the years. If you just wanted to do wedding shoots for fun or focus on your more artistic photography..." I trail off as her smile grows.

"I would like to get to that point. But I don't think I can do it over night. I am booked out a year in advance. It would be a slow transition." She chewed her lip as she thought. "Plus are you sure you could handle two mortgages, car payments, college tuition for not just Austin, but Ali and Bodhi too. Plus, Vet School?" Here is her practical side again. She is so whimsy and fun that when this alter ego shows up it makes me smile.

"I can cover it without a worry." I grin "But if you want to keep working, I will support you and your business and help you build it into whatever dream you imagine it to be. I love it here, but ultimately, I don't care where we are, so long as we are together."

"It would be nice to focus on photography for art's sake instead of to make ends meet." she says quietly. "If I'm not so focused on making my numbers to pay all the bills by myself, it could give us more time to spend here in New Mexico at your camp. I really love it here too. Maybe I could freelance around Taos a little? Or earn my keep taking those shots of the campground you asked for?"

Her mind is working to find ways to compromise and blend our lives. She is willing to give a little just like I am.

"All I want is for all of us to be together. You, me, Austin, Ali, Bodhi, Fluffs, Pippy... One big happy family."

"Mouse and Zoomie too." She smiles up at me as a tear falls from the corner of her eye.

"Yes. Mouse and Zoomie too." I kiss the tear away. "As well as any goats you want to adopt."

"I love you." she says laughing as another tear slides from her eyes. "This is all beyond my wildest dreams. You make me so happy, Cody, I want to make you happy too. I want to watch you grow and live out your dreams as well."

"You are my dream. Traveling the globe with you, watching our kids grow and explore life and the world. Maybe enjoying grandkids together one day. I love you so much, Ainsley."

With the amazing zing of her lips against mine, I experienced the manifestation of my dreams. Knowing that Ainsley will be by my side for the rest of my life.

# 41.

## Put a Ring on It

Ainsley:

We continue our walk hand in hand. Cody patiently waits, as I continuously stop to take photos of all the beauty surrounding us. We pass by the cottages Cody built with his father. A mixture of adobe style structures near the cliffs and pine and stone cabins near the creek. I am blown away by the craftsmanship and attention to detail which makes each of the dozen structures special and unique. There is also a small area for tents and camper trailers near a pool and small multi-use adobe structure. A large fire pit area set up for group gatherings is in the center of it all.

"I understand why this place means so much to you. It's amazing. Maybe we should have the wedding here? There would be enough space for everyone to stay, and we could say our vows under your tree."

"How do you read my mind so clearly?" he asks with a playful half smile. "Marrying you under my oak tree is what I have been manifesting for weeks now, and here you are putting words to my vision," he laughs. "You're perfect Ainsley."

Cody grabs a thin young branch from a birch tree as we walk. He starts twisting it round itself as we continue talking about the logistics of a wedding in this amazing place. As we round the path down to the creek, Cody pauses, grabbing my hand and bringing it up to his lips for a kiss. He then slides the little wooden ring he had been fashioning over my finger. The thin brown twig, braided around itself, is the most beautiful representation of love I have ever seen.

I start crying again.

Thank God I didn't put on any mascara today. My emotions are so full, *my cup runneth over.*

I hug him.

I kiss him.

I want to remove his clothes and devour him.

His hands and lips become more fevered too, as my tongue slides into his mouth and my hips press against his. His groan of desire makes me moan like a wanton slut. I am so happy I feel dizzy. Like I could evaporate in this perfect moment. Heart pounding, I hold onto his arms for support. My fingers grabbing onto his shirt just above his heart, pulling him closer, so that when I pass out, he can catch me. His arms wrap tight around my back, as if he knows what I need. His fingers climbing up the back of my neck, twisting in my hair, Cody makes me dizzy as he kisses me with his entire body.

Pulling back with a shuttered inhale, Cody rests his forehead against mine. I can feel his heart pounding just as wildly as my heart is.

"Thank you. I love it." I whisper, my hand releasing its death grip on his shirt, as my fingers wiggle the ring against his chest.

"We can pick out a real one in town today."

"This is a real one." I say indignantly. "Maybe we can find a way to preserve this, so it's not as fragile." I soften.

"Really, you don't want something more? Maybe we could work some diamonds into it or something?"

"You already bought me diamonds." I turn my blue diamond clad ear in his direction.

"This little twig is hardly six-months' salary; I feel like a cheap skate not drowning you in beautiful things."

"Cody, I am drowning in your beautiful campground. Besides, this is much more than money. This was made with your hands from the land that you lovingly tend. This little piece of wood has more light and fire in it than any diamond could ever hope to hold. It's all I want." I kiss him softly. "How about we make matching wood wedding bands? Perhaps we can have an artist set them in resin?"

He quietly nods his agreement at my idea. "But let me buy you something to wear next to it?"

I grin up at him. "Only if you teach me how to make your wedding ring the way you made mine." I bargain.

"Deal." He grins and kisses me again.

# 42.

## Charlie the Wise

Ainsley:

We continued our hike through the canyon and towards Charlie's house at the far end of the camp. Each turn displaying a new something amazing or beautiful. I truly love it here. I could live here. Although, I've never lived in snow. The idea of snow both scares me and excites me. I'm used to seventy-five degrees and sunny for Christmas in California. I wonder just how cold it gets here?

I fantasize about the fireplace in Cody's room lighting our shadows against the ceiling as snow falls outside. I'm not sure exactly how we are going to blend our lives yet, but I'm willing to bend mine for him. It wouldn't be much of a stretch to have to enjoy living here. And he is willing to stay in California too. We both want this bad enough to work for it. That's why I know we are going to have a beautiful life together. It's only been a month and a half, but I know this is right. I hope the kids don't freak out about us rushing things. But that's a problem for future Ainsley. I'm too happy to worry about anything right now.

"I love it here." I say spinning under the shade of some cottonwood trees. The sound of the wind ruffling their paper-thin leaves, sounds like the tree's agreeing with my thoughts of love. "You have created an amazing place."

"Thank you." Cody glows with pride. "Charlie had a lot to do with it also. He had already been the grounds keeper for over fifteen years here when I bought the place." he says bragging about his friend. "Much of this has been his vision too. He has been a real mentor to me, not just with the campground, but also after Nessa died. My Dad and I brought him in as a partner on the property about four years ago." He tells me.

"Does he still maintain the grounds?"

"Yes. But he has help now. He isn't as young as he used to be, and it's a big place. But the man is spry and I think working the yard keeps him young." he smiles.

"Charlie is really special to me. After Nessa died, I fell into depression and lost myself. I struggled with substance abuse for a short time: Cigarettes, alcohol, weed... Too much of anything that would take the edge off. I disappeared into myself a bit too long and a little too deep. Charlie pulled me out. He opened my eyes. Helped me heal myself through rebuilding my relationship with Austin. Taught me about metaphysics and manifestation." he smiled this warm amazing smile as he spoke about his difficult memories.

"Charlie and I joke that he was a Buddhist Monk in a past life, or a Shaman of some kind. But I don't really think he's kidding. I don't think I'm kidding about it anymore, either. The man is wise. You will see what I mean." he winks. "I have told him all about you. He already loves you, and I am really excited for you two to meet." I was not nervous about Charlie the way I had been when meeting Austin and John. Cody's excitement and joy had become mine, and without knowing anymore about Charlie; I already liked him too.

\*\*\*

We crest a small hill and I can see a charming stone cottage, nestled in a little meadow, surrounded by a small orchard of trees. Charlie is out tending his vegetable garden when we arrive.

"Charlie, this is my fiancé Ainsley!" Cody says with excitement. My heart flutters at the word fiancé.

"What's this, did my old ears hear you right? Fiancé?"

"She finally said yes!" Cody laughs as if he has been asking me for years.

"Then congratulations are in order." Charlie's smile is larger than he is, as he holds both of my hands in his, welcoming me to his home.

Bill arrives ten minutes later and we all sit down in the garden for a farm fresh brunch of homegrown fruit, fresh eggs, and scones.

"Charlie, this is the best OJ I've ever tasted." Bill complements our host.

"Picked the oranges and tangerines this morning. Grown and harvested with love."

"I can taste it. Mmmmm... Got any more?" Bill licks his pulpy orange mustache.

Bill is a stocky guy, with gray hair and a fantastic handlebar mustache. He looks to be in his mid-fifties, and wears a crisp white collared shirt with the sleeves rolled up and a bolo tie.

"There is plenty more. Especially if one of you volunteers to help harvest more citrus from the garden."

"I'll go." I raise my hand to volunteer as Charlie pours everyone a fresh glass. We each drink three glasses, it is so good.

Bellies full, Charlie walks me around his little orchard, telling me the names of all the trees, while Bill and Cody talk shop and go over a few details regarding a new client. Charlie's garden is beautiful, and his love for his plant babies makes me want to plant my own mini orchard.

"Have you and Cody chosen a place to settle down?" Charlie asks as we pick a few lemons.

"We are still trying to figure out all the details." I reply. "Next step will be introducing our families to one another."

" 'The mountain is not climbed in one giant leap, but with single footsteps.'- *Buddhist lesson

I think you and Cody have a clear path in sight. Even if you can't see all of it, due to the bends and turns, just yet."

"Thank you." I say smiling. "Cody and I are both willing to make changes to our current lifestyles; we just have to figure out what changes those should be. And I love everything you have all created here. It's so beautiful and peaceful. I would like to be a part of the camp ground too."

"Oh yes. Cody tells me you're an artist. We would be happy to have your sight as a part of our vision."

"Aspiring artist perhaps." I shrug.

Charlie pauses mid lemon pick and looks into my eyes. His deep brown eyes hold so much love and wisdom, I can feel it in my soul.

"You are what you say you are."

That hits me hard, and I understood Cody's comment, that Charlie is a reincarnated spiritual teacher, on a new level.

I know this lesson already, yet I haven't been living it. I needed Charlie to remind me not to lose focus of the path that leads to my dreams. I have been putting my artistic self in a locked room for future use. Why shouldn't I consider myself an artist now? Just because I don't have photos hung in a gallery somewhere, doesn't mean that I'm not creating something valuable. Sure, maybe the only people who see my work are my closest friends and family, but would it be so hard to post online or start a blog? And with so much new inspiration surrounding me, I wouldn't have any problem creating new things. My phone must already have fifty new pics just from this short visit. And more than a few of those are frame worthy. My heart buzzes warm with inspiration and a clear new sight, of not only what I want, but how to get there. And maybe, how to help Cody's dream for his campground in the process.

"Wow Charlie, you are so right. I'm going to take your advice. I am an artist and will gladly lend my talents to the team."

He smiles and gives a little nod. "I knew Cody would choose a wise woman to fall in love with." That made me laugh. I adore the people Cody surrounds himself with.

Like energy he had called it. And I really like all this energy.

***

Cody and I stay at Charlie's place chatting until a little after 2:00 pm. Bill, dons his white Stetson Cowboy hat, and leaves to get back to the office for a meeting. We walk back home to Cody's house along a different path. The new scenery here is just amazing. There is so much variety in such a small amount of space. I can't wait to test out all of the different trails and see how the earth changes with the seasons. I'm thrilled about this new adventure.

"I have an idea," Cody says, with a gleam, as his house comes into view on the horizon. "Austin's twenty-first birthday is coming up the first weekend in October. I was thinking of a trip to California. Take him to a show at the Pantages Theater in Hollywood one night, then perhaps we can hire Jordan for a comedy wine tour. He would love bougie wine country. We could invite Bodhi and Ali and Eric too. Put this final piece into the puzzle. Assuming they all hit it off, like I expect they will, we can tell them that we are getting hitched."

It was a great idea.

"How about your dad? Will he come out too? We could invite Lindi to be his date. I think Lindi will like your dad."

"I think my dad will like Lindi also." he squeezes my hand.

I grab my cell and open up my calendar. "I'm working weddings that Friday and Saturday, but Sunday and Monday are both free." I smiled at him.

"Maybe we will fly out Friday and stay in L.A. for a night or two, just us. Really make sure he knows and feels that the trip is about him. Let Austin experience Hollywood a bit. Then we can drive down for a night with you and wine tasting. Maybe a beach morning before we fly home?"

"This sounds perfect." I grin, kissing him soft on the lips. Then, I shoot Jordan a quick text to see if she is available that Sunday. She pings back a yes within seconds, while Cody calls his dad and Austin to make sure they are available to come out. Within thirty minutes, the entire trip is planned.

Everyone is available and we call up Brent and Sarah to check in and invite them along for the winery tour as well. This is our family. We want to share all of our love with all of them. I'm giddy with our next adventure planned.

Another step up that mountain.

It helps numb the sting of flying home alone the next day.

# Part Four

**Puzzle Pieces**

# 43.

## Wind Whipped Nerves

Ainsley:

I'm going to be sick. This is worse than when I met Austin and John.

So much worse.

I pace back and forth through the kitchen. I don't feel prepared for this, and it makes my anxiety spike. I hope Cody has a few ideas in mind about just how we are going to tell our families and closest friends that we are engaged. I'm scared of all of the worst-case scenarios that bounce around in my brain.

Being told I'm being irresponsible or rushing after lust.

Being accused of being selfish and not taking into consideration the kid's needs.

Anything, that causes me to doubt this choice. Because when I do doubt it, I feel sick to my stomach. But when I imagine my tomorrows filled with Cody and our happy families, I feel better. So, I try to imagine what I want to have happen instead of dwelling in my doubts. But my thoughts just fall back into worry with each lap of the room.

I glance out the window with each pace passed, to see if they are about to pull in the drive. Twisting my engagement ring around my finger until my skin is raw. I just got it back today and it's gorgeous. My work baby, Mia, has a roommate who is an artist, and he dipped it in resin for me. It's no longer fragile and it fits perfectly. I spin it around my finger nervously, peering out the window once more.

Cody called me at 10:15 am saying that they had checked out of their L.A. hotel and were headed south, ETA noonish. It's only 11:45 am now, but if traffic's light, they could make it in an hour thirty.

So, I'm pacing.

And I want to throw up.

Bodhi is still up in his studio with Pippy. I wish he would come down and join me. I imagine he is waiting for Cody and his crew to arrive before coming down. He's always been a bit of a homebody. He will go if invited, but never seems to initiate activity on his own. Preferring the company of dogs to humans most of the time. I'm grateful that he is a cool kid and his friends are always including him, so he doesn't become a complete hermit.

Today's plan is wine tasting in Temecula Wine Country with fabulously funny Jordan. Everyone else isn't due to arrive until 12:30 pm.

So, I pace. And I still want to puke.

I pour myself a glass of water, but barely take a sip. Staring out at the garden, I decided to go sit under my tree. I always feel calmer when I meditate out in nature. I don't want to get dirty, so I sit on the little wooden board swing that Bodhi and Brian made over a decade ago. The braided rope is worn smooth but the swing is still strong after all these years.

I feel the familiar rush of wind through my hair as I pump my legs gaining altitude, and the feeling has my nerves flying away. My eyes focus on the different colors of green in the tree and the way the light turns one leaf yellow and another dark green. Within moments, the distraction has worked to make my sick stomach completely forgotten. I fly through the leaves with a light heart and a much-needed release of dopamine.

Five minutes of pumping has my heartbeat up and my cells alive. My mind is clear and focused. I come to a stop feeling great and excited for everyone to meet. This is going to be a fun day. Never mind that I have no idea just how we are going to tell everyone that after only a few months, Cody and I have decided to get engaged.

It is crazy!

Not BrentRa crazy, but still kinda nuts. I'm just going to have to leave it up to God and the Universe to guide us on when and how to make the move.

There is a really good chance Ali is going to notice the ring. Fashion designer that she is, and all. But it's not your typical engagement ring, so she may not notice which hand it's on. I spin the ring around my chafed finger once again.

Ali likes him. I remind myself as my nerves threaten to bubble up the acid in my stomach.

He does dishes. I close my eyes and take a deep breath, feeling the memory of her approval of Cody.

"You can keep him."

She had said with a grin and gleam in her eyes. My heart warmed back then, just as it is warming now.

The sound of tires turning onto the drive has me wide-eyed once again. Cody's killer smile greets me and I wave and smile back. John gives a friendly wave from the front seat and Austin leans over in the back and starts blowing me kisses.

I really love Austin.

My heart, still warm and full from my brief meditation, the feeling triples looking at the three of them. Already, they feel like family.

As the car doors slam shut, Cody wraps me in his arms and kisses me a gentle hello. He notices the ring right away.

"It's done already?"

"Yeah, isn't it great."

"They did a wonderful job." He says, spinning it around my finger. "I love that you love it."

"Almost as much as I love you." I kiss a little peck on his lips. "Did you know birch tree rings were historically given to symbolize growing love when you made it for me?"

"No, I can't say I knew that little Jeopardy fact. Something you picked up in a book?"

"Uh huh." I smile up into his big, blue eyes. "Then I take it as a good sign from the universe that this was the wood you chose."

"I like that." He squeezes my hand, then turns to include Austin and John as they walk up to join us towing their luggage.

Hugs go around and I wish Austin a happy twenty-first birthday. Then the doggy door flap claps, and four paws can be heard running down the stairs of Bodhi's studio. Pippy joins the party with wiggles of excitement. She can smell Fluffs on our guest and starts smelling through their luggage looking for her friend.

"I think Pippy is wishing you had brought Fluffs with you again."

"So am I." calls Bodhi, as he exits his studio onto the balcony.

"Oh my God, who's the hottie?" Austin blurts out to his dad, as he watches Bods saunter down the stairs after Pips.

I do my best to hold in my laugh. This day might get really interesting.

***

We make introductions there in the driveway, then walk up to the house. I get everyone settled with some water, while we wait for Alice and Eric, BrentRah, and Lindi to arrive. Bodhi seems to be just as enamored with Austin as he is taken with Bodhi. John, Cody, and I all exchange looks of knowing, as the two boys go off into their own little conversation, forgetting about us old folks in the kitchen.

"Jordan is a doll and has offered to pick us up here at the house so that we don't have to worry about getting home tonight. She will be here between 12:45-1:00 pm." I tell the guys.

"I'm not a big wine drinker, any chance some of these places have a micro-brewery attached?" John asks.

"As a matter of fact, most of them do have beer offerings. I think one also does whiskey tastings."

"Now you're talking my language!" John claps his hands with excitement.

As if sounding along with John's enthusiasm for whiskey, three loud honks beep from the drive. I peek out the window to see Brent and Sarah pulling up behind the guys' rental car. Brent hops out, then rushes around to open the door for Sarah. They still look fabulously in love as he holds her hand helping her up.

"BrentRah is here." I tell the men. They join me as I head outside to greet our friends and introduce Sarah to John and Austin. Alice and Eric pull up as we are all talking in the yard, followed by Jordan in her cute trolley bus. Everything was happening so fast that I didn't have time to be nervous or worried.

"Is everyone here?" Jordan asked as we all grabbed our things for our day out.

"We are just waiting on Lindi." I reply

"Who is Lindi?" John questions.

"She's your blind date, Dad." Cody grins his evil up to mischief smile.

"For me? You're setting me up?"

"Lindi is my bookkeeper and one of my closest friends. No pressure. But she is single." I smile up at him sweetly.

"Ho, ho, ho. You two are trouble! He laughs. "Teaming up already, I see." John seems pleased with the idea of a surprise blind date. I just hope they hit it off as well as we think they will.

Lindi shows up about five minutes late, but looking like it was worth it. Her silver hair catches the sun as she gets out of her Prius wearing a pretty lavender sundress. Her make-up, perfect.

"You have pretty friends, Ainsley." John nudges my shoulder.

"She's funny and smart too." I beam.

## 44.

## Booz'n it up

Ainsley:

Our little group of ten clambers into the trolley bus. There is more than enough room for everyone to have a seat all their own, but everyone pairs up. Bodhi with Austin and John with Lindi. My people and Cody's people are quickly becoming our people.

"Everyone seems to be hitting it off nicely." Cody whispers in my ear, reading my mind again. Spinning my ring around my finger, I can feel the love growing. Just like the birch tree promised.

"Welcome everyone! I already feel like we are all friends here." Jordan opens over the speaker system. "Ainsley told me that we are celebrating Austin's twenty-first birthday, and his first wine tasting tour. So let me start by teaching you the secret to enjoying a good bottle of wine." Jordan pauses for dramatic effect.

"Open the bottle to let it breathe. If it doesn't look like it's breathing, give it mouth-to-mouth."

John and Brent let out real laughs, while the kids offer pity laughs at Jordan's 'Dad joke'.

"We have four wineries to visit today. Ending at Lorimar Winery which has live music this evening and a killer BBQ and pizza oven."

"Four wineries! Am I going to be tossed by the end of the night?" Austin asks.

"Yes!" half of the bus answers in unison, laughing.

***

The drive through wine country is beautiful. The sun kissed golden hills roll by with horse ranches mixed between the miles of vineyards.  Danza Del Sol is our first stop and after six healthy pours each, we are all starting to feel a little tipsy. By winery number two, funny stories from Austin's Hollywood birthday adventure have us all in stitches.

Austin is a true showman and storyteller. He is captivating and funny and Alice and Eric are enjoying his company almost as much as Bodhi is. But Bodhi also has stars in his eyes and a blush on his cheeks. The same star struck look that Austin keeps throwing his way. Austin's cheeks turn bright red each time he catches Bodhi staring.

Shit, they are adorable.

At winery number three, we lose John and Lindi for a good twenty minutes. We are all pretty tossed by now and the naughty jokes about Octogenarian sex started making the rounds.

"An eighty-year-old man is being examined by his doctor."

"Do you still have sex?"

"Yes, almost every day."

"Can you be more specific?"

"Sure. Almost on Monday, almost on Tuesday…"

"But John and Lindi are only Septuagenarians." I protest on Lindi's behalf. Her jaw would drop if she thought someone was calling her eighty!

"Do you know any Septaguaraawwwian jokes?" Austin slurs, butchering the word.

I think for a moment. "Nope." and I laugh right along with everyone else, feeling light hearted and giddy.

Bodhi and Austin offer to go find the missing grandparents, and disappear off into the vineyard in a totally different direction than from where Lindi and John had last been seen. Hand in hand.

"I bet it's going to be at least twenty minutes before we see those two again also." Alice teases. She and Eric making kissy faces after them.

"You two have a knack for hooking people up." Brent says. "First Sarah and I, and now both your dad and Lindi, and Austin and Bodhi seem to be hitting it off."

"Our love is contagious." Cody grins down at me. "I guess it's a good thing you didn't leave me your number all those years ago. Look at all the love that never would have had a chance to be." Cody is always saying the most perfect things. I hold his hand then give him a gentle kiss. Lifting our joined hands, he kisses my palm just below the ring. His blue eyes burning a hole into my soul.

"Mommmm. What's that?" Alice asks. Her tone of voice suspicious.

"What's what, honey?" I look away from Cody's drowning blue eyes over to Ali. The wine buzz slows my reaction and numbs my nerves as she points towards my hand.

"The ring, Mom."

"Oh, this!" I wiggle my fingers up in the air showing off the braided birch. "Cody made it for me when I was visiting him in New Mexico, isn't it pretty?" Cody smiled down at me, squeezing me around the waist and kissed my head, just behind my ear.

"He gave you a ring?" Ali starts to ask, just as Austin interrupts her coming into the clearing with Bodhi, John, and Lindi in tow.

"Hey folks, look who we found." The tension from Ali's unanswered question still hung in the air creating an uncomfortable silence.

"What is everyone talking so seriously about?" John asks, redirecting the attention off of his and Lindi's mysterious disappearance, and back onto Cody and I.

"Mom was just telling us about this new ring Cody gave her." Alice says with a smirk.

"He gave you a ring?" Bodhi questions quietly, a little in shock.

"Well, everyone is here. Now is as good a time as any." Cody whispers in my ear. I nod but don't speak. Instead, I plead with him silently to take over.

Thankfully he catches my telepathic message and looks out to our friends and family.

"I think you all know I'm pretty crazy for Ainsley. I knew she was special from the moment I saw her twenty-five years ago in Vegas and I never forgot about her. Turns out she didn't forget about me either." He smiles at our little group of friends, then redirects his attention just at me. "Every day I have spent with you my heart grows a little bigger. The beauty you see in the world, I now see. The love you have for your family and friends, I now have for them too. Your dreams are my dreams and I can't picture my future without you." Maybe it was the dozen plus wine tastings I have had so far that has the water works threatening in my eyes. Maybe it is the way he looks at me. I bite my lip trying to hold back and not mess my mascara.

"I love you Ainsley." he says as he wipes a lone tear from my cheek.

"I love you too." I kiss him, lost in the moment, half forgetting that our family is standing right there watching us.

"I asked Ainsley to marry me when she was visiting Taos, under my favorite old oak tree." He says, as his eyes scan the faces of our friends and family.

"And????" Austin yells impatiently.

"And she said yes." Cody finally tells the group as he directs his attention back to me with a gigantic smile.

"I knew it!" Sarah claps with joy.

"It's about time." Brent teases.

"OMG, I can officially call you Mom now!" Austin chimes in.

I laugh at all the good cheer surrounding us, as my eyes move to Alice and Bodhi to weigh their reactions. Bodhi is quiet but smiling a massive smile usually only reserved for dogs. Ali on the other hand is harder to read.

"He proposed and made you the ring?" she asks quietly.

I nod a yes as she walks over to take a closer look.

"That's so romantic." she whispers then gives me a gigantic hug. Alice isn't a touchy person and her hug is my undoing. I start crying like a baby. Having her blessing means so much to me. Alice then turns her attention to Cody and she gives him a hug too, which makes me cry happy tears even more.

"I think Alice must be drunk. She's getting all handsy" Bodhi teases.

Now I am laughing, and crying, and snot is threatening to run down my face. Ali sticks her tongue out at Bodhi, then punches him in the arm as he walks over to give his congratulations. Followed by love from Lindi and John, and Jordan too.

"I wish I had my Thousand-dollar bottle of Tequila for celebratory shots." Brent chimes in.

"I wish you had that too!" Austin jokes.

"Well, we have one more winery and they have a lovely sparkling wine we can all cheers to." Jordan suggests. "And it's probably time we got some food in your bellies to soak up some of the alcohol."

We all agree and leave for the car park.

As we file back into the trolley, ready to head towards our last stop, I snuggle into Cody's side. I have never felt so content and full of hope and joy for the future. Everywhere I look, I see love. I am so grateful to be right here, right now, and for everything in my life that has led me to this moment. I pray our next twenty-five years are as wonderful as the past few months have been. I can't wait to start life with Cody as my partner. We both want this enough to compromise and bend where we need to. And a little flexibility is a strong thing to have. It will keep us from breaking. This engagement may be fast, but I feel so sure. What good is waiting when the future can be now.

The universe knew what it was doing, giving us our twenty-five-year gap. And while I sometimes wonder about what life could have been like if I had only left my number with Blue, back in Vegas. That reality would not have given me this life I now have with Cody.

And I love this life, exactly as it is.

# Epilogue

**Six weeks later...**

# 45.

## The Next Chapter

Ainsley:

I sit all snuggly and warm, wrapped up in my favorite blanket. (One that Sarah crocheted for me two Christmas ago.) The fire gently crackles in the fireplace as I stroke my finger slowly along the warm body lying next to me on my right. Then, I lovingly graze the soft fur of the body purring to my left.

Zoomie paws at my right leg, requesting her turn again. So, I oblige and scratch under her chin. I am rewarded with her purr. Loud enough to drown out Mouse's motor still going strong on my left. The kitties have been my loyal companions these past few lonely weeks.

I look at my phone and see it's nearly 9:00 pm. Which means it's too late to call Cody in Taos. He said that they are expecting the first snow later this week. He and John have been busy winterizing the cabins these past few days, and he has been falling asleep before 10:00 pm, his time, the past few nights. I hope the storm coming in won't delay or cancel the guy's flight out to Cali later this week.

It's been nearly three weeks since I last saw Cody. And I miss him. We celebrated Halloween together this year by cliff diving in Maui in full costume. Cody dressed up as a pirate, and I was a mermaid. I smile over the memory as I look forward to seeing him again in just a couple of days. He is flying out with John and Austin to celebrate Thanksgiving with us. I'm excited to have my home filled with all the people I love. There is so much to be thankful for this year.

As I reach over Zoomie's head to plug my phone in for the night, it buzzes with a call. Excited, I look at the caller ID, expecting the name 'Blue' to pop up. But instead, it's Brent.

"Hey Brent, what's shaking?" I answer, almost as happy to talk to my new friend.

"Do you know where Sarah is? She hasn't come home yet and I'm starting to get a little worried." He sounded way past 'a little worried'.

"I haven't heard from her." I reply, my excitement gone. "I assume you tried calling her?"

"Yeah, nothing."

"Have you checked traffic?"

"Yeah, there isn't much." He says, sounding disappointed that Sarah isn't stuck in gridlock on the 405 freeway.

"Want me to try giving her a call?" I ask.

"Couldn't hurt."

We hang up, and I give Sarah a call. But after a few rings it goes to voicemail, just as Brent's calls had. I feel my nerves bubble up into my chest, but I push them back down. I stroke the kitties for a moment while I warm up a pep talk, before calling Brent back.

"Ainsley?" He answers with desperation in his voice. The man wears his heart on his sleeve for Sarah. Which I love for her. But all that love is a scary thing, when the worry of it being lost confronts you head on like this.

"Voicemail. Want me to come over?" I ask him.

I can hear him pacing back and forth across their apartment, and I imagine that he is biting his nails down to the numbs as he considers my offer.

"I don't know. Am I being ridiculous?" he huffs.

"How late is she?" I question.

"About two hours."

"Where was she driving from?" I ask, trying to piece the puzzle of Sarah's disappearance together.

"Irvine. But she left before 6:00 pm." It's almost 9:00 pm now.

"Have you checked the accident reports?"

"No, but I'm looking now." The line is silent for a good sixty seconds, while he pulls up the information online. I think my heart stops beating for those sixty seconds as memories of my late husband Brian's fatal car accident bombard my memory.

"Nothing." He finally tells me.

"That's good." I say in a great relief of breath.

"I'm going to go look for her." Brent says with determination a moment later.

"Where would you go? She is probably on her way home. Maybe her phone is just on silent and she doesn't hear our calls. Or she had to make a stop and is running late and forgot to call to tell you." I suggest.

Poor Brent is so worried, and it's not helping anyone. I hear him release a gigantic sigh and hope that he is calming down. It's sweet to witness this kind of love for my bestie. But it's also painful to see, because I know Brent is hurting.

"I'm coming over. I bet she will be home before I get there." I say, trying to reassure us both. "I'm not really sleepy yet anyway, and once Sarah gets home, maybe we can all make final arrangements for Thanksgiving." I suggest. Brent and Sarah will be joining us on Turkey Day this year too. I try to distract myself, and Brent, with thoughts of how I wish this evening to end.

"You don't need to do that." Brent says "I'm a big boy. I can wait by myself."

"I can be there in twenty minutes if I use my lead foot. Are you sure?" I kinda want to come over now anyway.

"Mmmmm." He mumbles into the phone.

"Let me know when she walks in the door, okay?"

"I will. Thanks for talking me down off the ledge."

"You're welcome, Brent."

"Bye Ainsley."

"Bye. Don't forget to let me know once she is home."

"I won't." He says before the line disconnects.

I hang up and extricate myself from in-between my fur babies. I head to the bathroom and splash some water on my face and brush my teeth. I run the brush through my hair, but it's wild and unruly, and doesn't want to play along. So, I tie it up in a messy bun instead. I throw on my chunky gray cable knit sweater, because it's warm and outside it's cold. Not Taos cold, but Cali cold.

It's only like 52 Fahrenheit outside right now! Burrrr.

I slip on my cozy socks and shoes, then grab my cell and throw it in my purse as I head towards the garage. I'm going over to Sarah's place anyway. Brent, didn't tell me Not to come, after all.

Besides, I'm lonely tonight. And despite my confidence that Sarah can't hear her phone ringing to answer, simply because she is too busy singing loudly in the car, I'm worried too.

***

Twenty minutes later, I pulled into the parking structure at Sarah's apartment complex. I pass by her car, parked in her spot, and smile. Glad my friend made it home. I luck out, finding a visitor parking spot just one aisle down and smile over scoring a primo spot.

Hopping out of the car, I text Sarah as I walk. Letting her know that I'm about one minute from knocking on her door and that she and Brent had better be decent.

But I never hit send.

Instead, I stand frozen like a block of ice opposite Sarah's car. I notice the blood covering the ground first. I follow it along the driver's side of her car, to the broken side-mirror, which is dangling at an odd angle from just a few cables and wires.

Dry, brown drips of blood appear doubled against the reflective surface, which seems to tease me with its warning that, "Objects in mirror may be closer than they appear."

The ice in my vein's melts into a pool of nausea in the pit of my stomach.

Ice becoming fire.

I feel like my skin is burning from the inside out. Rage, fear, anxiety…insert negative emotion here. I guarantee, each and every one is attacking my nervous system like a raging inferno at this moment. My mind spins in fear and guilt, as I hold my breath peeking inside the car; afraid of what I might find.

Thankfully, I found nothing other than her purse, still sitting on the passenger's seat.

I spin around looking for more clues. Looking for Sarah, or the boogie man; but finding nothing. So, I run. I run for the stairwell doors that will lead me to the third floor of the complex, and to Brent. I take the steps two at a time, as I race to bang on their door.

"Ainsley?"

Brent opens the door, surprised to see me. I don't waste any time with pleasantries.

"Sarah's car is in the parking garage. Her purse is still in it." I sputter, gasping for breath. "Brent, I'm scared." I grab the arm of his shirt to steady my shaking nerves and wobbly legs. "I think her ex may have come for her."

"Who, Wayne?"

I nod yes, as a new wave of fear cascades down my spine. "Brent, there is blood all over the fucking ground. We need to call the police." I say with a shaking voice.

I have never seen a human jump to action as quickly as that man, in that moment. Brent rushes past me and out the door, headed for the stairwell I just vacated. I take a deep breath, closing my eyes for three seconds while I compose myself. When I open my eyes, I notice Brent's wallet and phone on the coffee table. I grab them, adding them to my purse. I lock the door, then head back down to the parking garage. I don't run down the stairs this time. Instead, I take care with my steps, as I dial 911.

My hands shaking, as I hit the call button.

…Continue the saga with **Sarah's Story**.

Release date, Fall 2024.

# Semi-homemade

## Cinnamon Roll Apple Pie:

2 cans of cinnamon rolls,

1 cup chunky cinnamon applesauce,

8 apples,

A pinch of salt.

1/4 cup of fruit juice (any works)

8-9" Round pie tin

Butter or cooking spray

Preheat the oven to 325 degrees Fahrenheit.

Grease the hell out of your pie tin.

Unwind 1 can of cinnamon rolls, into one big roll, on the bottom and up the sides of your pie tin. Press down the dough, helping it to spread out and cover the pie tin. *It's okay to have space between your rolls of dough. It will rise and spread out some more while in the oven.

Pre-bake for 5-7 minutes. Press down the dough, while warm, with a big spoon or ladle. Set aside.

Skin and dice your apples into a microwave safe bowl.

Add your salt and whatever fruit juice you have available to the apples, coating them so they won't brown. Cover with a wet paper towel, and nuke in the microwave for about 2 minutes. Stir and nuke for another 2 minutes.

Add your apple sauce to your nuked apples, mixing them up all nice. Then pour on top of your pre-baked cinnamon roll dough.

Unwind can # 2 of cinnamon rolls on to the top like one giant roll. Leave space between the spiral for expansion of the dough.

Bake for about 15 -18 minutes on the middle rack, or until the top is brown and the smell makes you salivate.

Spread both frosting containers on top of the pie while it's still warm so it melts into the top.

Enjoy warm with vanilla ice cream.

# Thank you

A big heart filled thanks goes out to my husband Mike, who encouraged me to publish my novels.

To my children, Zoey and Gage, who allowed me the space to create.

To my parents, Judy and Ron Holte. Whom have always encouraged my creative endeavors, even though I will not let them read this book – it's too smutty.

Many thanks go to Vanessa Colwell, who is both an amazing artist and friend, for created the cover art.

A big thank you to my Beta readers:

Aspen Kelsey Clark, Christina Vujovich, Katie Silke, Vanessa Coldwell, Barbara White, and Amy Brown who helped with editing, format, grammar, filling in the plot holes, and my atrocious spelling.

Gisele Samaan, who was my very first reader and helped with character development.

Stefanie Castro, for sharing her publishing knowledge with me.

Deems Morrione, for suggesting I add something weird. Such as a one-handed ax thrower.

Catherine White, whos book club, *The Friends of Old Books Club* renewed my love of reading and encouraged me to try my hand at writing and giving me the confidence to hit send on the final draft.

## ABOUT THE AUTHOR:

S. Heather Carroll lives is sunny Southern California with her Husband, two kids, three cats, and a Beagle who refuses to be potty trained. She is a graduate of UC Irvine, with a BA in Fine and Applied Art. Heather loves hiking and nature photography, working in her garden, and nachos. But who doesn't love Nachos!

Want to learn more, leave a comment, or ask a question? Visit us at www.sheathercarroll.com. For upcoming events and new releases.

Fun Fact: This novel is exactly 77,777 words.